praise for

ALLY CARTER

'Ally Carter wrote a un[...] downable romance! I d[...] rom-com about grumpy/sunshine spies with amazing chemistry and a dash of amnesia, but it was exactly what was missing in my life. I'm wonderstruck by *The Blonde Identity*! (Also, this book needs to be a movie!)'

—ALI HAZELWOOD, *Sunday Times* bestselling
author of *The Love Hypothesis*

'Spies! Amnesia! And banter that'll make you chant, "Kiss! Kiss! Kiss!" No one writes an action rom-com quite like Ally Carter'

—RACHEL HAWKINS, *New York Times* bestselling
author of *The Wife Upstairs*

'A delightful, delicious joyride of a romp!'

—SUSAN ELIZABETH PHILLIPS, No. 1 *New York Times*
bestselling author of *When Stars Collide*

'*The Blonde Identity* was everything I wanted in rom-com and more! Full of brilliant banter, clever humour, and so many swoon-worthy scenes, this was a perfect book. I hope Ally Carter writes more stories in this world, because every second of this unexpected adventure made me smile. I can't remember the last time I had so much fun reading a book'

—STEPHANIE GARBER, No. 1 *Sunday Times*
bestselling author of the Caraval series

'Completely captivating – funny, fresh, and deliciously swoon-worthy, *The Blonde Identity* had me smiling over every action-packed page. I loved it'

—ANNABEL MONAGHAN, author of *Nora Goes Off Script* and *Same Time Next Summer*

'*The Blonde Identity* is hands down the cutest, most fast-paced wild ride of a rom-com I've ever read. Utterly impossible to put down!'

—LYNN PAINTER, *New York Times* bestselling author of *The Love Wager*

'*The Blonde Identity* is explosively funny and jam-packed with chemistry! I couldn't have loved this hilarious rom-com more. The story is full of humour, action, romance, and emotions that tug on your heartstrings. Ally is a rom-com genius!'

—SARAH ADAMS, author of *The Cheat Sheet*

'I absolutely adored *The Blonde Identity*! I loved the humour, Zoe and Sawyer were perfection, and the chemistry . . . I couldn't put it down'

—LORRAINE HEATH, *New York Times* bestselling author

'I am a Gallagher Girls fan, and *The Blonde Identity* satisfied *all* of my GG cravings! Ally Carter has that magic formula of the perfect amount of brilliance, fun, and sizzling banter down pat!'

—JESSE Q. SUTANTO, bestselling author of *Dial A for Aunties* and *Vera Wong's Unsolicited Advice for Murderers*

THE
BLONDE
IDENTITY

THE
BLONDE
IDENTITY

Ally Carter

PAN BOOKS

First published 2023 by HarperCollins, New York

First published in the UK 2023 by Macmillan

This paperback edition published 2024 by Pan Books
an imprint of Pan Macmillan
The Smithson, 6 Briset Street, London EC1M 5NR
EU representative: Macmillan Publishers Ireland Ltd, 1st Floor,
The Liffey Trust Centre, 117–126 Sheriff Street Upper,
Dublin 1, D01 YC43
Associated companies throughout the world
www.panmacmillan.com

ISBN 978-1-0350-3836-7

Copyright © Ally Carter 2023
Plaid illustration © Anya D/Shutterstock

The right of Ally Carter to be identified as the
author of this work has been asserted by her in accordance
with the Copyright, Designs and Patents Act 1988.

All rights reserved. No part of this publication may be reproduced,
stored in a retrieval system, or transmitted, in any form, or by any means
(electronic, mechanical, photocopying, recording or otherwise)
without the prior written permission of the publisher.

Pan Macmillan does not have any control over, or any responsibility for,
any author or third-party websites referred to in or on this book.

3 5 7 9 8 6 4 2

Printed and bound by CPI Group (UK) Ltd, Croydon, CR0 4YY

A CIP catalogue record for this book is available from the British Library.

This book is sold subject to the condition that it shall not, by way of
trade or otherwise, be lent, hired out, or otherwise circulated without
the publisher's prior consent in any form of binding or cover other than that
in which it is published and without a similar condition including
this condition being imposed on the subsequent purchaser.

Visit **www.panmacmillan.com** to read more about all our books
and to buy them. You will also find features, author interviews and
news of any author events, and you can sign up for e-newsletters
so that you're always first to hear about our new releases.

For the GGs. I'm so proud of you.

chapter one

HER

Here's the thing about waking up with no memory in the middle of the night, in the middle of the street, in the middle of Paris: at least you're waking up in Paris. Or so the woman thought as she lay on the cold ground, staring up through a thick layer of falling snow at the Eiffel Tower's twinkling lights.

She didn't know about the bruise that was growing on her temple.

She didn't see the drops of blood that trailed along the frosty white ground.

And she absolutely, positively didn't remember why she was lying in the street like someone who had tried to make a snow angel and fell asleep midswoop.

I should finish my angel, she thought.

I should get up.

I should go home.

But she didn't actually know where home was, she realized. So why not take a nap right there? It seemed like an excellent plan. After all, the snow was fluffy and soft, and the world was quiet and still; and sleep was such a wonderful thing. Really, the best thing. She didn't know her own name, but she was certain that sleep had to be her favorite hobby ever, so why not close her eyes and drift off for a little while? Really, no one would blame her.

But then she heard the low moan of the motorcycles—the shouts of the men. And a figure appeared over her, blocking out the Eiffel Tower's shimmering glow, casting a shadow in the middle of the night. Blurry. Dark. And shouting, "Get up, Alex! Run!"

So my name is Alex, the woman thought. Just before she realized she was probably going to die.

HIM

He was going to kill her. Yup. It was just that simple. At that place and time, he had two items on his to-do list: 1. Find Alex. 2. Kill Alex. The third item would have been *Save Alex*, but he'd decided to scratch that one off in Venice. By the time he'd tracked her to Marseille he had added *Maim Alex*.

But now they were in Paris. And Paris meant he was six days, three car chases, two shoot-outs, and one very questionable exit from a fast-moving speedboat into his hunt. So *Kill Alex* really was his only option.

As soon as he found her.

Luckily, he just had to follow the trail of blood to the body that lay, almost lifeless, in the middle of the street. He was so angry when he thought she was already dead. But then she stared up at him, a distant, dreamy look in her eyes. *Alive.* And for the life of him he didn't know whether he should be glad or disappointed.

But then he heard the roar of motorcycles, drawing closer and closer like a noose.

And he yelled "Get up, Alex! Run!" because Kozlov's men were closing in. Which meant that, soon, the badges would follow. Interpol. CIA. MI6. Maybe Mossad if they were especially unlucky. And he hadn't been lucky since Moscow. So he had to hurry. Because they all wanted to kill Alex, too, and he couldn't let them beat him to it.

"Alex, get up!"

"No, thank you," she said, turning onto her side like a little girl who had no interest in going to school.

"Get up. Now!"

"Five more minutes."

"Alex!"

That was when she saw the gun in his hand, cocked and ready.

Fear filled her eyes and, for a moment, she looked like a woman who had never seen a gun before—like she'd never seen *him* before. Which was the moment he knew something was terribly wrong. With her. With him. With this. Alarm bells were sounding—too loud—in his head.

"Alex?" he asked as shots rang out. Instantly, he spun and took aim, and by the time he turned back, Alex was already gone.

chapter two

HER

She didn't know how far she walked. Or how long she walked. Or even why she kept walking when the wind was so cold and the sky was so dark that it felt like even the moon was sleeping.

But she had to keep walking. Moving. Plodding along because the only thing scarier than walking was stopping. Because if she stopped they might catch up with her—either the men on the motorcycles . . . Or Mr. Hot Guy . . . Or even her own thoughts . . .

So she kept walking. And made a mental list:

THINGS THAT I DON'T KNOW
A list by Alex Whatshername

* My name.

Sure, Mr. Hot Guy had called her Alex, but she didn't have a last name. Or a middle name. Or even a real first name. Was she an Alexandra or Alexa or Alexis? What did her mother call her when she was in trouble? What did the teachers say on the first day of school and then she'd have to say, *actually, I go by Alex*? Alex had no idea. Which wasn't as worrisome as—

* Who is after me?
* Why are they after me?
* How long have they been after me?
* Exactly what are they going to do when they find me?
* Where am I going to go?
* What am I going to do when I get there?

4

All she knew for certain was that her head hurt and her stomach growled and yet the thought of eating made her belly ache for entirely different reasons.

So she kept walking, grateful for the snow that was falling in thick waves, blocking out the glow of the streetlights and filling up her footprints almost as soon as she made them. But she also cursed the snow because her boots were definitely *not* made for walking and her toes felt like icicles that might break off at any moment.

Her knees were bleeding, and her thighs burned; there was a hole in her black tights and a stitch in her side, and even her collarbones hurt. *Her collarbones!* Two bones that served absolutely no purpose beyond making a girl look great in boatneck sweaters.

So Alex leaned against a rough brick wall in a narrow alley and tried to focus on what she *did* know.

THINGS THAT I DO KNOW
A list by Alex Whatsername

* My name is Alex.
* I'm in Paris.
* The hottest guy I have (probably) ever seen is after me.
* He's not the only one.

For a moment, Alex wondered if maybe she should look for a police station or a hospital? Maybe she should lie back down and finish that snow angel? Maybe she should dig herself a snow cave where the temperature would never drop below thirty-two degrees (because she didn't know her own name but she'd somehow pulled that fun fact from her disastrously empty brain).

But, most of all, Alex wanted to cry. Because the one thing she was sure of was that she was having a very bad day, and it was probably going to get worse. So crying seemed okay under the circumstances.

Really, the only bright side was when she realized that her dress had pockets. Because (a) dresses with pockets are the best dresses, everybody knows that. And (b) her pockets contained a tube of lip balm, a few euros' worth of heavy coins, and a black plastic card that looked like a room key. But, sadly, there wasn't a hotel name on it anywhere—just a small golden C—which wasn't any help at all.

Oh, and there was also a crumpled tissue that she dug out and used to dry her runny nose.

It was still snowing, even though she was pretty sure it rarely snowed in Paris. But it wasn't as hard now, and the streets were suddenly too bright for the middle of the night. Shops were closed and apartments were dark, but the streetlights reflected off that pure white stillness, casting the city of light in an otherworldly glow. And Alex hated it. Partly because of Mr. Hot Guy and whoever else was chasing her. But also because there was a comfort in the darkness, of being lost in the storm. Isn't that why people go to Paris? Why they take long walks down unfamiliar streets, roaming for hours, trying to lose themselves? Trying to forget?

It was terrifying that, eventually, she was going to have to try to remember.

Somewhere in the distance, church bells chimed. Overhead, she heard a sickening crack and a big patch of snow slid off a steep roof and landed with a *splat* a few yards behind her. And still there was the low buzzing hum of the motorcycles circling closer and closer.

And closer.

She darted into the doorway of an empty restaurant. The window was a mirror in the darkness, and Alex gasped at the sight of the woman who stared back. Unfamiliar hair on an unfamiliar face, a bruise growing on her temple. Tearstained cheeks and grimy fingers, clothes torn and stained with blood that may or may not have been her own.

Alex was looking at herself. But she was also looking at a stranger. And the tiny smidge of hope that she'd been carrying for the past two hours faded away, because her memory didn't come back with her reflection. Not a speck. Not even a twinge. And Alex couldn't shake the feeling that the truth had fallen out along the way—was lying in the snow somewhere, waiting for a thaw.

On the other side of the darkened glass, a television flickered and glowed, and Alex watched as headlines filled the screen.

ALERTE! *Alert.*

DANGEREUSE! *Dangerous.*

N'APPROCHEZ! *Do not approach.*

"Ooh! I speak French!" Alex exclaimed, entirely too pleased with herself. But after hours of nothing, that felt like *something*. She wanted to make a T-shirt that said I SPEAK FRENCH. She wanted to stroll up to the first person she saw and stick out her hand and say, *Hi! I'm Alex, and I'm bilingual!* She wanted to pretend that her memory might come back as soon as she started thinking in the right language. But the past stayed blank, and the present stayed cold, and the future loomed before her, totally empty.

When the television changed, it took her a moment to realize what she was watching. It must have been some kind of surveillance footage because the picture was dark and grainy. It looked like some kind of fight. No. *An attack.* The word *fight* implies an even playing field, but this was one woman against a dozen men.

Except, Alex realized, *the woman was winning.* Punching and kicking and throttling men twice her size. *What's French for badass?* Alex was just starting to wonder, when the picture froze and it was like an echo.

Because the face in the dark window blended with the face on the screen, like a *before* and an *after*. The hair on the screen was red—not blonde. She didn't have any bruises and the clothes were different. But the face . . . the face was exactly the same, and for a moment, Alex couldn't breathe. Couldn't move. She couldn't even think until her brain translated the words beneath the picture: *Fugitive. Armed. Extremely dangerous.*

And Alex said the only thing that made any sense at all: "I'm a spy!"

chapter three

Jake Sawyer wasn't a spy. He loathed that word. Hated it on three continents and in four languages. Because it was the word a child uses, a novice, a civilian.

Sawyer was an Operative. Capital O. He wasn't some Hollywood actor with a stable of stunt doubles. He didn't have a fancy car with an ejector seat. He'd never even worn a tuxedo. This wasn't a facade for him. Not an act or a role or a persona. No. It was his actual, literal life, and he was tired. Of his life. And his job. And his missions and his enemies. And even his allies.

Especially Alex.

She'd looked half dead lying in the street, and for a moment, he'd thought he was too late. But then she'd stirred and looked up at him, squinting in the darkness, clearly concussed. And Sawyer felt something he hadn't felt in a long time. Pity. Compassion. Warmth even though it was cold enough to freeze off some of his favorite parts of his anatomy.

He had known Alex, worked with Alex, trusted Alex for almost five years. But that was the first time he had ever seen her look like that, weak and defenseless. Fragile. And that was maybe the scariest thing of all.

He had to find her. The only thing that gave him any comfort was that if he couldn't find her, then no one else could either. Probably. Hopefully.

She'd get to a safe house, lie low. Barricade herself behind a dozen walls and booby traps, because Alex was one of the most paranoid people he'd ever known. And he was a spy.

No. *Damn it*. Operative.

The snow wasn't falling quite as hard, and, soon, the city would wake up and start digging out. Already, there were lights going on in bakeries, vents blowing out steam that smelled like fresh bread. His stomach growled, but his feet kept moving. And, for once, he didn't bother checking his tail.

After all, if someone was back there, he'd already be dead.

HER

Sirens. Had they always been there, breaking through the chilly air? Alex wasn't sure. So she kept her head down and her steps sure. *Nothing to see here*, her posture said. *I'm no one to worry about.*

I'm no one.

But the snow was so deep she missed a curb, and the ground wasn't quite where she thought it would be, and that's how she turned her ankle and ended up lying in the middle of the street. Again.

"Are you okay?" a voice rang out, and Alex pushed upright to see a man rushing down the sidewalk, heading toward her. The street must have seen some traffic at some point, because the snow was packed down, pressed into icy tracks, so she had to be careful as she climbed to her feet.

"Here, let me help." Her first instinct was to scamper away, but her ankle hurt and her head swirled, and the man looked like someone's grandfather—like he couldn't wait for retirement so he could focus on his real passion: documentaries about World War II. "Are you lost? Can I call someone?"

"Oh, I'm fine!" (*She wasn't fine.*) "I know where I'm going!" (*She had no idea where she was going.*) "I don't need any help." (*She absolutely needed help.*)

She knew how she looked—ripped tights and snow in her hair, bruise growing at her temple and bloody knees. But she was committed now. No backing down.

"Just kind of a klutz!" She pantomimed sliding on the ice—which made her actually slide on the ice, catching herself at the last possible moment.

"I'll walk you wherever you're going," the man said helpfully. "You shouldn't be out here alone in this."

But she wasn't alone. She had a tube of lip balm and four euros; a soggy tissue and a voice in the back of her head—warning bells that were starting to quiver.

"Here. Allow me to—"

"You're speaking English," she said for reasons she absolutely did not know or understand.

He laughed. "Well, so are you."

She took a step back. And then another. And another, tripping on the curb again but managing to stay upright somehow. "Why? Why are you speaking English?"

He gave the slightest chuckle. "Because you are."

"You spoke first. You should have assumed I was French. Why didn't you speak to me in French?"

The warning bells were blaring now, too loud in her head—even before she felt the building at her back. Before she knew that she was hemmed in, trapped. Even before the man's face changed, that gentle, documentary-watching smile morphing into a sinister smirk as he said, "Because, Alex, languages never were your forte."

She wanted to run, but the man was too close. The sirens and motorcycles were too loud. And, overhead, there was a cracking sound, a splintering snap that she'd heard before, so she stopped thinking. And pushed.

It was untrained and unskilled and must have been wholly unexpected because he stumbled back and looked at her like *is that the best you've got*. But then the crack came again and, with it, a sheet of ice that cascaded down the steep roof and crashed into the man, knocking him off his feet. She could see him under a mountain of snow, partially buried. Totally stunned. And she didn't wait a single second.

She ran.

To the end of the block. To the end of the street. To the ends of the earth. But it wasn't far enough. It wasn't fast enough, because the sirens were deafening now. And when she turned, she saw the motorcycles bearing down. She turned again and tried the other way, but the street was a dead end. She could feel a wall of muscle and motorcycles and men closing in as she took a shaky step back, icy legs melting into a puddle in the street.

Okay, she told herself. She had this. Didn't she? After all, everyone knows that when spies wake up with amnesia, their brains might forget things like names and hotel room numbers, but their muscles always remember—hands moving independently from their bodies, years of training taking over. So when you think about it, Alex didn't have to *know* anything. She just had to wait for her body to go on autopilot, for her training to kick in.

As the men climbed off their motorcycles and stepped closer, she could see their black eyes and bloody lips, and Alex tried to remind herself that *she'd* done that. She'd seen herself on TV, beating these same guys to a pulp. She'd just have to do it again.

"Looking for me, boys?" she said with as much swagger as she could muster, and the goon squad looked around.

"Uh . . . yes?" Goon Number One said like it might be a trick question.

"Give us the drive, Alex," another goon barked.

Then it was Alex's turn to be confused. "Drive? What drive?"

They laughed like she was making a joke. They obviously didn't know that a half-used tube of lip balm was currently her most prized possession.

"Hand it over, and no one has to get hurt." The first goon looked at his friends and laughed again, a mocking sound. "Or we will make it hurt less. Which is better than making it hurt very much. It is your decision."

His voice sounded like vodka tastes, and a small voice in the back of her mind whispered, *Russian*. They were Russian. And for a moment she just stood there, waiting for her memory to come surging back. For something—anything—to feel familiar, but the only thing in her head was a dull, throbbing ache and the knowledge that she was outnumbered. But that was okay, Alex told herself. Her muscles would know what to do. Her muscles would remember.

"See? About that? Funny story. I actually don't have any drives. Really. Scout's honor." The men stepped forward, and Alex tried to sound as tough as possible as she said, "So I guess we're gonna have to do this the hard way."

And then she attacked.

Or . . . well . . . she *tried* to attack. Really. She did. She ran right up to the biggest, meanest-looking man of the bunch and kicked. Hard. But she slipped on the ice and fell. "*Ow.*"

For a moment, the men just stared at her, confused. Like maybe they were the ones locked inside a really bad dream. But Alex knew the clock was ticking. Soon they'd realize she was vulnerable, down there on the ground, so she did the one thing she could think of—she kicked again. Straight up between the biggest man's legs.

She heard him scream and watched him fall, and for a moment his buddies just stood there, staring. But then they pounced, and it was just like the movies: a blur. Head pounding. Blood spraying. Bodies dropping, one after the other. It was like she hadn't even moved and yet . . .

Wait, she realized. She *hadn't* moved.

But, suddenly, she could see the sky. The falling snow. And the look on Mr. Hot Guy's face as he stood over her, a smoking gun in his hand and bleeding bodies all around them as he said, "Damn it, Alex. I should kill you myself."

chapter four

Sawyer had a hold of her arm and he wasn't letting go. Not yet. Maybe not ever. They'd been walking for five minutes, but Alex still had that strange look in her eye—like she was going to turn around and bolt. Like there was anywhere she could go that he wouldn't find her. Like he didn't know all her usual haunts. Like they hadn't been his haunts first.

But she hadn't gone to any of their usual places this time, had she? From the looks of her, she must have been roaming the streets for hours. Which wasn't the dumbest thing he'd ever heard. Predictability was death, after all. And nothing about Alex had been predictable tonight. At all.

He took another look at her. Blonde wig. Plaid dress. A too-thin jacket and boots with a flimsy heel. Could she even run in that getup?

"Cool cover, Alex. Did you really think the sexy librarian look was going to keep the goon squad from recognizing you?"

"What's that supposed to mean?" She looked like someone who couldn't decide whether or not to be offended.

"It means *what the fuck are you wearing*?"

She gasped. "Don't use that language with me!"

He stopped. He stared. "Who the fuck are you to comment on my f—"

"Language!"

"—reaking language?"

"I-I-I-" She stammered. Her lip even quivered just a little. If it was an act, it was a good one. "I don't remember."

"What the hell . . ."—he started, but she glared— "*heck* was that back there?"

"Muscle memory."

"Oh yeah?" he scoffed but she just looked annoyed.

"You know, when your body remembers actions because of years of intense training and repetition," she said calmly—slowly—like he was the one who was off his game. So he flicked her on the end of her nose. "Ow!"

"You remember this?" he said, and then he flicked again. Not hard. But not teasing.

"Stop that." She smacked him on the arm—so weak it wouldn't kill a fly.

It would have been hilarious if it wasn't also terrifying. "Come on, muscles. Remember."

He flicked her ear. She slapped his hand. And that's when he realized that Alex would have had his nuts in a vise by now, but this woman . . . girl . . . person . . . She narrowed her eyes and bit her lip and looked up at him like she'd been drawn by Walt Disney. Like she was innocent and pure and good. Between the blonde hair and the big eyes it was like he was looking at a stranger.

"Will you take off the wig at least? I can't take you seriously in that . . ."

He reached up and tugged, but the hair didn't pull free. Instead, the woman shouted, "Ow!"

And then he *knew*. He just knew.

When he spoke again, his words were a whisper that echoed in the night.

"You're not Alex."

chapter five

HER

You're not Alex.

The words were still out there, floating like the snow and twice as cold. She looked at him—Mr. Hot Guy. And she thought about changing his name to *Mr. Annoying Guy*. Or *Mr. Just Shot a Dozen Men in the Street Guy*. She briefly considered *Mr. Just Saved My Life Guy*, but she didn't like that one as much for obvious reasons.

Because he was looking at her like he'd just remembered the gun was in his hand. And he was glad to have it there. Like it might be useful.

The hand flexed. The gun shifted. And his grip on her arm tightened. She thought she might bruise.

"Let me go."

She was definitely going to bruise.

"Who are you?"

"Let me go!"

In the next moment, a wall was at her back and the man was in her face. Chest against chest. Him breathing out while she breathed in, surrounded by a fog of warm breath and cold terror as his voice dropped lower.

"Who. The. Fuck. Are. You?"

Her lip quivered as she admitted, "I don't know."

He let go of her arm. (*Good!*) But then he moved his hand (as in the gun-free hand . . . as in the *best-case-scenario* hand) to her throat. (*Not* good!)

And he brought his mouth closer to her ear and whispered, "Try again."

He was so much taller than she was. Even in her uncomfortable boots. Broader too. Not bulky. Not like the kind of guy who thinks all his troubles will be over as soon as his neck and his biceps are the same circumference as his thighs. More like the kind of guy who owns a truck and everyone hints around whenever they need something moved.

He seemed . . . competent. Freakishly competent. Scarily competent. And strong. Really, really strong. A fact she couldn't help but remember when the hand around her throat began to squeeze.

"I'm not going to ask again." The words hinted at impatience, but he had the look of a man who could wait all day. Immovable object, meet very, very stoppable force.

"I don't know!"

Her eyes were hot, but she didn't cry. She wasn't exactly sure why she wasn't crying. She felt like crying. She felt like curling into a ball or maybe digging that snow cave. Maybe she was just too tired and hungry—and, let's face it, probably concussed—for a proper breakdown. Yeah. That was it. Everyone knows that to do a breakdown properly, you need snacks.

"I don't—"

"Stop lying."

"Do I look like I'm lying?" she shouted. "Your hand is on my jugular, how's my pulse? Look at my eyes. Look at my freaking tights."

"What?" he said because a pack of thugs in the street he could handle, no problem, but the word *tights* was throwing him for a loop.

"Do you think I'd be walking around like this if I had someplace to go? If I knew . . . I don't *know*!" she shouted even louder. Rage bubbled to the surface—like maybe there was a little fight left in her after all. Like there was a little of *her* left. If she could just remember where to find her.

She took a deep breath and met his gaze and was surprised, somehow, to realize that his eyes were blue. His eyes were pretty and soft and looked like springtime, but the rest of him was the coldest day of the year.

She tried again. "My entire memory goes back approximately"— she did the math in her head—"three hours? Four hours? When did you yell at me . . . the first time?" But she didn't really wait for an answer. "That's as far as I go."

He huffed then, a humorless sound. "So . . . amnesia? That's your story?"

"It's not a story." She turned her gaze away. "It's the truth."

He sunk his hands into her hair, cradling the back of her head in a way that should have felt really, really good. And sexy. And maybe kisslike. Yes. This definitely felt like a prekiss or midkiss or postkiss kind of situation, with those big strong hands running through her hair, except—

"Ouch!" Pain shot through her, sudden and quick, and she changed his name to *Mr. Doesn't Know His Own Strength Guy* because he kept probing, searching. "That hurts!"

And finally he stopped. "You have a head wound."

"Ya think?"

He didn't let go, but at least he stopped pressing where it hurt. His gaze dropped from her head to her eyes to her lips, and when he spoke again, the word was a whisper. "Fuck."

"Langu—"

"I thought she was lying." He squeezed his eyes tight and looked down at the icy ground.

"*Who?*"

"Alex." He looked at her like she was a puzzle and a missing piece. Both. "I didn't think she really had a twin."

He let her go and pushed away and, suddenly, it was colder without him blocking the wind and pressing all his muscly warmth into her. But then she processed what he'd said.

"Wait . . . Twin?"

He was looking at her oddly, like maybe he was the one who'd hit his head and woke up to find himself in a very bad dream.

"She used to say 'be grateful I'm the bad twin.' I thought she was lying."

She gave a nervous laugh. "Don't you mean joking?"

He glared. "Alex doesn't joke."

"But she lies?"

For the first time, he smiled. "Better than anyone."

chapter six

It wasn't Alex.

Sawyer believed her. He wasn't sure why. Maybe because no one—not even Alex—was that good an actress. Maybe because Alex had no reason to lie. Except no. That wasn't true. If the last few days had taught him anything, it was that he'd never known Alex at all.

"Excuse me, Mr. . . ." The woman started then trailed off, as if she was running through a long list of options in her head. "Gun Guy . . . Alex's Boyfriend Guy—"

But that made him laugh. Hell, that made him howl. He hadn't thought he was still capable of it, so he felt as surprised as she looked.

"I only mean . . . you have a gun. And you just shot a lot of people with it—not that I'm not grateful. I realize it was devolving into a *me-or-them* situation, and I'm very happy you chose me. So thank you. I'm sure you must be disappointed that I'm not the love of your life—"

"The *what*?"

"Alex," she said, like maybe he was the one who'd recently been unconscious. "I was talking about Alex."

"I know," he snapped. "But why the h—" She gave him a warning look. "—*heck* would you think *Alex* is the . . ."

"Love of your life," she reminded him.

"Yeah. You can stop calling her that."

"But—"

"Don't call her that. Ever."

"Okay. Um . . . partner? Significant other? How would you define your relationship?"

"Thorn in my side," he ground out then turned and started down the street.

"Ohhhhh," she said, falling into step beside him. "So you're in the early stages of . . . what? Friends to lovers? Enemies to lovers?" She looked a little concerned at that second one, but he had no idea what she was talking about.

"I don't have a lot of experience with head wounds, but you should probably get that checked out," he said, but then she darted out in front of him, surprisingly quick.

"It's clear that you're in love with Alex, and Alex is no doubt in love with you, but you're both fighting your obvious attraction, and—Hey!"

He was picking her up and pressing her against the side of a building, pinning her a foot off the ground so that they could see eye to eye. He couldn't take the risk that she would miss this. "Stop. Talking."

"But you clearly—"

He raised an eyebrow and she shut up.

"I'm only going to say this once. Alex isn't my girlfriend. She has never been my girlfriend. She will never be my girlfriend. She sure as hell isn't the love of my life." He didn't bother explaining that he didn't have one of those. Never had. Never would. There were some things that people with big Disney eyes would never understand, and the fact that love and covert operations don't mix was one of them. "And we are not"—he dropped her and made a gesture—"*anything* to lovers, whatever that means."

"There's no need to use finger quotes sarcastically here. Sarcastic finger quotes are not necessary."

"Alex is . . ." But that made him trail off. That made him think. And he didn't like what he thought about. At all. "Someone I thought I could trust. I was wrong."

All around them, streetlights were flickering off as the sky grew brighter, and he suddenly felt vulnerable there. Exposed. He needed to find cover, because the sun was rising and word was spreading and, soon, some people would come looking for vengeance and some would come looking for justice, but they were all going to bring a whole lot of trouble with them, and he wanted to be gone before they got there.

So he shoved his hands in his pockets and turned down another street, away from the sirens that were blaring in the distance.

"Yes . . . um . . ." He heard her running along behind him, stumbling in the snow and sliding on the ice.

"Are you sure you and Alex share the same DNA?" he tossed over his shoulder.

"No! Evil Twin is your theory. I did not throw out the option of Evil Twin."

"Stop saying Evil Twin."

"You're the one who said it!"

"But you're the one who keeps . . ." He trailed off and shook his head, longing for a small dose of amnesia of his own.

He looked back at where she stood in the snow, the horizon growing bright behind her as she stared at him like she wasn't quite sure whether he was a blessing or a curse. Which was okay. He didn't know either.

"Who are you? Who is she?" Her eyes were wet and her voice broke. "Who am I?"

Yeah. Alex never looked like that. Which was a shame. Doe eyes make for good cover. They were even working on him, and, just briefly, he wanted to take pity on her, put an arm around her—get her someplace warm and safe and off the grid. But he wasn't that guy. It wasn't his fault that she was that girl.

"Go home, Not So Evil Twin."

"I'd love to."

Well, that was easy. "Great!"

"How do I do that, exactly?"

"I don't know." He threw out his hands and spun on her, frustration seeping out of his pores. "I've been chasing your sister for six days across five countries. I've been shot at. Kicked. Punched.

Run off the road. Thrown out of a boat. Poisoned—but that was an innocent mistake. Never eat shellfish in Austria. In other words, I'm having a shit week, princess. And today's not looking any better. So—" He released his empty clip and slid in a fresh one. *Click.* "The Atlantic Ocean is that way." He pointed into the distance. "Start swimming for all I care."

He slid the gun into his waistband, pulled a bright orange cap from a pocket and tugged it on. Time to disappear.

"Not very covert, is it?" she said, and he almost laughed.

"That's the point, lady. Looking like you don't care if you stand out is a great way to blend in." He turned and started down the street, but she lunged out in front of him again, blocking the way.

"Are you going to find my sister?" she asked, and it was all he could do not to laugh. Or maybe cry.

"No." Sawyer shook his head. It was a relief to finally admit, "If Alex doesn't want to be found, I probably won't."

"But—"

"Look," he cut her off, too cold and too tired to pretend. "I've had one lead in the last week and she's right in front of me. *You* were my big break. But, lady, you were nothing but a waste of time and ammunition, so if you'll excuse me . . ."

He was almost free—he was almost gone—when a small voice came floating to him on the wind. "What's the drive?" He froze. "Those men . . . they said something about a drive, but I don't have it. I don't even know what it is. So . . . What is it?"

Sawyer took a deep breath. He really didn't have time for this. But for some reason he turned around anyway. "It's a flash drive."

"They want it. They think my sister has it. Why?"

"Because she has it!" On the other side of the street a man started shoveling the sidewalk, so Sawyer lowered his voice and pulled her into a darkened doorway. "Listen. Alex was a very bad girl."

"So you say."

"So *everyone* says. You know your friends from a while ago? The ones whose . . ." He trailed off as he looked down, noticing . . . "Oh hey. Their blood is literally on my hands. They work for Kozlov."

"Who's that?"

"Who's that?" He'd honestly forgotten there were people who didn't know. "You ever heard of the Russian mob? Evil oligarchs? How about gunrunners? Drug smugglers? Maybe a little human traffic—"

"I get the picture."

"Oh, I don't think you do. And I don't think you want to, but that's fine. Because he's not your job. He's mine. And up until a few days ago he was Alex's. She and I were *this close* to taking him down, but then your precious sister went rogue and decided to download his little black book onto a flash drive—*blow up the original*—and disappear." He let out a frustrated breath. "Alone."

"What's on it . . . this book?"

"Everything. Names. Contacts. Bank accounts. A veritable who's who of evil. The holy f—" *Glare.* "—freaking grail."

"What's it worth?"

He looked at her, cold. Impatient. And so fucking tired he could cry. "Her head." She gulped. "And I mean that literally. There's a whole John the Baptist component going on here."

"So a head that looks like . . ." She pointed to herself.

"Yup. That'll do."

He must have looked like he was trying to decide if it would be easier to transport her head *on* or *off* her body because she started slowly backing away, and with every dainty step he wanted to laugh.

"You just realized I can claim the prize and not kill your sister, didn't you?"

"I did indeed." Her voice cracked. "So, thanks for your help, but . . ."

"Stay right where you are, lady. I haven't told you the bad part yet."

Her throat worked while she gulped down a breath of icy air. "What's . . . the bad part?"

"Your sister was *supposed* to steal the black book and give it to her *other* bosses." It went against his training and his orders and about a dozen laws, so he couldn't actually tell her . . . Then he told her anyway. "At the CIA."

Something like triumph crossed her face, like she was on a game show and had just won a brand-new car. "So she *is* a spy!"

"No shit." He was running out of patience. And time. "But Alex didn't turn the drive over to the good guys, so now they're after her. And she pissed off the bad guys. Who are *also* after her. Basically, everyone with a gun in Western Europe is after her."

He took a deep breath and a long look at Alex's face and Alex's mouth and Alex's eyes, and he knew what the world would see: a fugitive. A target. A sitting-fucking-duck. So he had to admit, "And, I guess, you."

He watched her thinking, worrying, calculating until she realized: "So if I can't trust the good guys . . . And I can't trust the bad guys . . . Who else is there?"

He thought about it and huffed out a laugh, knowing he was going to regret the word long before he said it: "Me."

chapter seven

HER

He was lying. Definitely. Probably. He was almost certainly lying. But she was so tired she could barely stand upright. Her head hurt so badly she could hardly think. And the sun was so bright she could barely see, even though it was little more than a dot on the horizon.

"I'm a little concussion-y, so just to be clear . . . You're saying that my identical twin sister is a rogue spy who is currently on the run from the Russian mob and the CIA?"

"And MI6. Did I mention MI6? Oh. And Interpol."

"Is that all?" She was being facetious, but he shrugged.

"Probably Mossad." He noticed something on the street and turned his back, blocking them both from a passing SUV. "Make that an affirmative on Mossad."

The vehicle turned, and for a moment the street was empty. He glanced both ways, this total stranger with the bloody hands and blue eyes—and the gun . . . She couldn't forget about the gun.

She didn't know this guy. Heck, she didn't even know herself. So why was she thinking she could trust him?

Then he reached behind him and pulled out *another* gun, and, suddenly, that felt like two guns too many. She didn't know who she was or why she was there or how this had all come to be her problem, but she knew this wasn't her world—her life. And she knew what she needed to do.

"So . . . uh . . . where's the US Embassy?"

He didn't have to look as he pointed. "Six blocks."

She turned up her collar and shoved her hands in her pockets.

"Thank you for your help. I'm sorry to have wasted your time and ammunition."

Then she was off, stumbling down the icy street.

"Hey! Where are you going?" the deep voice called after her.

"Where do you think?" she said but didn't slow down.

"Okay. But just so you know, they'll shoot you on sight."

Well, that stopped her. Slowly, she faced him and tried to sound more confident than she felt. "No, they won't. I'm a US citizen. I think? Which means I'll be safe there. So thank you for your help, but . . ."

"Yeah. Okay." He shrugged. "They probably won't kill you, but they'll definitely assume you're Alex and ship you off to a black ops site that doesn't officially"—he did the finger quotes again—"*exist*. And that's assuming you can get past the ring of guys with names like Vlad and Igor who've been watching the embassy for the last two days. But, hey." He put his hands up in a move that screamed *don't shoot the messenger.* "All I'm saying is that if the embassy were safe, your sister would be there, but what do I know? I've just been her partner for the past five years. Have a nice walk, princess."

He pulled his cap lower and turned. He was leaving. He was walking away. She was almost free of him, when a little voice in the back of her mind whispered, *But what if he's right?* What if the embassy wasn't safe? What if there was *nowhere* safe? What if she was destined to wander those streets for hours—days? What if there was no place she could go or hide or . . . Wait, she realized. She had someplace to go.

"Do you know what hotel this is?" Suddenly she was digging in her pockets, trying to find the little plastic card.

He seemed extra annoyed when he turned back, looking at her like Alex must have stolen all the brains in the womb. "You have a hotel room? In your name? Is that where they found you? Do you have any money? What ID were you using? Have you been in touch with Alex?"

"Um, let me think . . . Amnesia. Amnesia. Amnesia. Four euros. Amnesia. And . . . amnesia. Any other questions?"

By that point she'd emptied her pockets and was standing on the icy sidewalk, hands cupped, everything she owned held out in front of her. She waited for his quippy reply, but he was too busy staring at the items in her palms like she hadn't spoken at all.

The key card. The euros. The tissue and the lip balm.

"What is it?" she asked because, suddenly, everything about him changed. His features softened and his lips parted and his breath fogged in the chilly air—it was the first time he had ever felt like flesh and blood. "What?"

"Alex uses that brand." He pointed to the balm like she'd just asked him to identify a body. "And no. I don't know a hotel with that logo. But I know you can't go there."

She tried not to feel too disappointed. Really, she tried not to feel anything. So she stuffed her worldly possessions back in her pockets and turned. "Great. Awesome. Now if you'll excuse me, I have a long swim ahead of me."

"Wait!" he called after her.

It took everything she had not to limp as she turned away and tried to climb over the big mound of snow that had been pushed to the side of the road. But she slipped because of course she did. And she ended up straddling the bank, which, it turns out, you can't really do gracefully. In fact, the only thing more awkward than getting *onto* a snowbank was getting off one.

"Hey . . ." He made a frustrated sound. "Let me—"

"Oh, don't worry about me! I'm *fine*!" she grumbled then just sort of . . . rolled. She staggered to her feet and winced but kept walking.

"You can't go to the hotel! Or the embassy. You can't go anywhere familiar!"

"Well, I have amnesia, which means *nothing* is familiar. So—" She gave him a double thumbs-up and wished it were a different finger.

"Hey!" He was jogging after her.

"I'm trying to make a dignified exit here!" she snapped back.

"Was that before or after you humped a snowbank?"

She turned abruptly, suddenly grateful for her anger. Really, it was the best medicine. Her body was full of adrenaline and rage.

"Hey!" he shouted. So much for the low profile. "If you want to get yourself killed, fine. You want to spend the foreseeable future being waterboarded? Be my guest. But I can help you. I am offering to help you. Come on." When he spoke again, his voice was soft and low. "Let me help you."

"Why?"

"So you'll be safe."

"What do you care if I'm safe?"

He looked up at the snowy sky and drew a deep breath. "I guess I'm just trying to be the good guy."

"I thought the good guys were trying to kill all the people who look like me?"

"Yeah." She started to change his name to *Mr. Looks Hot When He Smirks Guy* because she got a little dizzy when he said, "Well, lucky for you, I'm not all good."

chapter eight

HER

So that was how she ended up following a strange man with a gun through the predawn streets of Paris, stumbling along, trying to match his long strides with her own.

"Where are we going?" she asked.

"We have to get off the street." He pushed her down a snowy alleyway and glanced back over his shoulder. "Streets bad. Shelter good," he said like she was a kindergartner, which wasn't fair at all. Most kindergartners know their own names.

The wind seemed stronger then, snow swirling like a tiny blizzard, and she was momentarily grateful for his broad shoulders and deep voice. Even the slightly condescending tone she could handle because anger was like a fire now, her only source of warmth.

She wanted to ask him his name or his story. She wanted him to say it was going to be okay. She wanted to demand more details about this destination—this plan. But she also didn't want to jinx it because getting off the street meant no more walking and no more walking meant no more icy toes and uncomfortable boots. And maybe even no more shooting if a girl wanted to aim superhigh.

"So I don't suppose we can just . . . I don't know . . . *ask someone* where my hotel is and pop by real quick?"

"You want to *pop by* the hotel they may or may not know about?" He didn't actually laugh, but he gave the kind of breath that went with one. "Yeah. That's the one place we will *not* be going."

He peeked around the corner of the alley then took off walking down the snowy street, totally indifferent to the fact that she was probably down to six functioning toes by that point.

"But my clothes!"

"We'll get you new clothes."

"My passport!" she tried.

His laugh was as cold as the wind. "Yeah. You're definitely going to need a new passport."

"But—" She stumbled, sliding on the ice, and a strong arm wrapped around her, anchoring her against his side, and for a moment they just stood there, her trying to figure out why he smelled so good and him no doubt wondering whether or not he should just walk away. She was shaking and wet and half dead with fatigue. She wouldn't have blamed him.

"I . . ." *I want to know my name. I want to know where I live. I want to wash my face and brush my teeth and pull on at least three pairs of socks. I want stretchy pants and warm beverages and answers.* She wanted answers more than anything else, but he was right—of course he was right. She could keep complaining and die or she could keep walking and survive, and right then the choice seemed pretty simple. "You're right."

"I am?"

"Let's go." She could keep walking. She could do this.

But when he pulled her toward a patisserie on the corner she almost wept with relief. The air outside was warm and smelled like butter, but *Mr. I Don't Feel the Cold Guy* didn't even slow down. He just grabbed a long cashmere coat off a rack by the door and kept walking. He never even broke his stride.

"You just stole that!"

"Put it on."

"That's not mine."

"It is now. Put it on."

"But it's stolen property. I can't—"

"Look." He stopped in the middle of the sidewalk. "There wasn't a single customer in the place and employees would leave their coats in the back. So someone left it. I found it. Lost. Found. Put it on."

Suddenly, she remembered motorcycles and guns and John the

Baptist. Maybe stealing a coat wasn't the worst offense in the world? So she slipped it on and they kept walking.

When they passed another door, he reached inside and snagged a beret in the same shade of caramel.

"That I did steal," he said, but she put it on and didn't say another word.

She didn't know how long they walked down the narrow, winding streets of Paris, changing directions and dodging into alleys, doubling back and altering speeds. But they never, ever stopped.

"Should we get a taxi or something?" she tried after a while.

"Nope."

"Am I slowing you down?"

"Absolutely."

"I'm sorry." She was fully limping at that point. Her toes felt like bloody stumps.

So she wasn't expecting him to say, "Oh, no. The limping's fine. Limping's good, actually."

"Excuse me?"

"People notice gaits," he went on, more patient than she would have expected. "Posture. Body language. They don't know they're noticing it, but they do. You really want to lose a tail? Put a pebble in your shoe and something heavy in one pocket. But, hey, we don't have to because you're limping!"

"Uh . . . yay?" she said.

"That's the spirit!" He pulled her down another street.

"So if we're not going to a hotel or the embassy, where are we—"

"To a safe house."

"Oh, and we'll be safe there?"

"Yes," he said with exaggerated patience. "You can tell because the word *safe* is right there in the title."

She wanted to snarl at him. Or shout. Or cry. Or curl up in the snow and wait for the plows to come and push her away, but the man had blood on his hands, so the least she could do was keep walking.

It wasn't the nicest street or the shabbiest. Not the newest or the oldest. The apartment building was utterly nondescript in every way. But he was careful as he approached it, and she let herself have a small glimmer of hope that safe houses might come with soup and cocoa and tiny marshmallows. And also Band-Aids. She really, really needed a Band-Aid.

But as they neared the door, he shifted suddenly, steering her into an alley as if that had been their destination all along.

He was always cautious, but he was practically pulsing with awareness as he pulled out his gun. "Here. Hold this."

"I don't know what to do with that!"

"I didn't say *do* something with it. *Geez!* No! The last thing I want is for you to *do* something. Just"—his tone was especially gentle, like he was handing her a newborn baby—"hold it."

So she took it. The gun was heavier than it looked and warm from his hand and she was so focused on not accidentally shooting them both that it took her a moment to notice—

"Are you making a snowball?"

"Yup." He pressed the snow together, packing it tight; then he rose and tossed it at a third-floor window. But the alley was narrow and the window was high, and the snowball landed against the underside of the sill with a splat.

"Shit," he said, then he bent down and made another one, aiming for the tall window like they were at some kind of carnival and he was trying to win her a prize.

"Um, just out of curiosity, why are we throwing snowballs at a window?"

"The paint on the door was chipped. I just need to check on something," he said as the third snowball crashed into the glass.

The sound was so loud it almost echoed, and she worried someone might come investigate and find her holding a gun that had recently shot a very large number of very large men.

But he just stood there for a long time, quietly staring up, until—

"Hey!" He sounded almost hopeful and more than a little bit relieved. "I guess we're clear." He gave her a smile that could fire the sun.

And then the apartment exploded.

chapter nine

"Shit. Shit. Double shit. Shit."

"Language," the woman beside him said, sounding far too prim for someone who still had a Glock in her hand and—*Oh shit*, he realized. She still had his Glock in her hand.

"I'll take that." Sawyer grabbed the gun with his right hand and reached for her with his left, felt her delicate fingers interlace with his even though that had to be sloppy tradecraft. Hand-holding. It served no purpose whatsoever and slowed reaction times by at least a second. But her fingers were like ice and her eyes were huge, and she was shaking despite the orange-red flames that were breaking through the—

Oh right. *Flames. Windows. Explosion.* That's what made Sawyer pull his gaze from hers and drag her to the end of the alley.

"Uh . . . what just happened?" It was a fair question, but he was still too mad to answer.

"Shit! That was my second favorite safe house."

And that seemed to be the thing that threw her because she blurted, "You have *two* safe houses?"

"Oh, don't kid yourself, lady, I have way more than two. That was just my second favorite."

Black smoke billowed behind them, and sirens blared in the distance, coming this way fast, so Sawyer let go of her hand and tugged off his cap—crammed it in his pocket—and threw an arm around her shoulders because that *was* actual tradecraft.

Covers come in all shapes and sizes, and right then the best place to hide was in the middle of the sidewalk. Head down. Beautiful woman beside him. Looking to all the world like two lovers taking a stroll through falling snow."

"Just try to look natural," he told her.

"None of this is natural!" she shouted, then gave the quietest scream he'd ever heard.

"Okay. Maybe try a little harder than that."

He pulled her tighter against him and felt her sink into his side. Maybe because she understood the cover but more than likely because she was simply exhausted. Hell, even he was tired and he wasn't walking around on stilts and with a concussion.

He wouldn't have blamed her for complaining or arguing or just lying down in the street and giving up, but she kept walking on those impossible heels, and he knew, suddenly, that Alex wasn't the only tough one in the family. With every icy step his respect for her grew a little more.

"So what was that back there?" she asked when they reached the end of the block.

He didn't let himself look back. "Kozlov likes motion-sensitive booby traps—the kind that go boom with a little vibration."

"Boom?" she echoed, sounding very young and very sleepy. Damn concussions.

"Boom."

"So now we go to one of your other safe houses? Maybe one that's close? And warm? And full of food and first aid essentials?"

She sounded so hopeful—like there was some place on Earth where they'd both be truly safe. But Sawyer had learned a long time ago that safety wasn't just an illusion—it was a lie. And it would get you killed.

"Now we go to Plan B." He steered her toward a sidewalk café. The tables had been cleared of snow and set with crisp white linens but no one looked twice as he pulled a butter knife from a tray and slid it up his sleeve in one smooth motion.

"Plan B requires a knife!"

"Calm down. It's a butter knife. On a scale from one to machete, butter knife is down . . ." He gestured toward the ground and risked a glance at her.

"That's what has me worried."

Honey-colored hair fell across her shoulders in a wave, and the beret sat on her head at a jaunty angle that served to hide her growing bruise. She was bundled tightly inside that cashmere coat, the belt tied with a flourish, so all in all she didn't look like a woman on the run. She didn't even look like Alex, which was the idea, of course. But it made him forget who she was and why she was with him.

That's the risk you run with covert operations—not that you'll forget your lies but that, someday, you'll start to believe them.

They weren't a couple out for a walk in the snow. They hadn't woken up naked and sated and spooned together beneath the weight of a warm duvet. And yet there she was—gazing up at him with her big green eyes and rosy cheeks . . . She looked so pure and good that it was like biting into something way too sweet. Sawyer wasn't used to it. He felt his breath catch. But that was probably because of the cold. Or the smoke. Or both.

She pulled the balm from her pocket and ran it across her lips—rubbed them together for good measure.

Yeah. It was definitely both.

"Trust me, there's no need to be worried," he told her.

"Oh?" She brightened.

"You should be terrified," he said then pulled her toward Plan B, praying like hell that he still had a few tricks up his sleeve.

chapter ten

HER

When she saw the signs for the Metro she felt a small glimmer of hope. Metros have seats, after all, and shelter and vending machines. And she had some euros burning a hole in her pocket. "Ooh! Are we going to take a train?"

But *Mr. Never Gets Tired Guy* didn't even answer. He just kept walking, past the escalators and over a bridge and down a steep embankment. And then he was pulling at a chain-link fence, squeezing between the rusty wires like this was the most normal thing in the world.

"So that's a no on the train then," she said, numbly following him to the underside of the bridge. The snow was deeper there, blown into drifts by the wind. But they were out of sight, at least, and she leaned against the cold stone arch, shivering with her hands in her pockets, admiring the view. Turns out, in Paris, even the graffiti was lovely.

She could feel his gaze on her, though. Appraising and more than a little warm as he ducked his head and looked at her over the turned-up collar of his peacoat. There were big flakes of snow in his dark hair, and everything about him looked like he'd just stepped out of an ad for really expensive man perfume. She could see it now: *Covert—the new fragrance by Calvin Klein.*

Maybe in her real life she was used to handsome men looking at her. But probably not. She felt her face go hot in the cold air. She was half dead and who knew when she'd last brushed her hair, so she felt pretty certain this wasn't the good kind of staring. But there was no use trying to read a face that the Central Intelligence Agency had trained to be unreadable.

"What? I'm just resting. Is resting allowed?" she asked because even though she didn't want to sit in the cold, wet snow, she could lean, so she was going to lean as long as possible.

She didn't expect him to say, "You're doing great, you know?"

His gaze was more intense now, and something about the kind words and gentle tone . . . They broke her. "Then you must have a concussion, too." Her voice cracked. Her eyes burned. And, suddenly, his face morphed from *wry appreciation* to *dude who is terrified a woman is going to start crying*.

"Don't . . . No. It'll come back. Your memory . . . It'll . . . Don't worry."

"Yeah." She wiped her eyes and forced a smile. "I'm sure once I see something familiar . . . I mean, as soon as we find Alex . . ." She let the sentence trail off, waiting for him to say something. *It was obviously his turn to say something!* But he stayed quiet. And somehow the silence was a warning. "We *are* going to find Alex, aren't we?"

"Sure." He pulled the knife out of his sleeve and turned his attention to a big metal box covered with scary-looking stickers. Which was better than looking at her, evidently.

"Wait. You *do* have a plan to find my sister, don't you?"

"Of course."

"Then what is it?" She pushed off the wall and prowled closer, but he stayed silent. "Well . . ."

He exhaled a weary breath. "We don't have to find Alex. When the time comes, Alex will find us. Okay?"

Except . . . it wasn't okay. It wasn't even a little bit okay. "So just to be clear . . . the plan is you have no plan."

"Look." He wheeled on her, and for the first time, he seemed just as cold, just as tired, just as cranky as she felt. "Alex doesn't need us. Alex doesn't need anyone. While we're out here getting our asses handed to us, Alex is curled up somewhere warm and dry, sharpening her knives and biding her time, which is exactly what we're going to do just as soon as we get someplace safe."

And that's when she realized he wasn't just looking at the big metal box, he was using the butter knife to unscrew the lid.

A lid that was covered with stickers that said things like RESTER DEHORS!

Keep out, her tired brain translated.

HAUTE TENSION!

High voltage!

DANGER!

Danger!

Okay, so maybe the last one wasn't all that impressive, but that didn't keep her from blurting, "Did I tell you I speak French?"

"Congratulations," he said, but he didn't even glance in her direction. He was too busy prying open the box that *obviously wasn't supposed to be opened*. And, suddenly, she was terrified for entirely new reasons. She took a wobbly step back.

"So . . . uh . . . those signs say that this box is very, very dangerous, and, oh, that is a lot of wires . . ." Yes. Dozens of wires. Hundreds of wires! "So maybe you should put the lid back on the scary box and—"

He looked at her. "Or I could do this."

And then he slammed the metal knife into the wires and circuit boards. Screams filled the air, echoing off the stone archway and dissolving into the snow as terror shot through her veins like the electricity that was shooting through . . .

Wait, she realized a moment later, *he* wasn't screaming. He wasn't shaking or falling to the ground or smoking. Really, he should have been smoking by that point! But he wasn't. No. *He was laughing!* And she realized that he might still die because she might kill him.

"You!" she shouted as he used the knife to pry the guts out of the big Box of Death. "Why aren't you dead? How? That's—"

"Fake," he said, still chuckling while she just stood there, gaping like an idiot. "Lady, there are very few things that are universally feared, and death by electrocution is one of them." He gave a rueful smirk as he revealed a compartment that was hidden behind all those (evidently fake) wires. "Which makes them a great place to hide . . ."

He made a *ta-da* kind of gesture as he pulled out a backpack and unzipped it, pausing to inspect giant wads of cash and passports. And guns. So many guns.

"What is that?"

"It's a Go Bag," he explained as he slipped it on. "So go." He gestured for her to lead the way, but she just stood there.

"That was mean," she said and he gave her the kind of grin that had probably been working for him for ages, little boy charm on a hot guy face. Forget the guns, that combination alone was lethal.

"I know. I'm sorry." He smirked again and glanced down, looking up at her from beneath his dark lashes.

"I thought you were being fried like an egg. I thought you were dying. I thought . . ." Her voice cracked again and, suddenly, his expression softened. The little boy smirk faded into genuine remorse-slash-guilt-slash-regret-slash-*oh shit! Please tell me she isn't going to cry again.*

"Hey. It's okay." He reached for her and she pulled back.

"You've probably been waiting to play that joke on someone for ages, but—"

"No," he said quickly, but the look that crossed his face wasn't anger or impatience. It was surprise. Like he'd only just realized—"I don't joke. With anyone." He gave a quick, quiet laugh like *I'll be damned* then looked at her. "I guess that makes you special."

His grin was warm and soft, but when she spoke, her voice trembled. "Just . . . don't die on me, okay? Fake or otherwise."

"Hey." He reached out—hand lingering too long in the air—like he might want to hug her but he didn't know how, so he rubbed the back of his neck instead. "I'm sorry. I won't do any kind of dying. I promise."

And, like it or not, she believed him.

chapter eleven

HIM

Paris was having a snow day, or so it seemed. Ladies in cashmere sat beneath portable heaters at sidewalk cafés. Kids filled the streets, dragging sleds and shouting taunts.

The world was bright, and the sky was clear, and it would have been so easy to believe in clean slates and second chances. Sawyer felt the woman beside him turning, taking it all in like she was one of those little kids, racing toward the park, savoring the feel of snowflakes on her lashes.

So he had no choice but to pull her close, hand on the back of her head, looking to the world like he wanted her within kissing distance at all times.

"Oh! Are we going to make out so no one gets suspicious?" she asked, and Sawyer almost fell on his ass.

"What?" he asked.

"You know?" she said with exaggerated patience. "When two people are about to get caught, so they kiss suddenly and—"

"No!" he said a little too sharply. "We're not doing that."

"Oh. Well. We could. If we need to. For our cover. I'm here for whatever we need to do, cover-wise."

She was so matter-of-fact, gazing up at the stretch of skin between his jaw and his throat like she didn't know that's exactly where you'd need to cut to make him bleed. So he weaved his fingers through her hair and pulled her closer.

The shell of her ear was cold against his lips as he whispered, "Fun fact: facial recognition software only works if it can see your face."

"Oh. Right." She gave a little shiver and tucked her chin low as if bracing against the chilly wind.

And walked right into a streetlight.

"Ow."

"Here." He sighed and slipped an arm around her shoulders, suddenly missing the cover of darkness. But at least now they had the cover of people. People on their way to work. Kids playing hooky from school. Tourists stumbling along, not knowing if being in Paris during a blizzard made their luck incredibly good or exceptionally awful.

"Well, now that we have the official bag of going—" she started.

"That's not what it's called."

"—*where* are we going? Exactly? I mean, what's Plan C? Or Plan B-point-one? Because . . ."

She was looking up at him with her too-big eyes again, so he glowered down and pushed her head toward his shoulder.

"We keep our *heads down* and we walk. We don't make contact with anyone we know and we don't go anyplace we've ever been before. Predictability is death."

"Well, that's convenient," she muttered. "Because I don't know a soul."

He felt the weight of her head against his shoulder, the soft brush of her hair blowing across his cheek—and Sawyer, who had been alone in the world for more than a decade, wondered what it would feel like to wake up with no friends and no enemies, no ghosts and no regrets. He wondered if he'd miss them.

"That's not true." He couldn't help glancing down at her. "You know me."

He was just getting ready to chastise her for looking up at him again. And smiling at him. Again. It was sloppy, sloppy tradecraft and he needed to tell her to stop it, but that was when he saw the blue jackets and swirling lights. A police car was inching down the street and two cops were on the sidewalk, pushing through the crowd. Looking for something. Someone.

And, suddenly, Sawyer wanted to turn. Run.

Up ahead, the officers were examining every face, scanning every tourist. He felt the Glock at the small of his back as he scanned the crowd. He could get her out of there, but not without a whole lot of collateral damage.

"What's wrong?" She was looking up at him. Again. He could see the cops out of the corner of his eye, coming closer, so suddenly, he stopped thinking and pushed her against a shop window.

The glass was cold but her skin was warm as he pressed his palms against her cheeks, cradling her face, blocking her from view and looking into those green eyes that seemed to be asking a question there was only one way to answer.

"For the cover," he said.

And then he kissed her.

Except he didn't. Actually. Technically. Mouths didn't touch. Lips didn't part. But his nose brushed against hers and their heads tilted, faces fitting together—his body leaning against hers like a shield and a blanket and a promise, saying *I have you; I'll protect you; I'll keep you warm. And safe. And more* . . . It almost certainly looked like more.

It was the kiss equivalent of the junction box—something fake and deceptive, screaming *Keep away! Don't look too closely!* But he could smell the scent of her lip balm (cherry) and the moment was thick with foggy breaths and roaming hands and the privacy that comes from being lost inside another person. She gripped his shoulder and shifted her hips like she preferred him to the cold pane of glass at her back, and so he held her tighter. Longer. And when she gave a quick little intake of breath that faded into a long, deep sigh, a jolt of lightning went through him—like he was finally feeling a spark.

It couldn't have lasted more than a few seconds, but when he pulled back, it took an embarrassingly long time for him to remember—"There were . . . uh . . . cops."

"That's okay." She was tugging on her beret. She was rubbing her lips. But when she spoke again, she sounded smug. "I told you that was how you undercover."

By the time they reached the Seine the streets were thick with tourists, and Sawyer felt himself start to breathe.

"Keep your eyes peeled for a taxi," he told her.

"Really?" She looked like he'd just said he'd buy her a pony if she was a very good girl, and Sawyer, a known curmudgeon, bit back a grin.

It was the most exposed they'd been and yet it felt safe for that split second, with the gilded statues standing guard at the edges of the bridge and the Seine rushing beneath them and the tourists all around.

They were almost okay. They were almost safe. They were almost gone. But the alarm bells that lived in the back of Sawyer's mind—the ones that had kept him alive for the last ten years—were starting to quiver. Then vibrate. Then blare. Because two Range Rovers were turning onto the bridge.

Instantly, he ducked his head and whispered, "Don't panic. And don't engage. If we get separated, go to the nearest Metro station. Take the first train east, three stops. Get off. Wait."

"Why?" Her eyes went wide and terror filled her face because she might have been a civilian, but she wasn't a fool. "What are you—"

Which was when the shooting started. The sound of gunfire didn't belong on that snowy street, but it was there, reverberating off the bridge and icy water. Windshields shattered and people screamed. Vehicles started pinging off one another like bumper cars as they tried to escape, stalling the progress of the SUVs. But Kozlov's goons were already out and heading their way.

"Go!" The Glock was heavy in his hand as Sawyer pushed her toward the far end of the bridge, dodging behind the blocked cars for cover, clinging to some hope that this wasn't the way he was going to die. He had hoped for something far more noble and much, much later.

But then the motorcycles appeared on the other end of the bridge, blocking the way. They were officially surrounded.

"Uh . . ." She grabbed his arm and backed away. "That's bad, right?"

"Yup," he told her as he pulled out a second gun because sometimes quantity beats quality and he was all out of ideas.

As they hunched behind a Mercedes, he studied the woman who hadn't asked for this, trained for this, chosen this life at all. It wasn't her fault. But she was going to die there just the same. She was going to die unless he saved her. And, suddenly, he really, really wanted to save her.

"Get low. Stay low. And run like hell."

Then he rose and started to fire. A moment later, he risked a glance in her direction but she was already gone. He fought against the wave of unexpected disappointment, reminded himself that it was a good thing—the right thing. That maybe she'd get clear. Maybe she'd survive. Maybe . . .

But then he felt a presence at his back and saw a shadow on the snow—rising, blocking more and more of the sun until he found himself turning, staring up at the woman who was standing on the icy railing, looking to all the world like some kind of avenging angel. Or crazy person. Really it was a toss-up.

Kozlov's goons must have been as surprised as Sawyer felt because, for a second, no one fired—no one moved—as she stood surrounded by the blinding white light of sun on snow.

"Or I could do this," she said.

Then she threw out her arms. And jumped.

chapter twelve

HER

It had seemed like a good idea at the time. Really, it had. After all, if both ends of a bridge are blocked, then the only options left are the sides, right?

But that was before she found herself standing on the icy railing, realizing for the first time she might be afraid of heights. And sharp falls. And water? *Oh no. What if I'm afraid of water? What if I don't remember how to swim? Or, worse, what if my lifelong fear of water meant I never even learned how to swim? What if . . .*

But then she noticed the silence. All the Russians had stopped shooting and started staring. It was just a matter of time until they remembered that they were supposed to be shooting *at her.*

So she threw out her arms and jumped, flying through the air and landing with an incredibly unladylike splat. But not a *water* splat. Oh no. More like a *bug on a windshield* splat in which she was most definitely the bug.

Or so it felt as she looked down through the glass-covered roof of a boat full of tourists who were staring up at her. One man even picked up his camera. She forced a smile as he took a picture—*click.*

Her body hurt. Her head hurt. Her pride hurt. Then her whole body bounced as—*splat*—someone landed right in front of her, spread-eagled, a gun in each hand.

"Hi," he told her.

"Hi," she said back.

And that's when the tourists started to scream.

And that's when the Russians started to shoot.

And that's when the big pane of glass that half his body was lying on shattered and *Mr. Looks at Her Like She's Crazy Guy* started to fall. She grabbed his arm and held on, helping him swing onto her section of glass.

"Go!" he shouted, and they both got up and started running down the very long, very narrow boat that looked like a floating greenhouse. There was so much very clear, very shatterable glass that was . . . well . . . shattering behind them as Kozlov's men fired and the boat took off, racing farther and farther away from the bridge and the Russians and the guns.

"Are you going to yell at me?" she shouted over her shoulder, breathing hard even though she'd only gone thirty feet.

"No!" he yelled. "Yes! I don't know. Ask me again later."

Which seemed like an okay plan because, at the moment, she had a lot on her mind.

Like how some of the tourists were still screaming and others were still taking pictures, not to mention the sudden realization that anyone beneath her could totally see up her skirt.

"Hey!" she shouted at a man who was aiming his camera in a most undignified way. She stomped on the glass. "Pervert!"

Mr. Hot Spy growled and made a gesture that, considering he had a gun in each hand, made the guy turn as white as the snow, and she felt warm all of a sudden.

"Aw. Thanks."

"Any time." Then he growled again because it was a very growly kind of morning.

"Okay," she said as a big gust of wind came rushing down the Seine. Her hair blew wildly around her as the boat sped up, roaring away from the Russians and the bridge.

With every passing moment, Kozlov's men got a little farther away. But it was just a matter of time until they jumped on those motorcycles and chased after them. Streets ran along the river, after all. And there were other bridges. It wouldn't be hard to get ahead. They'd only gone two hundred yards.

"What do we do now?" she asked just as the wind caught her stolen hat and whipped it off her head. On instinct, she lunged for it, but she lost her footing on the sloping glass. In the next moment, she was sliding. She was falling. Until, suddenly, arms like steel bands wrapped around her waist and hauled her against a hard chest, blue eyes staring down at her, colder than the wind.

"Damn it! Are you trying to drown? Are you trying to die? Are you trying to—"

There was a shadow over his shoulder, long and dark and coming this way fast.

"Duck!" she yelled, shoving and tackling him to the top of the boat as they passed under another bridge.

So that's how she found herself straddling a stranger on top of a floating terrarium while two dozen tourists took photos from below.

"At least the . . . uh . . . shooting stopped?" she tried.

"For now," he warned. And he was right, she remembered, as they floated out from underneath the bridge and back into the sun. It was just a matter of time until the goon squad caught up with them. They'd be exposed. They'd be dead. Or nearly. They would most assuredly be pre-dead!

He must have sensed it, too, because he pushed her off him and cocked both guns.

"Any more bright ideas?" he bit out, but all she could do was lie beside him, watching as another—even lower—bridge passed overhead, old beams and arches close enough to reach.

Wait. Close enough to . . .

"Yeah. Actually. This."

She let go of her beret, let it flutter to the icy water below as she reached up and grabbed hold of one of those ancient beams—wrapped her arms and legs around it and held on for dear life as the big glass boat moved on.

Without her.

She looked at Mr. Spy Guy . . . Hot Guy . . . Gun Guy . . . watched him drift away, and all she could think to call him was *Mr. Please Don't Make Me Do This Without You Guy*.

Then he cursed under his breath and shoved his guns into his pockets and reached for one of the braces overhead and held on.

And the boat floated away.

Without them.

chapter thirteen

"Well, this was just an excellent idea."

"Thank you," she said, sounding mildly pleased with herself until she turned, staring at him through the shadows. "Wait. Are you being sarcastic? Because it might be the brain injury, but I'm finding it really hard to tell if you're being sarcastic."

Given that they were both clinging to a pair of old, rusty beams, feet scraping and scrambling for purchase as they held themselves horizontal over the icy water of the Seine while eight-to-twelve Russian mobsters with semiautomatic weapons searched the streets overhead . . . Yeah. Sarcasm seemed okay under the circumstances.

"Well?" she asked, sounding impatient.

"Give me a minute. I'm trying to decide."

For a moment, he savored the silence, but it didn't last long. There was yelling up above, deep, guttural shouts that carried on the wind and seemed to echo through the old stone and rusty metal.

"What are they saying?" she whispered.

"Keep searching," he translated softly. "Find them."

Motorcycles roared to life and took off, probably chasing after the boat full of tourists. But Sawyer knew they might not all go. And some would certainly circle back. Soon, the banks of the Seine would be swarming with mobsters and badges. He wasn't certain, but he thought he heard her gulp. He knew exactly how she felt.

"So we've got a small window." She winced and shifted and almost lost her grip. The sharp edges of the beams were cutting into his arms. They had to be cutting into hers, too, as they held on, forearms wrapped around the metal. He felt ridiculous. But also . . . alive.

"So what do we do now?" she asked.

"I don't know," he admitted. He could hear traffic overhead and feel the cold wind blowing down the river. A few minutes before, he'd thought they were going to have to carry him away in a body bag, so it wasn't that he wasn't grateful. It was more that this felt like a classic frying pan/fire situation.

"Do you have any ideas?" he asked as the air around them seemed to change. Another boat was passing below. And, suddenly, her eyes went wide. Her whole face glowed. She didn't look at all like Alex when she said, "Yeah. This."

And then she just let go.

He tried to lunge for her, catch her, pull her back and hold on tight. But she was too far away and he felt her slip through his fingers. He looked down, expecting to see her disappearing into the icy water, but, instead, she was rolling across the deck of the ship that was moving in the opposite direction from the boat full of tourists. And, presumably, the Russians.

So he dropped down beside her, onto a deck that looked like it had been put in a press and squeezed flat. Everything was horizontal, collapsed. Smushed. There were disassembled deck chairs and tables, and *was that a big umbrella*? But it didn't matter what kind of ship this was, all he cared about was that it was still moving and, in three seconds, they'd be exposed unless . . .

"Ooh! What's that?" she asked, but he didn't have time to think, or look, or debate the strategic advantages of hiding under patio furniture because he was too busy pushing her under that giant tarp, pressing against this total stranger and squeezing in—lying perfectly still.

Waiting for the danger and the world to pass them by.

chapter fourteen

HER

Really, as escape plans went, they could have done a lot worse. The tarp was thick and the water was smooth, and to the world at large, the deck no doubt looked entirely empty. The sounds of Russian curses and police sirens were growing more faint by the moment as they lay side by side in the bright sun that filtered through that piece of off-white canvas, casting them in a hazy kind of glow.

They'd been together for hours, but somehow it felt like she was seeing him for the first time. Probably because he was close. *So very, very close.* It would have been rude not to admire his dark eyelashes and strong jaw, or how he kind of needed a shave but in the way that actually looks really, really nice.

She wanted to curl up and cry, but he was barely breathing hard—as if he did this every day. And, hey, maybe he *did* do this every day? She didn't know him. She didn't even know . . .

"Uh . . . can I ask you a question?"

"Yes. That is a gun in my pocket."

"Uh . . . okay. Good to know. But I was just going to ask . . . Uh . . . What's your name? I mean I'll understand if you can't tell me. You probably go by a number like Agent Double-O-Forty-Seven or—"

"That's not how it works."

"I mean, you probably have a code name. So if I have to call you Falcon or Dragon or the Denominator—"

"I think that's for math?"

"—or something I totally will. It's just . . . what *should* I call you? Or, well, is there something I can call you that won't make you have to kill me? Because I'd really prefer it if you weren't trying to kill me, too."

They were close enough that she could feel his breath, the rise and fall of his chest. She could see that his eyes were really two shades of blue—a ring of navy surrounding the light, clear blue that she had noticed on first glance.

So it was no surprise that she was close enough to see the little muscle in his jaw tighten. She just didn't know what to make of it.

"Sawyer." His voice was as warm as the sunlight that glowed around them. "Call me Sawyer."

"Okay, Mr.—"

"Just Sawyer," he said with a little more edge—like he wasn't in the mood to be prodded with questions just to fill the very long stretch of very awkward silence.

"Yes. Absolutely. Just Sawyer it is. You can call me . . . Well, I guess that's TBD. But that would be a terrible name, right? T-B-D? What kind of name—"

"I'm gonna go out on a limb and say you ramble when you're nervous?"

She had to smile; she might have blushed. Because, turns out, awkward silences weren't her thing at all. "Well, now there's at least one thing we know about me. Or two, I guess. After all, you know Alex, so you already know me better than I do."

He looked like he wanted to say something, but he shifted instead, trying to get comfortable on the very hard deck. She started to scoot away and give him his space, but an arm shot around her waist and pulled her closer.

"No. Don't. The tarp can't move and we don't need your foot sticking out, so . . ." He shifted, and suddenly, parts of her were intertwined with parts of him, and she felt herself stop breathing for reasons that had nothing to do with covert operations.

"Right. Yes. Thank you for the reminder that we are currently in the middle of a slow-speed getaway. Did they teach you how to do this at spy school?"

"There's no such thing as . . ." He trailed off and shook his head, but she saw the corner of his eyes crinkle—just a little. His jaw ticked again. And there was a note of wry amusement to his voice when he said, "No. Nothing in my training prepared me for this. Exactly."

"Great. So we're the same then."

"Well, I wouldn't say we're *exactly* the—"

"Just winging it. Sawyer and the Denominator."

He was looking at her like her head wound might be far more dangerous than he'd previously thought, but then his jaw did that thing again—that little tic. And, suddenly, she was warm for the first time in her entire memory, with the tarp blocking the wind and the sunlight filtering down and the heat coming off the man beside her.

She thought about giving him a little more space but didn't. Because when cuddling with a hot guy is a matter of life and death, you just go with it. And, soon, her cheek was resting on his shoulder and her feet were nestled between his and the world felt quiet and still, despite the gentle rocking and listing of the boat.

"We're probably to the Eiffel Tower by now," he said softly.

"Really?" She desperately wanted to peek out and look, but his grip around her tightened.

"Don't. Move," he warned, shifting until her hand ended up resting on his chest because where else was she supposed to put it?

"We'll just wait here until we get some distance," he told her.

"Right. Good."

So she lay there in that golden light, still and warm and oddly comfortable for the first time in her entire memory, while Paris passed her by.

chapter fifteen

HER

"Hey, lady. Hey . . . you. Alex's sister . . ." The words filtered through her hazy mind, as soft and warm as the light. "Hey, Denominator!" he said a little louder, and she bolted up just as a strong arm pulled her down and pinned her to the deck beneath him, and that was how she came awake, staring up at the most beautifully rugged face she'd ever imagined.

"*It's you.*" She didn't even try to hide the wonder in her voice.

"Yeah." He chuckled softly. "Who else did you expect it to be? As far as I know . . ."

"You're the only person I know?" She remembered gunfights and bridges and snow falling through streetlights. And him. He was the only thing in her entire memory that didn't make her want to cry.

"Well, yeah." *Well, duh.*

"I thought you were a dream. I thought this"—she gestured to what she'd started to think of as their *Tiny Cocoon of Not Dying*—"was a dream. Or a nightmare."

"That's understandable," he said then inched away. "Anything coming back yet?"

She stretched as much as she could without really moving and racked her mind, but it was as blank as the canvas that covered them. She shook her head and bit back a yawn. "How long was I out?"

"Thirty minutes or so."

"Oh." She didn't know why she felt so disappointed. Did she want it to be longer or shorter? She had no idea. "How far have we gone?"

"I'm not sure. But probably far enough."

He was careful as he lifted the tarp and peeked outside, but the sunlight cut across her face, blinding her. The wind sliced across the deck, freezing her. All she wanted to do was curl up and go back to sleep, but the man who was crouching on the deck, surveying the scenery and assessing the threats, didn't agree.

"Come on." He pushed the tarp back a little farther. "It's safe to stand—no more bridges."

So she made herself crawl out into the sun. It felt good to stretch, at least. To look around at the outskirts of Paris and feel semi-confident that no one was going to shoot at her. Because, well, the bar . . . it wasn't all that high, but a girl has to have some standards.

It was the first chance they'd had to really examine the boat. Ship? Maybe in her other life she was a nautical badass, but in this one she was a woman with a sore head, ragged tights, and a full bladder. So she was perplexed to see something that looked like a putting green. Dozens of collapsible tables and chairs. The tarp they'd been lying under seemed to be a massive shade of some kind. Someone would probably come up there and raise it eventually, but for the moment, they were alone.

"Is this a giant yacht?" she asked, confused, because it had to be hundreds of feet long but it was also low enough to pass under all those bridges.

"No." He shook his head. "I think it's a river cruise."

"Ooh! I've always wanted to go on one of those!" she exclaimed but he looked at her.

"How can you possibly know that?"

"Because everyone wants to go on one of those," she said, feeling indignant.

"I don't . . ." he started but trailed off. "Never mind." Then he quietly headed toward the back of the ship. When they reached the edge of the top deck, he said, "Give me a second," then dropped to his belly.

So she dropped to her belly.

He sort of army crawled toward the edge.

So she sort of army crawled toward the edge.

He peeked over.

So she—

"Stop doing that!" he spat.

"Stop doing what?"

"Just . . . wait there," he said with exaggerated patience before leaning over to peer at the deck below.

It extended farther than the top level, with at least fifteen feet between them and the frothy strip of water that spread out in their wake.

"Ooh," she said, and he spun on her.

"I thought I told you to stay back." He was whispering, but he was also kind of shouting. She wasn't sure how that worked exactly but she guessed it was something they taught at spy school.

"What are we looking for?" she asked just as a voice drifted up from down below.

"Melanie! What should we do with the luggage for the Michaelsons?"

She and Sawyer scooted back just as a woman came up a staircase, a young man on her heels.

The woman, Melanie, stopped on the little deck and looked back at the younger man. "The Michaelsons' flight was canceled because of the storm."

"But they shipped their luggage ahead. It's here. What should I . . ."

"Take it to storage. Oh, and bring up a case of white? Lorenzo's running low."

The young man must have said something, but the words were lost on the wind and soon there was nothing but the sound of birds overhead and the water lapping against the hull and . . . silence.

The deck below them stayed empty, and Sawyer studied her, a *now-or-never* look on his face as he slid over the edge. Maybe she really was afraid of heights, she realized as she looked down and he looked up, impatience all over his face.

"Come on," he whispered.

"It's high."

"It's not even ten feet."

"That's high!"

"You've jumped off two bridges in the last ninety minutes!"

"People were shooting at me! Guns are scarier than heights. It goes *guns*"—she drew an imaginary line in the air then dropped her hand ten inches—"*heights*. Everybody knows that!"

"I have a gun," he mumbled under his breath. For a moment, he looked like he was considering pushing her overboard. But instead he held up both arms like she was a toddler who was refusing to go down the slide. Oh, how she wished there were a slide.

"Come on." He cast a nervous glance in the direction of the disappearing woman. "I'll catch you."

Maybe it was the words . . . Maybe was the gesture . . . Maybe it was the tone . . . But somehow she believed him. Sure, it was probably just because a sprained ankle or broken leg would slow them down even more. But *why* didn't matter. It was enough that it was true, so she inched toward the edge.

"Any day now . . ."

And rolled onto her belly.

"Oh, we're doing it this way," he said, stepping closer.

And lowered herself down as far as she could go.

She was just starting to contemplate how long her arms could hold her when she heard a chuckle and felt the cold wind on the back of her thighs.

"Uh, you may want to drop . . ."

"In a second."

"Okay. But just so you know your skirt got caught on something and I'm looking at your—"

She let go. She fell.

And, sure enough, he caught her.

chapter sixteen

HER

The balcony led to a vacant room that must have been a restaurant. It was all glass and chrome and rich, soft leather. She wanted to lie down in the round booth in the corner and sleep for a thousand years. She wanted to make snow angels on the plush carpet.

Carpet angels, she thought. Those had to be a thing.

But she stayed behind Sawyer because if she was in front of Sawyer there was no guarantee he wouldn't look at her butt again and he'd probably seen enough of that for a lifetime. So behind Sawyer it was.

And Sawyer kept moving. Through the nice, empty restaurant and out the doors, then down the walkway that ran along the edge of the ship, water rippling beside them.

"Okay," he said, voice low. "Stay on my six. Keep your head down and don't engage. The water is cold but not freezing. If you have to, jump. Then—"

"Head to the nearest Metro station, take the first eastbound train three stops and wait."

He looked back at her, an annoyed gleam in his eye. "I'm trying to decide if you're being sarcastic."

She actually had to think about the answer. "You know? I think I might always be a little sarcastic?"

He looked like he preferred being shot at as he mumbled, "Great."

They crept farther down the deck, but eventually he raised a fist into the air as if she was supposed to know what that meant.

"What does that—" She heard it then, the tinkling of glasses and the low hum of small talk floating up from somewhere below.

"Back up," he said and she spun, but it was too late. The woman from before was already heading toward them, a very skeptical look on her face.

"Hello. I'm afraid you're on the wrong deck, the captain's reception is in the promenade lounge—one floor down."

She saw his hand inching toward his waistband—and the gun. Not that he was going to use it . . . Surely he wasn't going to use it! But it was probably like breathing to him. Like saying *excuse me* whenever you heard a sneeze. But still . . . *gun!* And she couldn't help herself, she lunged between him and the woman who was carrying a tray of . . . *ooh! Shrimp!*

"Yes. Right. We were just exploring the boat. Or ship? You call it a ship, don't you? I get so confused. Jet lag! Isn't that right, sweetheart?" She cast a too-big grin over her shoulder at Sawyer.

"Yes," he said coldly.

She watched the woman—Melanie—take in her ripped tights and too big coat. Their tired eyes and windblown hair. "I thought I knew everyone on board, but . . ."

"Oh!" She didn't know where the words came from—she just knew it was too late to hold them back. "We were running soooooo late. First, our flight was canceled. The weather! Who knew Paris got blizzards? Then we got a different flight on a different airline into a different airport. But the car service had a flat tire—we are never using them again, let me tell you. And, well, long story short, we made it! Didn't we, sweetheart?"

She gave Sawyer a pointed look, but his reply was the same flat, "Yes."

"*Whew.* Needless to say, we are so glad to be here! Are you Melanie? They told us we'd need to talk to Melanie?"

But Melanie looked leery. And confused. "I'm sorry, who told you?"

"Oh, I don't think I got his name." She looked back at Sawyer like, surely, between the two of them they could remember. "It was a man. And he was European."

She was willing to bet her life savings—all four euros' worth—

that most of the staff was European, and the beleaguered look on Melanie's face told her she was right.

"Oh, well, yes. I usually greet most guests, Mr. and Mrs. . . ."

"Oh, didn't I say?" She didn't have to turn around to know that Sawyer was reaching for his gun again—or maybe he was just getting ready to toss her overboard. In any case, she didn't see any choice but to exclaim, "We're the Michaelsons!"

chapter seventeen

The first time Sawyer ever went undercover he had to live with a group of violent extremists whose leader hadn't left their own private mountain in six years. Eventually, Sawyer got what he needed but his exfil went to hell and he ended up sleeping in a cave for nine days.

Damn, he missed that cave—would have given anything to be there rather than here. There was no polite chitchat in the cave, no nosy women saying things like "I'm so glad you made it! Welcome aboard the *Shimmering Sea!*" which, he gathered, was the name of the ship that, as far as he could tell, was strictly a river vessel and wouldn't go out to sea at all.

Well, at least the *Shimmering Sea* came with booze. And . . .

"Food!" His *wife* practically dove for a tray of crab puffs.

Cramming one in her mouth, she turned her back on Melanie and whispered, "For the record, if I'm allergic to shellfish, and this kills me? It was how I wanted to go."

The woman—Melanie—couldn't have heard, but she was still staring. Maybe it was their windblown hair and bloodstained clothes, but she had a curious gleam in her eye as she said, "Well, you must have had quite the ordeal."

"You have no idea." Sawyer reached for a glass of something that looked very old and very expensive and took a nice, long swig.

But then Melanie's expression changed. There were practically little hearts in her eyes as she exclaimed, "It would have been a shame for you to miss your honeymoon!"

Sawyer choked on his thirty-year-old scotch. "Our . . ."

"Honeymoon!" his *wife* said, reaching for him. "Because we're married. And in love. So in love! And—Ooh!" She reached for a tall glass of champagne. The little bubbles were still floating toward the top, trying to escape. He knew exactly how they felt, he thought as he plucked it from her hand.

"Hey! I was drinking—"

"Concussions and alcohol don't mix, darling," he said, and then he drained it.

Melanie's eyes went wide as she noticed the bruise on his *wife's* temple—the streak of dried blood in her hair. "Oh no! What happened there?"

And for once his blushing bride had the sense to ... well ... blush.

"Oh ... I ... See, it was ..."

"The Mile High Club," Sawyer cut in. "Harder to join than it sounds." Then he commandeered a whole tray of tiny meatballs.

"Oh. Well." Melanie turned bright red. "If you'll excuse me, I'll just ..." She stepped away. Which was just as well because his *wife* was staring at him like maybe looks really could kill after all.

"I can't believe you did that!" Her hand connected with his stomach and he winced.

"Ow. You know, I think you're getting stronger."

"That nice woman is going to think that you ... That I ... That *we* ..."

Sawyer didn't even try to hold back his laugh. "You should have thought about that earlier, *Mrs. Michaelson.*"

He shouldn't have loved the blush of her cheeks—that rushed little intake of breath. A part of him was still looking for his exits and sizing up the crowd, but another part couldn't take his eyes off the woman who had turned the approximate color of cocktail sauce.

He'd never tried to tease Alex. Probably because Alex would have cut his tongue out. But he liked making this woman blush and stammer and squirm. Luckily, he didn't have to think about why because Melanie was heading toward them, a pair of room keys in her hands.

"Here you are. Sorry we didn't have them for you right away.

We're just so glad you made it! You both seem so . . . in love?" Melanie probably didn't mean for it to sound like a question.

"Oh, yes," his blushing bride said. "I love being Mrs. Michaelson. Gonna make him carry me over every threshold on this ship. Really, I'm just so happy I could pee myself." But then she stopped, inched closer to Melanie, and lowered her voice. "No. Seriously. I could pee myself."

Melanie straightened, back on the job. "Well then, let's show you to your suite."

chapter eighteen

Sawyer peered through the crack in the draperies, looking over the banks of the Seine. The Eiffel Tower was far behind them by that point, the Louvre and the Ritz a million miles away. Hopefully they'd left Kozlov's men in the *Shimmering Sea*'s glistening wake as well, but he wasn't going to bet on it. He didn't bet with anything but his life.

So Sawyer stayed behind the gauzy curtains of the honeymoon suite, listening to the sound of water. And humming.

In the five years he'd known Alex he had never heard her hum, but her sister did it all the time when she thought no one was listening. Also when no one was shooting at them. Which, to be fair, hadn't been terribly often in the hours that he'd known her. But now she was locked away in a bathroom that looked like something from a very old movie about very rich people, so she must have felt safe because she'd been humming for five minutes.

But Sawyer . . . Well, Sawyer checked his Go Bag and his guns.

When the bathroom door opened, he had just finished reloading the Glock and was sliding it into his coat pocket.

"Good timing. You ready?"

He headed for the door. According to the ship's itinerary, they wouldn't dock until tomorrow morning, so they were either going to have to jump or hitch a ride on another low-hanging bridge. There should be one coming up and he didn't want to miss it.

But the new Fake Mrs. Michaelson was stumbling out of the bathroom, looking a little more alive but a lot more exhausted and he had to remind himself that adrenaline might be a powerful drug, but the crash was a kick in the teeth if you ever let it happen.

So he grabbed the backpack and repeated, "You ready?"

"For what? To sleep a hundred years?" She threw out her arms and crashed onto the king-size bed and sighed. "Ooooh. *Thread count* . . . Can you make sheet angels?" She moved her arms and legs out and together over and over . . . soft sheets against bare skin. She sighed and moaned. "Ooh, this is nice. You've got to feel—"

"No!" His voice was rougher than he intended. "Come on. We gotta . . . Where are your shoes?" He started looking around for them. "Get up. Stay with me. Come on."

"*Noooo*." She sounded like a petulant child and he felt like a cranky stick-in-the-mud but that didn't change things.

"We've got to keep moving."

She pushed herself up on one elbow. "We are! We are literally moving right now. See?" She pointed to the countryside that was drifting past those gauzy curtains. And she was right; of course she was right. They were moving. And they were sheltered. But that didn't change the fact that Kozlov was the least of their problems.

"We've got to go. Now."

"Why?" she asked.

"Because Kozlov might not know where we are at the moment, but the guys who work for him? They're not gonna give up. And if that's not bad enough, any minute now a whole lot of agencies are going to retask a whole lot of satellites and, lady, once that happens, there won't be anywhere to hide. So *we can't stay here*."

"Why not?" She sounded wide awake and ready for a fight. "Is this one of your safe houses?"

He looked around the opulent suite. There were mirrors on every surface and literal mints on the pillows. He'd never been more insulted in his life.

"No."

"Is this someplace you'd come on your own?"

"No."

"Someplace you've been before?"

"Of course not."

"Is this something a seasoned undercover operative would do?"

He tried—and failed—to bite back a laugh. "Not hardly."

She narrowed her eyes. "Then this is *exactly* where we should stay. Predictability is death, right?"

He prowled closer to the bed, but she just smirked up at him—like this was some kind of verbal Krav Maga and she could use his own force against him.

"Now look—"

She scrunched up her face and lowered her voice. "Streets bad. Shelter good."

"Hey, I don't sound—"

"I thought we were supposed to keep moving?" She climbed up on her knees as he leaned down, the two of them suddenly eye to eye, skin flushed, heat pulsing between them.

"We are!" he said a little too loudly.

"I thought we were supposed to find shelter?" She was shifting on her knees and inching closer, like she might launch herself at him at any minute.

"We are!" She was just right there—so close he could smell a hint of mint on her breath. Her lips were plump and the color of cherries, and for one brief moment he wasn't sure if he should kiss her for real or smother her with a pillow.

But before he could do either she fell back onto the bed so hard she actually bounced. "Well . . . we are literally moving right now. And we're sheltered. And—" She pushed up. "Maybe I *am* a spy!"

"You're not a spy."

"I'm *good* at this."

"You're not that good at—"

"Ooh! Tiny cheeses!"

He wanted to lecture her about countersurveillance and evasive maneuvers, but she had already plucked a plate off the bedside table and was taking a bite of a soft white cheese. She gave the kind of moan that should never be associated with dairy, and Sawyer felt his pulse tick up.

"Oooh yesssss."

"Don't—"

"Here. Take a little bite." She offered him the plate. "Just a nibble."

"No nibbling. There's no nibbling in covert operations!"

She picked up an olive and took the world's daintiest bite then looked at him from beneath her lashes. "Your loss," she whispered, and Sawyer's mouth went dry.

"Come on." He coughed and choked. "We've got to . . ." But she was already pulling the bedspread around her and turning over and over before giving another long, low sigh.

"Oh, this feels good."

"Stop. You're messing it up."

"Of course the bed's getting messed up." She flashed a cheeky grin. "We're on our honeymoon."

"No. We're—"

"It's so warm"—she kept rolling—"and tight and—"

He made a sound that was part groan and part moan and, suddenly, she wasn't the only one feeling tightness in the lower half of their body. "We have to get off this ship!"

"Why?" She tried to sit up, but she'd wound herself into the middle of a blanket burrito and now she was stuck. Which served her right. At this rate, Sawyer was going to need a cold shower. "Why can't we stay right here?"

"We just . . . it's not safe."

"Fine." She pulled her arms free and propped herself up on her elbows. She'd stopped making those erotic cheese and blanket noises and was, instead, staring daggers. He almost longed for the time when she was deeply in love with a piece of brie. It was better than being on the receiving end of a look that reminded him of Alex. "Do you know where my sister is?"

Because Alex. It would always come back to Alex and his mission and his job and his life. Beautiful women with pink cheeks and doe eyes had no place in Sawyer's world, and he couldn't let himself forget it.

"Well, *do* you?" She crossed her arms.

It was hard to make himself admit, "No. I don't."

"Do you know where we can find that flash drive?"

He was a little too quiet for a little too long before he swallowed. "No."

"Do you have access to a nearby safe house that absolutely, positively will not blow up when we get there?"

That time, Sawyer had to think about the answer. There was a place they could go—a place that was secret. And safe. And a day's drive away. But he hadn't been there in decades, and he was really hoping to keep the streak going a little longer—preferably for the rest of his life.

"Well . . . is there?" she prompted, and slowly, he shook his head. "No."

"Do you have any idea how to stop this Kokopov—"

"Kozlov."

"—person and end this thing?"

She sat there for a long time, willing to wait him out and make him say it. "No. I don't."

"Then where are we going to go? Huh? What are we going to do when we get there? We don't know *anything*! Except my feet hurt. And my head hurts. And right now—at this moment—one hundred percent of my memories are about running, and I can't . . ." Her lips quivered and her voice cracked and, with it, his defenses, his resolve—maybe even part of his soul. "I just can't . . ."

"Hey." He dropped down on the bed, but she was still too far away and wrapped up in way too many layers.

"I don't know who I am!"

"I know." He inched closer but she didn't fall into his arms, which . . . well . . . he didn't want her to anyway.

"I don't know what happened to me or how I got to Paris or why or . . . I don't know anything except this bed is very big and these sheets are very soft and those little cheeses are very good, and I just need something good, Sawyer. I just . . ." She wasn't crying. It was like she'd lost her tears when she lost her money and her memories and her name. "I don't know who I am."

There were several hours of daylight left, but it was suddenly dark inside the honeymoon suite. Shadows lined her face, and he'd never felt more defenseless than when he sat there, watching her demons win.

Sawyer couldn't tell her who she was. He couldn't track down her memories. He might not even be able to track down her sister. But that didn't mean he couldn't do something.

He looked around. There was a pad of paper and a pen by the phone, so he got up and grabbed them, tossed them on the bed beside her. "Do me a favor and get this pen to work, will you?"

At first, she just sat there, looking up at him like he was very much a useless man. Then she pulled the lid off with her teeth and spat it halfway across the room, a *do I have to do everything?* look on her face, but he leaned against the table, crossed his arms, and tried not to smile and call her a smart-ass.

"So let's say we go with your plan, what then?" he asked her.

"I don't know," she whined. "What were we going to do if you hadn't blown up your second favorite safe house with a snowball?"

"The snowball didn't actually . . ." He rubbed a hand across his face as he trailed off. "I don't know. I probably would have kept checking safe houses. Called up some old friends . . . or enemies." He gave an ironic laugh. "Maybe her archnemesis has heard from her."

Her eyes went wide. It was her *excited* face and he was starting to fear it.

"Ooh! Alex has a nemesis? Are they enemies to—"

"They are *nothing* to lovers!" Sawyer blurted, and her face fell. "Besides. He got out of the game five years ago and Alex hates his guts."

"But you think he might have heard from her?" she asked.

"I think she's got to be somewhere," he told her softly, wishing like hell he didn't have to say the next part but knowing she needed to hear it. "But the clock's ticking. The agencies have unlimited resources. And Kozlov? If she has a weakness, sooner or later, he'll find it. And his guys will use it."

"You mean sooner or later, they'll find me." He wanted to go to her, hold her, tell her it would be okay, but she just threw the pen and paper at him. "Here. It works. Weirdo."

He looked down at the paper and didn't try to hide his grin. "Watch who you're calling a weirdo . . . Zoe."

Maybe it was the adrenaline crash or just the aftermath of her quiet, indignant rage, but it seemed to take her a moment to hear it—to realize what he'd said.

He tossed the paper back onto the bed, watched her scramble for it then look down at the pretty writing in wonder.

Zoe.

"How . . ."

He didn't want to smirk but that didn't mean he was able to stop it. "Ask someone to test a pen and nine times out of ten they'll write their own name."

"I don't remember my name."

"Your muscles do."

He thought he heard her mumble something about *butt kicking* but he was too busy watching the smile bloom on her face to ask.

"*I'm Zoe.*" She looked younger than she had five minutes before, and the light was back in her eyes, and Jake Sawyer, a man who had spent the past decade doing very bad things to very bad people, couldn't bear the thought of putting it out.

"No, you're not." He looked from the banks of the Seine to the woman on the bed and resigned himself to what he had to do. "Until you're rested up and we have some kind of game plan . . . You're Mrs. Michaelson."

chapter nineteen

Sawyer let her sleep. At some point in his training he'd been lectured about head wounds and concussion protocols, but she couldn't keep her eyes open and between her full stomach and the gentle swaying of the ship and the knowledge that she had a name—*Zoe*, he reminded himself; Zoe had a name—she must have felt safe enough to roll back up in her blanket burrito and drift into the deepest sleep he'd ever seen.

He hated her for it.

Sawyer couldn't remember the last time he had slept—had dreamed. *Sleep with one eye open* was a cliché but it was also a way of life. And his way of life was killing him. Probably sooner than he hoped.

So he sat on the world's most uncomfortable chair and watched her sleep because he couldn't stand the thought of letting her out of his sight, and he didn't dare stop to wonder why.

After a while, there was a knock on the door and Sawyer bolted across the suite before the sound could wake her.

Peering through the fish-eye lens he saw a man dressed in the uniform of the *Shimmering Sea*. He looked like he belonged, but the good ones always did, and Sawyer wasn't in the mood to take chances. The man was raising a fist to knock again when Sawyer opened the door and realized a little too late that he still had a gun in his hand.

"Shi— Hi." He leaned against the door. *Nothing to see here. Nope. Just your regular honeymoon dude who is worn out from all the enthusiastic boat and airplane sex.*

"Mr. Michaelson?" the man asked like he didn't already know the answer.

"Yes."

"I'm Ramon, your butler. I have your luggage, sir. My apologies that it wasn't waiting in your room, but we were told you wouldn't be here."

"Yeah, storm messed up our flights," Sawyer said easily because that's what happens when your whole life was a lie. Eventually, it's the truth that you can't tell with a straight face.

"So sorry about the confusion, sir. Shall I bring it in and unpack?"

"What?" *These people unpack for you?* "No. I mean, my . . . uh . . . *wife* is sleeping."

He glanced back at Zoe: bare foot sticking out from under the blankets, hair fanned around her. She looked well and truly debauched and a knowing grin spread across Ramon's face. "Yes, sir."

Sawyer wanted to defend Zoe's honor, but he didn't know why. And the cover meant letting Ramon think it. If anything, the cover meant raising an eyebrow in a way that said *yeah, I'm a stud but don't make me knock your teeth out for leering at my woman.*

But Sawyer didn't have a woman—and he never would—so he just said, "I'll take those bags now."

He never moved away from the door. He never took his eyes off the man. And it wasn't until the corridor was empty that he realized he'd clicked off the Glock's safety.

"Who was that and did they want to kill me?" Zoe's voice was soft from sleep and the words sounded like they were coming from a mile away, but he could see her face in ten million reflective surfaces because, evidently, honeymooners on the *Shimmering Sea* are really into mirrors. Kinky bastards. The whole room looked like the inside of a disco ball.

She raised her arms and stretched. Hair smushed. Cheeks red. She'd gotten hot, he realized, but that must have come as a relief after twelve hours of freezing.

"So are they going to kill me *now* or did you talk them into coming back to kill me later?"

If it hadn't been for all the damn mirrors he wouldn't have even known he was smiling—wouldn't have known to stop it.

"No." He rolled the massive suitcases into the room. "It was the butler."

"We have a butler!" She shot upright but swayed a little.

"Hey." He bolted toward the bed.

"Head rush," she said. "I'm fine." And he believed her because she was already clawing her way out of the blankets and heading toward the suitcases.

"Darn it. They're locked," she said, like that was that—no force on earth can possibly bust through the locks that come standard on overpriced luggage. Then she remembered. "Wait! *You're a spy!* You can pick locks! Ooh!" She was already pushing the smaller of the two bags in his direction.

"Twelve hours I keep you alive and the thing you're impressed by is that I might be able to get into those suitcases?" he complained but reached for his kit.

"First, I'm pretty sure that we kept each other alive. I was very instrumental in plans B, C, and D-point-one. Second, are you saying you can't get into these suitcases? Because—"

The first bag was already opening with a *pop.*

"Ooh! Excellent." She dropped onto the floor—onto her knees. "You know, you're more helpful than you look." She was staring up at him with her bed-mussed hair, and it took him three full seconds to remember that he should have been insulted.

"This is what you consider helpful?"

But she was too busy throwing clothes across the bed to answer. Pants and blazers and ties. She was like a tiny tornado ripping through a department store that caters to dudes who have a regular caddy at the club.

"Shoot. This one's yours." She reached for the other, even larger, suitcase and—with otherworldly strength—pushed it in his direction. "Do me. Do me."

He audibly groaned. "You need to—"

"What?" she asked, looking way too innocent for a woman who was currently eye level with his crotch.

74

"Never mind," he said, and two seconds later, the lock sprang open.

What followed was a whirlwind of silks and cashmeres and satin. A whole lot of satin. He tried very, very pointedly *not* to look at the satin. But it was hard, what with the low sounds of pleasure that were coming from the back of her throat. "Ohhhh. Yes . . . Oh, that feels so good. Oh, look!"

"I'm not looking!" he said a little too quickly.

"Flats!" She was pulling a pair of shoes to her chest and rocking them like a baby.

"Are they your size?"

"I don't care. They'll fit me. I'll make them fit me." She closed her eyes. "I love being Mrs. Michaelson."

He had to admit, as covers went, he'd had worse. They were warm and dry and had plenty of food and water. And they were technically moving. For now. Plus, he hated to admit it, but there's a limit to what the human body can take. Every operative knows that fatigue doesn't just make you slow, it makes you sloppy. And in Sawyer's world, sloppy almost always makes you dead.

Zoe must have read his mind because she eyed him. "Did you sleep?"

He bit back a laugh. "Wasn't sleepy."

Maybe he was losing his touch—or maybe she was just getting to know him—because she arched an eyebrow. "Liar."

She gave him a mocking side-eye glance, and, damn, she looked better. Alive. Skin flushed and eyes bright. And a part of him couldn't shake the feeling that she should have looked more like Alex now that she wasn't dead on her feet, but somehow, she looked even less like her sister.

Alex always looked like she was in on a secret. But Zoe looked like she was in on a joke—like at any moment she was going to say *knock, knock* and the whole world was going to lean close enough to whisper *who's there?*

He'd never known anyone so alive, and he suddenly felt it like a weight in his chest—like he'd never be able to forgive himself if he couldn't keep her that way.

"Do you mind if I take the first shower?" Zoe was already grabbing a tiny green bottle of mineral water from the tiny fridge and pulling together an armful of Mrs. Michaelson's tiny clothing.

"Knock yourself out," Sawyer said. A moment later, the door clicked shut and the water turned on and he just stood there, trying not to think about a wet, naked Zoe on the other side of the wall. It might not have been so bad if he hadn't noticed the tuxedo staring back at him from the pile of clothes, taunting him, like it was waiting for 007 to come and claim it.

"Fuck James Bond," Sawyer said to no one but ten thousand versions of his own reflection. He wasn't going to be that kind of spy—that kind of man. He wasn't going to seduce Zoe—*use* Zoe. Not if his life depended on it.

But then a sound echoed through the quiet room. A crash. Breaking glass.

And a woman's scream.

A moment later, he was vaulting over the bed and bursting into the bathroom only to be hit by a cloud of steam. Zoe was just a blonde blur in the haze.

"What—" he started, but as he stepped toward her, he heard a crunch and looked down. The floor was wet and covered with shards of green glass. *The bottle broke*, his mind filled in, but Zoe looked like she didn't hear a thing, see a thing, as she stood there, staring at a mirror that was completely fogged over.

Oh, and she was naked.

Well, not *precisely* naked. Just mostly naked. She was seventy-five to eighty percent naked, a part of his brain calculated. But she was alive. And even though a part of him realized he could uncock the gun, another part of him knew that the thing that had made Zoe cry out was still in there. And Sawyer was going to kill it.

"What happened?" He expected her to grab a towel—maybe one of the plush robes hanging by the shower doors—but she just stood there in her bra and panties, staring at that fog-covered mirror. "Zoe—"

"I don't know," she said—to him or to her own reflection, he wasn't really sure.

"You don't know what?"

He turned off the shower and the room was suddenly too quiet—the air too clear—and he saw what Zoe would be seeing for hours—days. Maybe the rest of her life.

"I don't know how I got them."

She tentatively reached up to touch the scar that ran in a line between her breasts. There were others too. Along her ribs. Down her back, skirting along the edge of her bra. She probably hadn't seen that one, but he could. He wanted to reach out and trace it, smooth it away with his fingers, but he was too afraid to move—to speak. You shouldn't wake a sleepwalker, they always said, but no one ever talks about what to do when you catch someone having a nightmare while wide awake.

"I don't remember. Doesn't this seem like the kind of thing . . . I don't remember!" she screamed, but she wasn't scared—she was furious. At her body and her mind. "I—"

"Stop!" he blurted when she started to move, and she froze, embarrassed. It was like she suddenly realized that she was seventy-six percent naked in front of a man who was more or less a stranger.

"I—"

"Don't move," he said, softer now, as he grabbed a robe and threw it over her shoulders. Then he scooped her up into his arms. They were eye to eye in the steamy room and her body was like a coil that was wound way too tight. He was afraid she was going to snap. "Broken bottle. Bare feet."

So she didn't fight him as he carried her into the bedroom and sat her gently on the bed. She looked a little nervous, though, as if suddenly worried that being carried in a bridal suite might make them married in truth.

"Can't have you injuring yourself again." It was meant to be a joke. It was meant to make her smile. And she did, but the light didn't reach her eyes.

"I'd only slow you down."

"That'd be a shame." Then he went to clean up the glass because he'd rather throw his favorite gun overboard than call housekeeping, but when he was finished, he couldn't decide if he was supposed to sit beside her or kneel in front of her or just get the hell out and let her be alone.

"I . . . I don't remember." She was still staring into those blasted mirrors like maybe the story was written on her skin and if she just looked hard enough, she might figure out how to read it. "I keep thinking I'm going to see something or hear something and it's all going to come back, but . . . They scared me. I turned around and saw something, and . . . My own skin scared me." She looked up at him. Her voice cracked. "And nothing came back."

"Hey. It will." He'd spent a lot of time learning how to kill, but right then he needed to know how to soothe and so he just sat there, afraid to touch her. He didn't want to be the thing that made her shatter.

She looked down and suddenly realized that the robe was gaping, scars peeking through.

"Oh." She jumped to her feet and tried to pull the robe closed.

"No. Don't." He didn't mean to stand—to reach out—but he was already grabbing the edges of that robe and holding them tight, wrapping her up in a cocoon of soft cotton and not letting her move an inch until he'd told her, "Something tried like hell to kill you, lady. And you survived it." He turned her to face the largest mirror—her back to his front—as he looked over her shoulder and into her eyes. "You *won*. And nothing on this earth is sexier than a woman who told death to fuck off."

She closed her eyes, like she didn't just need to hear the words— she needed to *absorb* them through her skin and into her bloodstream, like that was the fastest way for them to reach her heart.

But when she finally opened her eyes, her gaze met his in the mirror. "Does my sister . . . Does Alex have . . ."

He shook his head and didn't make her finish. "Alex has the kind of scars you can't see."

chapter twenty

HER

Mrs. Michaelson had taste. Mrs. Michaelson had money. Mrs. Michaelson had . . .

Teeny. Tiny. Boobs.

Seriously. Zoe had never—in all eighteen hours of her memory—considered herself especially voluptuous, but as she stood in the bathroom, looking at the mirror, she couldn't help but wish she could take three inches off the hem of this little black dress and add them to the chest. Luckily, the dress was A-lined, so it fit pretty much everywhere else. Unluckily, it didn't have pockets, which was a pity. Always.

Maybe I'm a hotshot political operative running on the platform of Pockets for All, she speculated absentmindedly. She would win reelection in a landslide every time. It was something to consider as soon as her life went back to normal. Whatever normal looked like.

But right then she had a growly tummy and squished boobs, and she was finally clean and rested and wearing something that didn't smell like gunpowder. So she was going to look on the bright side. And no one would notice that the built-in bra was two sizes too small. Right?

Wrong.

"It's a little tight in . . . er . . . places?" she had to admit as soon as she stepped out of the bathroom. Sawyer, bless his covert heart, tried to act like nothing was wrong, but he choked when he saw her. And he wasn't even drinking anything!

"It looks"—he swallowed hard around the stuff he wasn't even drinking—"fine." He gulped again.

"It's not zipped yet."

"It's not?" His voice actually went up an octave. Because of all the choking, evidently.

"No!" She sounded upset. She *was* upset. All she wanted was to wear a pretty dress and eat a nice meal and have random strangers congratulate her on her nonexistent marriage while *not* shooting at her! Was that too much to ask?

"I couldn't twist that . . ." She pantomimed twisting and stretching and reaching for the zipper she couldn't, well, reach, and he just stood there being no help at all because, again, *no one was shooting at her*, which was really Sawyer's time to shine. Dress zipping, not so much, evidently. He was looking at her like he'd never even seen a woman's back before.

"Do you mind?" She tried not to sound too terribly impatient, but those tiny cheeses had been hours ago and Melanie had told them that dinner was served at eight and she didn't want to miss it.

So she pulled her hair over her shoulder and turned her back to him, hoping that a hot guy who probably had a lot of experience *un*zipping dresses could figure out how to do it in reverse. But for a long time he just stared at . . . something, and she remembered the scar she'd seen in the mirror.

"That's fine." She turned back quickly. "I'll . . ."

But then she felt a touch, whisper soft down the line of her spine. Her whole back tingled. "No. I'll do it. It's just . . . You don't appear to be wearing a . . . uh . . ."

"Bra?" she finished for him because even though he seemed fluent in several languages "girl" obviously wasn't one of them. "No. It's built in. There are these little cups that hold—"

"Great," he blurted a little too quickly. "Here. I'll . . ." He tried the zipper, but it barely budged. "I can't . . ."

"What if I suck real hard—"

"Please don't say that," he ground out.

"What?" She glanced over her shoulder. "I'll—" She drew in a deep breath.

"That's not help—"

"Here. Let me try . . ." She leaned over and stuck a hand down the dress and wriggled. "Maybe if there's less boob *inside* the dress . . ." She started, then went to work on the other side.

"That's"—he swallowed hard one more time—"a plan."

And when she stood, sure enough, her cleavage was spilling out and Sawyer was choking . . . again.

"Do you need some water or something?"

"What?" His eyes came back to hers in one of the mirrors. "No. Here."

That time, the zipper slid smoothly into place, but the room must have been way too cold because, when she felt his knuckle run between her shoulder blades, she shivered. And when she turned, he was looking at her oddly—like there was something on her lips.

"Just tell me the truth."

For a moment, she thought he hadn't heard her because it seemed to take forever for Sawyer to shake himself free of some thought and say, "I'm sorry. What?"

"Can you see my nipples?"

chapter twenty-one

HER

Sawyer never did answer the nipple question, but Zoe wasn't too concerned. She tried to remind herself that Mrs. Michaelson was a high-powered political operative on her honeymoon with her handsome husband. Mrs. Michaelson had a bold and daring sense of style. And, most of all, Mrs. Michaelson was hungry.

But as they walked toward the dining room, Sawyer's thumb made slow circles on her back and Zoe felt her skin come alive. She risked a glance over her shoulder. Mr. Michaelson also had money and taste, but the sleeves of his expensive blazer were a little too short and the shoulders were a little too narrow, but Zoe told herself that no one would notice—not with her boobs in the vicinity.

"What?" he asked when he caught her looking.

She wanted to tell him he looked nice. She wanted to ask again about the nipples. She wanted to run onto the deck and hurl herself into the water because that had to be better than admitting what she was thinking: that he was handsome. And sexy. And hot. Too hot. And she didn't remember how to talk to hot guys. In her whole life, she'd probably never spoken to a single man who looked as good as—

"*Mr. Michaelson! Mrs. Michaelson!*" The voice was very loud and the accent was very French and the man at the front of the restaurant was wearing a tuxedo and smiling like he was about to break into a song accompanied by dancing dishes. "*The lovebirds! We've been expecting you!*"

"Table for—" Sawyer started, but the man was already turning and leading them through the opulent room. They'd probably gone ten steps when Sawyer stopped and blurted, "No."

"Pardon?" the man asked, clearly confused.

Even Zoe wasn't sure what the problem was until Sawyer said, "We'll need a table for two."

Then she realized the only empty chairs were at a table where six other people were already seated.

The maître d' looked confused. "But Mr. Michaelson . . . On the *Shimmering Sea* there are no private tables. That way our guests can form lifelong friendships that—"

"We're on our honeymoon," Sawyer said flatly.

"Well . . . if you would like . . . eh . . . *priv-a-cy*," he said with a lascivious and very French emphasis on the last word, "we offer twenty-four-hour room service."

Sawyer looked like that was the greatest news he'd ever heard, but something was coming over Zoe. She didn't know what or how or why but, suddenly, she felt herself striding toward their new table-mates, calling out, "Hi, y'all! We're the Michaelsons!"

Suddenly, the hand was on her back again and lips brushed against her ear. "Did you just become spontaneously southern?"

"*I think I did!*" she whispered back, her accent even stronger. "But who's to say I wasn't already?"

"Me. I say—"

"So sorry we're late!" Zoe exclaimed as they reached the table. "I don't know what came over us. Jet lag, I suppose. And, well, we are on our honeymoon and we only have eyes for each other. Isn't that right, honeybunch?"

Sawyer missed his cue so she pinched his butt, which, fun fact, was like a gently rounded piece of granite.

"Yes . . . sweetheart?"

There were six other people at the table. The Fitzpatricks—two brothers in their eighties who were from Edinburgh and had been on thirty-seven cruises in the past nine years. *Retirement, eh! The world is our backyard!*

There was a couple in their sixties, Thomas (call me Thomas) and Tammy. They'd been married for forty-five years and had apparently been miserable for forty-four of them. *Her eyes are on her head, darling.*

Marc and Anthony (*no Cleopatra jokes, ha ha*) were also on their honeymoon. "Just five years too late." Marc might have sounded just a tiny bit bitter.

"I'm in construction," Anthony explained.

"He's a workaholic," Marc clarified.

"Well, some of us can't do our jobs anywhere there's Wi-Fi," Anthony shot back.

"I'm in tech," Marc added.

"It's not like I can pack up the bridge and move it. It stretches between two countries!"

"Not again with the bridge . . ." Marc mumbled.

"I'm building the world's longest high-altitude glass-bottomed bridge," Anthony explained.

"Well, that's a mouthful," Zoe murmured.

"It's not technically glass," Marc confided. "Some kind of polymer something something—"

"Do you know how few people can work at that altitude?" Anthony stared icily at his husband and Sawyer leaned closer to Zoe.

"So glad we left our room for this," he whispered just as a series of waiters approached the table. "Actually . . ." His tone changed considerably when a waiter slid a perfectly cooked filet in front of Zoe.

Her mouth watered. Her hands shook. She thought she might weep in appreciation until she heard, "What the hell is that?" and glanced over at Sawyer, who was staring at a plate of . . . well . . . Zoe wasn't exactly sure what it was.

Something white. And green. And kind of clumpy.

"Your entrée, sir," the very confused waiter said.

"That's not what she . . ." Sawyer turned and Zoe froze, a big chunk of filet hanging in midair. He was glaring, so she plopped the steak into her mouth before he could stop her.

Then she moaned because she couldn't help herself. "Oh, that's so good."

"For the love of—" Sawyer was grinding his teeth, which couldn't be good for oral health. And possibly spying.

"Is something not to your liking, Mr. Michaelson?" the waiter asked, confused. The entire table was watching, as if this was the most exciting part of the cruise so far. "You did request the vegan, gluten-free, sugar-free, lactose-free, low-sodium option, is that correct, sir?"

Zoe had a brief moment of panic, wondering exactly how many guns Sawyer might have stashed under Mr. Michaelson's suitcoat.

"Oh!" she exclaimed with her mouth full. "Trust me, y'all. You do not want to see this man on gluten!"

He looked like he had other uses for her steak knife, but Sawyer managed to grin and hand the plate back to the waiter. "It's a special occasion. Just bring me what she's having."

"Right away, sir," the waiter said as Sawyer grabbed a piece of asparagus off Zoe's plate, and she couldn't help but look up at him, savoring the warmth and comfort and safety of being Mrs. Michaelson, wondering if it might be better than being herself.

chapter twenty-two

HIM

"Well then he said, what's the use of having an emotional support goat if it's not going to be in the wedding?" Mrs. Michaelson said and Mrs. Michaelson's new friends laughed and laughed and laughed, utterly enchanted.

She'd been telling stories for two courses, so it was a relief when she paused to take a sip of the very pink drink that Lorenzo, her new BFF-slash-waiter, had brought her. But then she took a deep breath and lowered her voice. "But what we didn't know is that no one had fed Beatrice yet that morning, and *that*"—*dramatic sigh*—"is why I don't have a wedding ring."

Zoe held up her bare hand and a chorus of *boos* and *oh nos* echoed around the table.

It wouldn't have been so bad if Sawyer hadn't felt her leaning against his side—fitting them together like a puzzle. "But I told him, you don't have to worry about someone trying to steal me on our honeymoon because it's gonna be so obvious that I"—she *booped* him on the nose—"belong"—*boop*—"to—"

In a flash, he grabbed her wrist and tugged until she was sprawled across his lap, resting in his arms. Close. So close. Entirely too close! There was no tactical reason for them to be that close, but he didn't trust her not to *boop* him again. And if she did, well, he wouldn't be responsible for what happened. But that didn't change the fact that their lips were inches apart and her tongue was peeking out to swipe at a spot of wayward chocolate.

He'd almost forgotten they weren't alone until the traitors of table seven started tapping their glasses, chanting, "Kiss! Kiss! Kiss!"

He should have let her pull away—lose herself in her second helping of chocolate mousse—but she needed to learn her lesson about life in deep cover. That any lie you tell becomes your truth. So he leaned closer.

He could feel her breath on his lips when he whispered, "You did this to yourself, Mrs. Michaelson."

Then he kissed her. Because covers. And lessons. And, really, they'd almost kissed once already. This wasn't that much different than the street. Except in all the ways it was. Because, this time, she tasted like chocolate and she smelled like raspberries, and she was a soft, pleasant weight against his chest. And that dress was serving her breasts up like they were his actual dessert, so he stopped fighting and let himself taste her, feel her, breathe her in until her fingernails scraped against his scalp and she gave a sharp little intake of breath. His lips parted and her tongue peeked out and . . .

"Well, someone's having a real honeymoon," Marc muttered, and Sawyer jerked away. But Zoe was still blinking up at him, and he couldn't tell if she was mad or disappointed. The band began to play and people were starting to dance, but Zoe just sat there, staring.

"What?" he asked, but she was quiet for the first time since he'd known her. Her fingers brushed against her lips and there was a dazed look in her eyes. "Your head okay?"

"Who . . . who are you?" The other couples had all taken to the dance floor and the brothers had dozed off on the other side of the table, so Sawyer and Zoe were more or less alone when she said, "Where did you grow up? How long have you known Alex? When did you become"—she cast her eyes around in a textbook example of what *not* to do—"*a spy*? Why did you become a spy? How—"

"Let's dance." Sawyer pulled her to her feet and she tucked into him without missing a beat. He could practically feel her smug smile against his shoulder—like this had been her evil plan all along.

But then she gazed up at him, eyes hazy in the dim room. "Is Sawyer your real name?"

Sawyer didn't want to think about the answer. She was the one with amnesia, but he'd spent his whole life being other people. Arms dealers and mercenaries, smugglers and thieves. He'd spent five long years working his way into Kozlov's inner circle—a place where even the good guys have to be bad. Zoe was pink drinks and funny stories and what the world feels like after a rain. He was nothing but a long list of names and backstories, legends and lies.

He was no longer sure where the covers stopped and the man began, so he just told her, "It's one of them."

She made a sound that was twenty percent anger and sixty percent frustration and one hundred percent Zoe. So he dipped her.

"Five years . . ." he said to her upside-down face. "I met Alex five years ago." He pulled her slowly upright, felt her nestle back into his arms. "And at the time I thought she was the most beautiful woman I'd ever seen."

"Oh." Her voice was rough. "But she's not anymore?"

He brushed a piece of hair out of her face and told himself to stop talking, stop sharing, stop breaking protocol and taking chances, but it felt like the most obvious thing in the world to say, "Now she's second."

Then Zoe blushed and pressed her forehead against his chest.

When the band changed to something slower, he should have told her the night was over. They had eaten. They had danced. No one would ask questions if the newlyweds slipped away. But for some reason he pulled her closer because, well, a spy learns to trust his gut.

When she put her head on his shoulder, he whispered, "Just so you know, the more lies you tell, the more you'll have to remember."

But she sighed into him, chest rising and falling in time with the music and his own breath. "I won't forget. Right now, my fake life is the only one I have."

chapter twenty-three

Thirty minutes, three dances, and one more tiny pink drink later, Zoe was holding on to Sawyer's arm and waving goodbye to her best friends in the world.

"I'm gonna text you and get that recipe, Anthony!" (It turns out, Mrs. Michaelson liked to cook.) "Gute nacht, Petra!" (She also spoke German.) "Ciao, Lorenzo!" (And a little bit of Italian.) "Ooh, the boat is moving." She stopped and planted her feet wide as if to feel the sway. (There was no sway.)

"Boats tend to do that. Come on. Let's get you to bed."

He would have picked her up and carried her if he hadn't thought her fan club would burst into applause at his "manly vigor." Because, seriously, at some point she had actually used the words *manly vigor* in conversation. It was enough to make him miss the cave again.

But as they reached the elevator the ship really did sway, and so did Zoe, right into Sawyer's arms, which wasn't nearly as romantic as it sounded.

"Now this is just a theory," she said clumsily, "but I'm starting to wonder if maybe I'm not much of a drinker?" It was a valid question, he thought, right up until she belched. Loudly. After, it was a certainty.

"Yeah. That's my theory too," he said as she stood on one foot, leaning against him as she took off her shoes.

"You're a grouchy bear." She was listing a little to the right.

"You have a head injury." He was mad at himself for letting her have even one tiny pink drink, even if he had told the waiter to water them down.

"I know," she whined. "And it's sooooooooo annoying."

"So your judgment is off. Obviously. I am not grouch—"

"And you keep getting grouchier. And grouchier."

"I'm not grouchy. I'm just tired."

She seemed like the soberest person in the world as she stopped and looked at him—a hint of understanding in her eyes—and he hated that this woman could see him so clearly.

"You know who never has to say that? Nongrouchy people." She pushed the button, leaning more and more of her weight against him.

But there was a mirror in the elevator and when he looked up at the man beside her, he was smiling.

HER

Twenty minutes later, Zoe was standing in the bathroom, hydrated and showered and feeling a bit more like herself. Or the person she wanted to be. Someone who was fun but together, cautious but playful, friendly but subdued. But what she looked like was a stranger.

She'd scrubbed off Mrs. Michaelson's makeup and brushed out Mrs. Michaelson's curls. She'd washed away the cover—the lie—she had built for herself and she wasn't sure she liked the woman who was left.

"What were you doing in Paris?" she asked the reflection.

The reflection didn't answer back.

So she had no choice but to put on Mrs. Michaelson's nightgown . . . Which Mrs. Michaelson had planned to wear on her wedding night . . . Which meant it wasn't much of a nightgown. But surely it wouldn't be that bad, would it?

She was wrong.

It was worse.

So, so, so much worse.

Because the nightie was very short and very sheer. Too sheer, really. So sheer it might as well have not existed at all. At least it came with a robe, she told herself. But the robe was . . . yup . . . also incredibly sheer, so she stood there, fully clothed and extremely naked and told herself not to panic.

She'd just crack open the door and ask Sawyer for a T-shirt or something. But when she peeked into the room, it was empty.

The only light came from the tiny sconces by the bed, but thanks to the nine million mirrors, it looked like the room was full of fireflies. And it was gorgeous.

"Hi." She heard his voice at the same time she felt a gust of cold wind and saw the curtains billow out.

Sawyer. Balcony. Doors. Nightie. Nipples! So many words filled her (admittedly empty) brain at the same time that she thought she might black out from the overload.

"I . . . What were you doing out there?" she asked, but he wasn't listening—she was pretty sure because he wasn't looking at her eyes, or her lips. And her brain shouted *nipples* again. "Honeymoon!" she said a little too sharply then dove for the big, fluffy robe that had been hung on a hook by the bed.

The bed that was currently covered in . . .

"Are those . . ."

"Rose petals?" He smacked his lips and nodded. "Yes, yes they are. Because . . . honeymoon."

"Yes, honeymoon. Very, um, romantic."

"Yes."

"Except no," she said for reasons she couldn't start to name. And then she named them. "What if you're allergic?"

"Right?" he exclaimed. "And they just get everywhere . . ."

"And won't they stain the sheets? And . . ." She trailed off as she looked between the bed half covered with rose petals and the sliding door . . . and him. "Wait. Were you tossing rose petals overboard?"

"No. Yes." He had that little boy look on his hot guy face again. "I panicked, okay?"

"You panicked?"

"No."

She wanted to laugh. Was he blushing? It was hard to tell between the dim room and the five o'clock shadow. "You have multiple firearms, and rose petals scared you?"

He grimaced and grabbed a blanket from the bed, dragged it to the balcony and tossed the remaining petals overboard.

When he came back, she had a full-on smirk. She wasn't even trying to hide it. "You were scared!"

"This is my first fake honeymoon, okay?" He actually pouted as he closed and locked the door.

"Well, at least you're mostly clothed." She tried to laugh, but he didn't make a sound. He just stood there, a dark look on his face as his gaze slid from her eyes to her lips to her nearly nonexistent nightie and then landed on the bed. The *one* bed. And leave it to her brain to yell *nipples* again for good measure.

She grabbed a pillow and held it in front of herself and tried to keep her voice nice and even. "So there's only one bed."

"Yeah." He didn't sound bothered by that fact, probably because they'd been in the suite for hours and he'd done this math ages ago.

"So obviously we're in an only-one-bed situation."

"Yes?" It sounded like a question but he looked at her like he was starting to wonder if she'd lost her good sense as well as her memory.

"So this is a classic only-one-bed scenario . . ."

"I'm confused," he said.

"There's only one bed."

"Yeah. I can see the bed. It's right there. And . . . oh." Suddenly, it must have dawned on him. "You can have it."

"Oh! No!" She couldn't do that. She was ninety-nine percent certain she was a feminist and also a heavy sleeper, so . . . "You take the bed. It's only fair. I had it all afternoon. I can sleep on the floor. You can sleep—"

"I don't," he said quickly then added, "sleep. I don't sleep."

She ran the words back, sure she'd misunderstood them. "Of course you need your sleep."

"No. I don't." He was so matter-of-fact that she was starting to second-guess tiny pink drinks two through five.

"Of course you will. You have a very dangerous occupation and sleep is essential for motor function and reasoning and decision-making and—"

"Take the bed, Zoe."

"No! You need your—"

"I. Don't. Sleep. I never sleep. Ever."

"Ever?" Moonlight filtered in through the curtains and surrounded him in a shimmering glow. She saw pain on his face but no worry. This was just his normal, as odd as that may be. "That is biologically impossible," she told him.

"I sleep some." Sawyer gave a shrug. "But not a lot. So please. Take the bed. I'll sleep just as well on the floor, trust me."

Zoe wanted to fight but knew she wouldn't win, so she crawled beneath the petal-less sheets and stretched out in her basically non-existent nightie. She turned off the sconces and all that was left was the moonlight.

"Are you a vampire? A zombie? If you are in any way undead, I have the right to—"

"No." The word was hard but the tone was soft. She might have even heard a chuckle in the shadows.

"Are you a werewolf? Is there a full moon?"

"Good night, Mrs. Michaelson."

But she couldn't stop from rolling over and staring down at the man who had taken off his shirt and lay bare-chested on the soft carpet beneath a blanket that still smelled like roses. In the glow of the moonlight, his skin looked soft but his muscles looked hard, one arm crooked behind his head, bicep bulging, like at any moment he might spring to his feet and take on the world, and Zoe was tired just thinking about it.

"You can take the night off, you know." She wasn't teasing anymore. "You don't have to be on duty."

She actually thought he might have drifted off because it was a long time before she heard, "I'm always on duty."

chapter twenty-four

HER

Maybe it was the jet lag or the three-hour nap or the many, many, many pink beverages, but sometime in the night Zoe had to get up and use the bathroom. Sure enough, eyes were staring back at her in the dark. She would have apologized for waking him, but as she made her way back to bed, he was smirking, a look that said *told you so*. So Zoe stayed quiet as she crawled beneath the covers.

It was her first memory of silence. There had always been shooting or running or talking. Even the sounds of the ship—room service carts, and guests passing in the halls—had gone dormant in the middle of the night. But now Zoe could hear her own thoughts. She wasn't sure she liked them.

Because the longer she lay there, the more they piled on top of one another, a wall of questions with no answers. Like *where was she supposed to be sleeping*, and *what was she supposed to be doing*, and, most of all, *who was she supposed to be doing those things with?* She couldn't stop wondering if someone was out there—missing her, needing her, wondering why she hadn't come home? What if—at that very moment—there was someone going crazy without her?

Or, worse, a tiny, terrible part of her wondered, *what if there wasn't?*

"You okay up there?" Sawyer asked because clearly the CIA had next-gen brain reading technology implanted in all their operatives.

"Yes. No."

"Well, that's clear."

She didn't turn. Didn't look. It was enough to feel him, a calming presence in the night. He was four guns, three knives, and six-foot-two inches of dangerous. And he was on her side. But this wasn't something he could kill, so she just whispered, "It's nothing."

"Hey." His voice was gentle. "That doesn't sound like nothing."

Her eyes were a little too wet, all of a sudden. "It is. It's silly."

"Then you should definitely tell me. I could use a laugh."

But she was the one who giggled softly. "I . . . It's just . . ." She'd been terrified the night before, stumbling through the snow and the shadows, but lying in that beautiful room, something about the darkness made her brave. That's the only reason she had the strength to ask, "Do you think I'm in love?"

It sounded so silly when she heard it, and immediately, she wanted to take it back, roll over. Pretend like she was asleep, but it was too late. She heard the rustle of the blanket as he sat up. "What?"

"Nothing." She turned on her side, away from him; but they were in a hall of mirrors and his gaze bore through the dark.

"Hey." The bed dipped beneath his weight. "What did you say?"

Fingers brushed against her shoulder, faint and whisper soft, and, suddenly, her eyes felt hot again. She didn't want to face him.

"I said . . . Do you think I'm in love?" Suddenly, the weight of the silence was too heavy, pressing against her, pushing out the words she should have kept inside. "I mean, do you think there's someone in the world who makes my heart beat really fast and my fingers tingle? I remember tingly fingers. But I don't know if I have them or if I just *want* to have them? Do you think I'd know it? Because love isn't a memory, right? It's a feeling. So do you think I've forgotten being in love? Or am I just not?"

She felt fingers in her hair, a slow, gentle stroke that made her eyelids heavy. "I think . . ." The words were as soft as the moonlight. ". . . that you've had a shit day, lady. And you'll feel better in the morning."

She felt warm breath on her shoulder and the quick brush of soft lips on her skin before he pulled away and returned to his place on the floor. But a few minutes later, she heard, "You know, most people would ask, *do you think someone loves me?*"

Zoe closed her eyes. She pretended to sleep. She didn't want to admit that, deep down, she already knew the answer was no.

He was a liar. A lying liar who lies. She could tell because people who don't sleep don't dream, and people who don't dream don't scream "No!" as they toss and turn.

"Sawyer."

She slid out of bed and crawled across the carpet toward the man who was a tangle of blankets and flailing limbs, sweaty skin and—

"Helena!" he shouted, and Zoe froze, knowing she shouldn't be hearing this—seeing this. She didn't want to be an intruder in his dreams.

But he was lashing out again, sheer anguish on his face, and, on instinct, she reached for him. As soon as she touched his bare shoulder he pounced. Like an animal—an apex predator—something strong, and territorial, and alpha—as he twisted, pressing her against the floor and—

"Sawyer!"

She saw the moment he drifted from mostly asleep to mostly awake—the second he saw her—that he *knew* her. The second she was safe.

"Hey, sleepyhead," she tried to tease, but he didn't smile. Not even the crooked one that he probably didn't know he had. "Did I wake you?"

"What . . ." He shook his head, like he couldn't quite remember where he was. "What happened?"

"I'm no expert, but I'm pretty sure it's called *dreaming*." She was more smug than scared by that point. "It happens sometimes. When people sleep, which all people do."

He was lying over her—*on* her, technically. His body long and lean and pressing into hers; and she was still wearing the great invisible nightie—a fact that he seemed to remember a split second later because he rolled away. But there was a dark edge to his voice when he asked, "Did I hurt you?"

"No."

"Are you—"

"I'm sure." She was careful as she touched him, a gentle brush against his skin. "I'm fine. I feel guilty, though. You take the bed for the rest of the night. I can—"

"No."

"You exasperating man! You obviously need your sleep way more than I do. Whatever happens tomorrow, I won't need to shoot guns or judo chop—"

"I do *not* judo chop . . ."

"—bad guys. I'm expendable, so—"

She thought he was scary with a gun in each hand and dead Russians all around him, but she had never seen Sawyer look as lethal as he looked then. "You are *not* expendable. Don't ever call yourself that. Ever."

Suddenly, he was too close and his gaze was too hot and it was all way too much. She hated how badly she wanted to look away but she knew he'd see her—he always saw her.

"I'm serious, Zoe. You're not expendable. And you never will be."

He was so much closer then, and her throat was so much dryer as his hand cupped her cheek. It was all she could do to choke out the word, "Okay."

The boat took that moment to rock slightly, and he swayed— away from her and the moment—so she climbed to her knees and said, "Come on. It's a king-size bed. I'll put a row of pillows between us. That ought to protect me."

She gave a saucy glance over her shoulder, but there was a look in his eye—something hot and dark and hungry. And Zoe felt like she had when she was flying off the bridge—like her stomach wasn't where it was supposed to be.

"Lady, nothing can protect you from me."

Then he got up and went to the bathroom, flicked on the light, and closed the door. Zoe sat there for a long time, wondering what had just happened.

When the light flickered off ten minutes later, she felt the other side of the bed dip; she heard the covers rustle. And Zoe kept her gaze on the moonlit countryside passing outside their window.

She never said a thing.

chapter twenty-five

Sawyer hadn't been lying. He really didn't sleep. Except when he did. It was always like that—bits of the night like black holes where stars used to be, moments where he lost his hold on the present and got sucked into the past. And he hated it. Because, to Sawyer, nothing was more exhausting than what happened in his dreams.

So that was how he ended up back on the floor the next day, shirt off, pushing himself as far and as fast as he could while lying still.

"Eighty-nine. Ninety. Ninety-one . . ." His arms burned. His chest ached. And he knew he was only halfway through the minimum when the covers rustled, and a small voice said, "You're up early."

He lost count and laughed, a sound he didn't quite recognize when he first heard it. "You're up late," he corrected, and she glanced at the clock by the bed.

"Is that three . . ."

"P.M.? Yes. That's why the sun is shining."

He pointed to the bright light behind the gauzy curtains, but Zoe was unflustered and unconcerned as she stretched. But then she stopped suddenly, looking down at where he sat, sweaty and shirt-less on the floor.

"Did you really do a hundred push-ups or did you start counting at like eighty-five?"

He didn't laugh. Nope. Not at all. But it was all he could do to bite back a smirk as he pushed himself upright. "Now I have to start from one . . . again. Since someone made me lose count."

"Mm-hmm."

"One. Two."

"Are you flexing your muscles right now?"

"No. I'm using my muscles."

"He said," she went on, "*flexally*."

"That isn't a word."

"He said, *glisteningly*."

"Still not a—"

"Ooh! Breakfast!" She must have spotted the croissant and fruit he'd pilfered from the buffet and brought back to the room.

"More like lunch," he said, but she just groaned in response.

"This is so good. How long have you been up?"

"I didn't—"

"Sleep." She actually rolled her eyes. "Which is a lie. But I'll allow it. When did you get out of bed?"

"Sunrise. I searched the perimeter."

She looked at him like he was an idiot. "Do you mean you walked around the boat? Is that what that means?"

"I can take my croissant back, you know."

"No." She scooted to the other side of the bed. "I need this. I'm working out too." She brought it slowly to her mouth. "It's so heavy. I should do a few more reps."

He didn't know whether to laugh at her words or groan at the sight of that nightgown in the light of day, so he crashed to the floor again, push-ups totally forgotten.

"I . . ." She started then trailed off as he took a towel and rubbed it over his sweaty chest. He'd have to take a shower soon and pray Mr. Michaelson packed something other than stuffy blazers.

"What?" he asked.

"Uh . . ." She shook her head and jerked her eyes away from his chest.

"Zoe?" he prompted.

But she looked like maybe she wasn't sure if she should admit it, share it, like maybe she trusted him with her life but not her secrets. Sawyer totally knew the feeling. His whole life was classified.

So she peeled off a layer of fluffy croissant and shrugged. "I was going to say I never sleep this late, but maybe I do? Maybe I never rise before noon because I'm up all night doing brain surgeries. Or fighting fires. Or . . . I don't know . . . managing a sex club!"

He coughed as he took a drink of water.

"A classy one," she added, sounding defensive of her nonexistent sex club. "*With masks.*"

Yeah. Sawyer was definitely going to need that shower soon. He wanted to turn away, but everywhere he looked he saw her. Damn mirrors. Sawyer had spent his whole life looking over his shoulder, but right then he didn't want to know what was behind him. And he sure as hell didn't want to think about what was in front of him, so he just sat there, trying not to think about anything at all.

Not Kozlov or the drive or Alex—definitely not the woman who was (*finally*) pulling on a robe. Because the one thing he knew for certain was that Zoe probably wasn't going to be safe without him and she sure as hell wasn't safe with him and so Sawyer genuinely didn't know what to do.

"So what's on the agenda for today?"

"Oh no," he told her as he jumped to his feet. "Don't put this on me. This is your plan."

"Fake dating is a good plan. It's very good spying."

"You say that like it's a real thing."

"It is!" she exclaimed then cocked her head. "Except, technically, we're not fake dating. We're fake *married*. And double technical—"

"That's not a real term."

"—we're not *faking*. We're *undercovering*—"

"That's definitely not a real—"

"So we're not a trope. We're a *mission!*"

How could she do that? Sleep in another woman's clothes in another woman's bed—on another woman's honeymoon—and wake up beaming and glowing as if she wasn't the meat in life's shit sandwich?

"If you say so."

"I do! But for the sake of argument, let's say we were doing it your way—assume we spent the night on the dirt floor of some safe house and roasted a raccoon over an open fire for supper. What would your plan be then?"

"Well, first of all, I wouldn't eat raccoon. Ever."

"You might," she shot back and he tried not to roll his eyes.

"Second of all, we'd need to lie low. Keep moving."

She pointed to the lavish suite and the countryside beyond the balcony doors. "Check. And check! Gosh, I'm good at this! Spying is obviously genetic."

He wanted to tell her she was wrong—that families have no role in covert operations, but that wasn't true, and he knew it.

"So what would you do . . . if you weren't burdened with me?"

You're not a burden he wanted to say. He wanted to tell her again that she wasn't expendable or collateral damage. But if he wasn't careful she was going to be all those things, and it was just a matter of time until she got hurt—one way or the other.

"Well . . ." she prompted.

The problem was that he knew exactly what he'd do if he didn't care about her. But at some point in the past thirty-six hours his priorities had shifted in a way that made him a worse spy but a better person and he wasn't at all sure how to feel about the trade-off.

"Sawyer . . ."

He collapsed onto the carpet with a groan. "If it were just me, I'd shake a few trees. See what falls out."

She dropped onto the bed and exclaimed, "Okay! I'm rested! I'm ready! Let's go shake trees!"

"The last thing I shook literally exploded, so . . . no."

She crossed her legs and looked at him. "Okay. The ship will dock sometime today, and we'll get off and—"

"The ship was supposed to dock this morning but it got rerouted because of ice."

"Oh." She bounced again, coming up on her knees. "Then Plan B! We'll—"

"No!" He didn't mean to snap. He didn't want to yell. But there's only so much optimism a man can take before it breaks him, being that close to something he can never have and never feel. Sawyer was in the Worst Case Scenario business, and he couldn't let himself pretend otherwise, no matter how tempting it might be—how tempting *she* might be.

"We have to find my sister." That time, Zoe's voice was soft. "We have to find her before they—"

"They already have her!" He hadn't meant to say it, and he really hadn't wanted to shout, but she had to know . . . She had to brace herself because . . . "The CIA probably had her before you even woke up from your nap yesterday. And that's the literal best-case scenario—that she's tied up with a bag over her head in some government facility that doesn't officially exist, because . . ." He trailed off because there were some things even he wasn't callous enough to say.

"What's the other scenario?" She drew the robe tight around her in a way that had nothing to do with skimpy nighties.

But he was shaking his head. "Nothing you need to worry about."

"What's the other scenario?" She looked like someone bracing for a hit, trying to convince themselves they're tough enough to take it.

"Don't, Zoe—"

"What is it?"

It was harder than it should have been to admit, "Kozlov has her."

"And she's dead?" Her voice cracked.

She wanted the truth—needed it on some level—and that's the only reason he said, "And she's not."

She was silent for a long time—perfectly still—but then she bolted off the bed and across the room. She reached for the sliding glass door and tried to open it, but the safety latch was on, and no matter how she tried, she got nowhere. Story of his life.

"Zoe . . ."

"This darn . . ." *The door rattled and banged.*

"Zoe . . ."

She slammed her palm into the glass, so he reached around her to release the latch. The door slid open, and she rushed outside and gripped the rail.

"I could be wrong," he told her, but she just stood there, pulling frigid air into her lungs like she wanted to freeze herself from the inside out.

"That happen a lot?" She cut a look over her shoulder.

"More than I'd like." He wasn't making a joke and he didn't smile.

"Is there anything . . . Is there anything I can do to help her?"

He'd lain beside her all night, listening to her breathe and coming up with plans—dozens of them—one after the other. But there wasn't a single option where she wasn't likely to get hurt, and Alex would hate him if he got her sister killed. Worse, he was pretty sure he'd hate himself. So that's what made him say, "No."

His hands were on her shoulders then, turning her, making her look at him—making her see.

"I may be wrong, Zoe. Alex is smart and ruthless and . . . If I was going to bet on anyone, it would be her. They may not have her. Hell, she may have them, for all I know. I just . . . I just want you to know that in this business . . . in this life . . . people like Alex—and me—we don't get a happy ending."

She looked at him with more pity and compassion than he'd seen in decades. "Then what do you get?"

Not you, he thought. *I'll never get you.* He wasn't sure where that thought had come from but, in the end, it didn't matter.

"If we're lucky? Another mission."

"Okay." She belted the robe tight and looked out over the icy landscape. "And us?" *Us? Us? There is no* . . . "Then what do we do? What do *I* do? Where do I go? What . . . What do I do?"

As a spy, there were three questions Sawyer asked every moment of every day.

Who can I trust?

What do I need?

And how do I get out?

What he hated more than anything was that, when he looked at her, the answers to those questions were as blank as her memories.

So he drew a deep breath and said, "Does Mrs. Michaelson have anything besides skimpy lingerie and backless dresses?"

She choked out a laugh, her breath foggy in the cold air. "You have something against lingerie and dresses?"

Sawyer bit back a grin. "I do not. But they're not exactly appropriate for what I want to do next."

She sounded genuinely leery when she asked, "What's that?"

chapter twenty-six

"You want my hands where?"

"You heard me."

"I'll hurt you."

"Lady, you wish you could—"

And then she hurt him. Not that she meant to. But she was stronger now that she was rested, and the kick, well, he didn't exactly see it coming.

They were back on the top deck, but the crew had raised the sunshade and set up the folding chairs. A few people dozed while others chatted, but no one paid any attention to the honeymooners sparring at the front of the ship. The wind was stronger up there with nothing to break it, but Sawyer didn't mind. He liked being able to see what was coming.

But as he looked at the woman in his arms, he couldn't shake the feeling that the real danger was already there.

"What if I try this?" Zoe swung her elbow and he ducked, dragging her hands behind her back and pulling her close. It wasn't the first time he'd shown her a type of hold. But it was the first time he didn't want to tell her how to break it.

"How do you get out?" he whispered in her ear.

"Kick to the knee?" She tried it. "Headbutt?" He evaded.

Then he whispered, "You could flip me."

"Noooooo." Zoe glanced over her shoulder, wind in her hair, cheeks pink from the cold and the exertion. She didn't look like Alex then, not even a little bit. And, suddenly, he knew that she was far more dangerous to him than her sister would ever be because, sometimes, when he looked at her, Sawyer forgot. His mission and his training and his life. She made him forget he wasn't Mr. Michaelson and he never, ever would be which made her the most lethal twin of all.

"Show me! Show me!" She practically bounced she was so excited.

"You have to get close. Closer." He pulled her toward him. "Grip tight."

"Here?"

He felt her smaller hand on his arm. "Yeah. Tighter. Now step in and—"

In the next moment he was flying through the air and landing with a thud on the deck, staring up at her.

"Oh my gosh! Maybe I am good at this. Maybe I'm a professional cage fighter. Maybe—"

He swept her leg and brought her down—hard—landing on top of his body.

His hands cradled her ribs, and he could have sworn he felt her shiver. He wanted to hold her tight and keep her warm, but he just said, "You aren't a cage fighter."

She looked down at him from beneath the curtain of honey-colored hair. "Well, my job is definitely dangerous with a lot of authority. Like FBI agent. Or junior high school principal."

"Yeah." His hands itched to slide—to move. He watched her lips as she licked them. "That's probably it."

Slowly, she pushed away. But instead of crawling to her feet, she settled down beside him, her head on his shoulder like he was a soft place to land.

She actually nestled a little closer as she said, "Maybe tomorrow you can teach me how to kill a man with a telephone cord."

"A telephone cord?" He forgot to bite back his laugh.

"Yeah. You could do that, right?"

He didn't even have to think about it. "Of course, but—"

"And an ink pen. Or a shrimp fork. Do you think we can sneak one out of the dining room to—"

"No."

"Okay. Regular fork it is. Maybe a hand towel? Can you kill a man with a hand—"

"That would be better for defense, but—"

"Right. We'll get you a knife and me a towel and—"

"No." He didn't know he was rising, rolling, pinning her beneath him on the cold deck until he was staring down at the way her hair fanned out around her like a halo. "Don't joke about that. Never joke . . ."

"I know."

"This isn't a game, Zoe. It's not a joke."

"I know," she said, softer.

"I don't want you to *ever* have to kill a man—to live with that. But, sweetheart . . ." Her eyes went wide at the word, but it was too late to take it back. It was more important to make her see. "If that ever happens . . . if it's ever *you* or *them* and I'm not there . . . Then you need to promise me, Zoe. Don't *wound. Kill.*"

Sawyer didn't realize how cold he was until he felt her warm hand on his cheek, brushing away the tears that were never going to be there. The part of him that could cry had died a hundred years before. It was the first part to go and the last part he'd miss.

"I promise."

The world was suddenly too cold and too quiet and too still, so he rolled away, but not far enough because he could feel the back of her hand against his—a gentle brush—and they lay sprawled on the deck for a long time, looking up at the sun that was setting in the distance. He wasn't sure what time it was. He didn't even know where they were. But the scariest part, Sawyer had to admit, was that he didn't care. Which was how he knew he had to leave her. Soon. Before he got any sloppier—before they both got killed.

"Hey, Sawyer," Zoe said, her voice breaking through the peaceful calm. "Thank you. In case I haven't said it, thank you for saving my life and giving me the bed and letting me try to kick you where it hurts."

Her hand slipped into his, and his throat burned a little when he said, "Any time." Then that hand oh so gently squeezed, and he didn't want to let her go.

He had to let her go.

Because he had to keep her safe and he had to find her sister and he had to get the drive and stop the bad guy and figure out why Alex ran—from the CIA and from him. He had so much to do but the only thing he wanted was to lie there, holding her hand, and that was the scariest thing of all. He would have stayed there forever if she hadn't let go and climbed to her feet.

"Now if you'll excuse me . . . It's formal night, so I'm going to go take a very long, very hot shower and put on a very slinky, very fancy dress."

He tried not to grin. "I'll be down in a bit to help you zip it."

"Oh, that's okay." She pulled her hair into a knot on the top of her head, exposing the long, graceful line of her neck. "This one is really stretchy. And super low cut, so . . ."

He gulped. "Uh . . . how low cut?"

"Low enough," she tossed over her shoulder and he tried not to groan as she walked away.

After that, Sawyer took his time, walking around the perimeter and double-checking their route and trying not to think about the clock that was ticking louder and louder in the back of his mind. He needed to stay with Zoe. And he needed to let her go. He needed to hide her somewhere. And they needed to start running and not stop until they reached the other side of the world.

All Sawyer knew for sure was that, right then, he had two choices: do his job or keep Zoe safe, and never before had the smart call and the right call been so diametrically opposed.

She wasn't his job or his mission. She wasn't *his*, and Sawyer couldn't let himself forget it.

But as he passed the shops that lined the lobby, something caught his eye, but he didn't reach for his gun. He reached for his wallet.

Predictability is death, he always said. Well, if his new post-Zoe life was any indication, he was going to live forever.

chapter twenty-seven

HER

Okay, the dress wasn't that stretchy. But it was more than a little low-cut, so Zoe threw on a wrap as she headed toward the dining room and joined the table by the window, trying not to worry about the empty seat beside her.

"No Mr. Michaelson tonight? Don't tell me, you wore him out?" Marc asked with a wink.

"Oh, he'll be . . ."

"There!" It was Tammy who pointed to the man in the tuxedo on the other side of the dance floor.

Zoe had seen Sawyer looking at that tux like it was some kind of straitjacket, but he walked into the room like it had been custom made for him. By angels. His shoulders had never looked so broad, and his jaw had never looked so chiseled, and . . . had he shaved? He must have. But . . .

Her thoughts trailed off as she realized he was looking at her, too. Like she was beautiful and precious and *his*. He was looking at her like she belonged to him and it did funny things to her insides. She had to remind herself that it was just the cover—that it was all pretend.

But it was easy to forget when he said, "I believe they're playing our song."

Blue eyes staring down at her. Hand reaching out for her. Heart somewhere between her throat and her stomach but definitely not where it was supposed to be. Then he was pulling her out of her seat and into his arms and all Zoe could do was stammer, "Th-this is our song?"

"I suppose it is now." He seemed almost distracted, looking at her like maybe—

"Did I miss a boob or something? Is that how I got this dress on?"

"No," he said a little too quickly. "It's just . . . You . . . you're . . . beautiful." Wait. Was Sawyer being *awkward*? Was *Mr. I Only Lie on Floors and Never Actually Sleep Guy* uncomfortable? He swallowed hard. "You're beautiful. And I saw this and thought maybe . . . I mean, I'd understand if you don't want it, but . . ."

He reached into his pocket and pulled out a very small box.

A collective "Whooooooooo" went up from their table as Sawyer presented her with what could only be described as something ring-shaped and ring-colored and ringlike. Yup. It was ringish in every way, but in no universe was—

"It's a ring," he said. She knew for a fact the man spoke at least three languages, but he seemed at a loss for words. "I saw it at the gift shop. Thought you should have it. You know . . . for our cover," he added in a whisper.

She nodded. "Yes. For cover purposes."

But as he slipped the thin silver band onto her finger it didn't feel fake at all. And that was the part that scared her.

chapter twenty-eight

He got her a fucking ring.

Like a fucking moron.

Never mind the dent it made in their emergency cash, he should have felt like a fool standing on that polished dance floor, slipping a ring onto the finger of a stranger. But as they walked toward the honeymoon suite, Sawyer couldn't bring himself to get mad about it.

She couldn't go undercover without a ring, and if she smiled when she saw it—well, that wasn't his problem.

"Oh, hello, neighbors!" Marc and Anthony were unlocking the room next to theirs. "Now you two keep it down over there tonight." Marc gave them a wink as Sawyer put his hand on Zoe's back and ushered her inside.

"Oh. Uh . . . Okay!" she called back as the door clicked shut and her cheeks turned pink.

She blushes, Sawyer reminded himself. When was the last time he had known someone who could actually, literally blush?

"Well, I guess we convinced them." She held up her hand and the ring caught the light. "Good job with this. It looks almost real."

"It is real," he said a little too quickly.

"Oh. Well . . ." She was stuttering and stammering and, if possible, turning even redder. "I'll give it back to you. When it's over. You can use it the next time you need a fake wife."

But Sawyer was never going to have another wife—fake or otherwise. That wasn't how his life worked—how his world worked—and, suddenly, the honeymoon suite felt too small and the boat felt too hot and something was wrong. His gut had kept him alive for years, and he could feel it then—the absolute certainty that if he stayed there he was going to get hurt. He was never going to recover.

So he headed for the door. "I need to check the perimeter."

She smiled the smile that meant he was an idiot. Because he was. Only an idiot would have gotten her a fucking ring.

"Do you mean you're going to go walk around the ship?"

"Yes." He stepped toward the door. He should sleep on a deck chair, that would show her.

"No!" she called. "It's freezing out there!"

"That's okay." He grabbed the long cashmere coat he'd found in Mr. Michaelson's suitcase. "I won't be long." He looked at her. "I promise."

Zoe went into the bathroom and he slipped on the coat, lingering for a moment over a small pile of things on the dresser. She must have emptied her pockets after Paris because he saw the tube of lip balm. A few euros and a crumpled tissue. And that little card she'd thought they should use to find shelter at her old hotel. Had it really just been two days before? It seemed like a lifetime. He'd felt like another man then.

And that's exactly what scared him.

HER

It was impossible. Literally. There had to be some law of physics that stated that if last night's negligee was the teeniest, tiniest negligee in the world, then *tonight's* negligee couldn't be even teenier or tinier. That had to be a law! Didn't it?

But that didn't change the fact that it appeared to be true. Very, impossibly true.

And, worse, it didn't change the fact that she . . . uh . . . liked it? A lot. And there was a small part of her that wondered if maybe Sawyer might like it too? Maybe he'd stare? Or stammer? His jaw might tick and his hands might flex and then . . .

She caught sight of the ring in the mirror and tried to remind herself it was all pretend.

Pretend ring and pretend husband. But the tingles in her fingers were very, very real. And they were terrifying. And she knew she had two options: crawl beneath the covers and pretend to be asleep when he got back? Or—

She fluffed her hair and walked into the bedroom, strategically positioned herself on top of the covers—just a little bit—and told herself she might as well enjoy being Mrs. Michaelson. For a little while. Because eventually, she was going to have to go back to being herself. Whoever that might be.

##

The deck was empty and the moon was full, but the wind really was freezing. Sawyer turned up the collar of Mr. Michaelson's coat and walked beside the railing, trying to outrun his thoughts.

So much of his training was about not having to think, to stop, to process. He had spent years honing his instincts and perfecting his skills, but somehow he'd ended up on a luxury river cruise anyway. In a tuxedo.

Fuck. His. Life.

From the front of the ship he could see a bridge approaching. Maybe it would be low enough that he could just reach up and grab on? He could leave. He *should* leave. Write a note telling her to stay in the cabin and order enough room service for two. The crew would believe it. He'd seen the knowing looks on Marc's and Anthony's faces. No one would question a thing if the honeymooners stayed in bed for the next six days.

Zoe could go on being Mrs. Michaelson. She could be safe inside their moving bubble. For a little while.

He should do it.

But bubbles burst. Always. And then what? She'd reach her destination and wander straight into Kozlov's arms or a CIA sting. Or both. He really couldn't rule out the possibility of both.

A shadow passed overhead, temporarily blocking out the moon, and he looked up at the bridge that he didn't even try to grab, at the lifeline he didn't take, wondering if his biggest threats were out here or in there. With her.

He was heading to the other end of the ship, trying not to think about the answer, when he slipped in some water on the deck. No. He looked down. *Snow.* There was snow on the deck.

No.

His blood went cold.

There were footprints.

He turned and let his eyes follow the snowy steps to where they began, right in the center of the deck. Then he looked back at the snow-covered bridge disappearing in their wake, and Sawyer didn't think. Didn't plan. Didn't theorize or strategize.

He just ran like hell.

HER

She fell asleep.

Zoe didn't know much about her real life, but she clearly wasn't a great seductress because when she finally heard the door open she was definitely asleep and there was definitely a little drool on her chin and she had definitely gotten cold at some point and pulled the edge of the bedspread over her teeny tiny nightie, covering up all the good parts.

"I was starting to think you forgot about me." She stretched but had to smile when the bed dipped behind her and a hand caressed the delicate skin of her neck, whisper soft and smelling like snow.

"I could never forget you . . . Alex."

And then the hand on her throat began to squeeze.

chapter twenty-nine

HIM

Sawyer was going to wake up the whole ship and he didn't give a single, solitary damn as he ran the length of the deck and down the stairs, feet pounding on teak and then plush carpet, room numbers flying by fast but not fast enough.

He was probably wrong, he told himself.

It was probably nothing, he swore.

There's no way Zoe was actually in danger.

He lied.

And he knew it. He knew it like he knew his heart was fire and his blood was gasoline. Like he knew it was his fault for staying in the safe, cushy confines of the ship. He'd stopped running. He'd stopped hiding. He'd stopped listening to the voice in the back of his head that told him there were no safe places or happy memories, only the missions you live through and, ultimately, the one you don't.

So Sawyer kept running.

And he prayed he wasn't too late.

HER

The good thing about being an amnesiac is that when your life flashes before your eyes it doesn't take very long.

So when the big man began to squeeze, what Zoe felt were Sawyer's hands on her throat that afternoon, gentle but strong. What she heard was Sawyer's voice, saying, *Tuck your chin down to protect your windpipe. Put your hands here. Put your foot there. Leverage your hips up and—*

"Flip."

Zoe's voice was full of gravel as she watched the big man fly off the bed and land on the floor. She tried to scramble away, but she was still tangled up in the blankets and a calloused hand grabbed her ankle, pulling her back.

She reached for the bedside table. Clawing. Grabbing. She had to try something . . . She had to do something . . . So when her hand landed on a solid object, she didn't think. She just grabbed it and swung.

Russian curses filled the air. Blood splattered, red dashes across dark mirrors. But then the door flew open and Sawyer was standing in the dim light of the hallway, looking from Zoe, breathless on the bed, to the big man bleeding on the floor.

"Did you just break an assassin's nose with a telephone?"

Her eyes were wide. "I think so?"

He absolutely beamed. "*Good girl.*"

And then he pounced, but the dude on the ground rolled, and the next moment a gun was in the man's hand and his hand was pointed at Sawyer's chest.

Sawyer dove as the gun fired. It must have had a silencer, because the noise wasn't enough to bring security or alert the guests. If it hadn't been for the shattering of one of the mirrors, Zoe might have thought she'd dreamed it, but the glass was cracking, breaking, and she hoped the bad luck wouldn't rub off on them. Because the man was turning . . . And firing again—right at Zoe.

She dove behind the bed as the patio doors shattered.

Freezing wind gushed inside, curtains whipping and snapping as Sawyer lunged for the man, pressing him against the bed while the two of them hit and kicked. The headboard banged against the wall, a rhythmic *thump, thump, thump* that led to someone banging back— Marc's low voice shouting, "Keep it down over there, you lovebirds!"

Sawyer had a hold of the assassin, and the assassin had a hold on the gun, and the gun was pointed right at . . .

"Zoe!" Sawyer yelled as the shot fired.

In the next moment, Zoe was rolling over broken glass, but she didn't feel the pain somehow. She was too busy remembering how Sawyer had told her that Kozlov and his men will always find a person's weakness, exploit it, use it, kill them with it if they have to.

And Zoe knew that, right then, Sawyer's biggest weakness was her.

When she saw the backpack on the floor, she stopped thinking and dove for it.

"Sawyer!" she yelled, standing and tossing one of the guns in his direction, but she missed, and as he lunged for the weapon she realized her mistake.

Because she was in front of those broken doors now, glass cutting into her feet, curtains and hair whipping around her, and absolutely nothing else standing between her and the railing, and the river.

And the Russian launching himself in her direction.

Beefy arms around her waist like a vise. Railing slamming into her back like a bat. And freezing wind on all her skin not covered by an almost nonexistent nightie.

"Zoe!" Sawyer bellowed, but Zoe could feel herself bending over the rail. She was going to break in two. She was going to black out. She was going to die.

Which was her very last thought before the world turned upside down. And black. And very, very cold.

chapter thirty

HER

Apparently, Zoe *did* know how to swim. But she was going to drown anyway. Or at least that's how it felt as the cold sent a shock through her system, freezing water like fire on her skin, numbing her fingers and burning her toes. Her whole body wanted to curl into a tiny ball and sink to the bottom of the river. Zoe had to make herself kick. She had to make herself fight. And fight. And fight some more because she hadn't gone over that railing alone.

The man's fist was tangled in Zoe's hair. She'd liked it so much better when Sawyer had done it—back when her biggest problems were no money, and no memory, and no name. She hadn't appreciated just how much she'd gained in forty-eight hours, but Zoe didn't even know where her next breath was coming from as the man pushed her head underwater, and she felt . . . nothing.

Not her hands or her legs, not her skin or her bones, just the overwhelming sense that she was about to explode if she couldn't breathe.

She had to breathe!

She'd spent all afternoon learning hand-to-hand combat from an actual spy but he hadn't covered "How to Not Drown in a Freezing River" in the intro course. Zoe wanted her money back.

So she made herself stop. And think.

The current was just as strong for him. The sky just as dark. The water every bit as cold. Zoe had nothing to stand on, but neither did he, so she pulled her legs up, twisting them around his arms and his neck, using every ounce of her strength to break his hold and surge to the surface.

She gasped for air, desperate to fill her lungs, but she couldn't stay there. Staying there meant dying there, so she took the deepest breath she could and dove, desperate to hide, to escape.

But hands were groping in the darkness, and Zoe felt herself jerked back against the current. She couldn't even feel him except . . . wait. He didn't have *her*. He had a fistful of that skimpy nightgown. So she kicked and clawed and twisted, trying to get free. But the man was too strong and Zoe was too weak—too frail. And she was all alone. She was all alone, her broken brain said. And that was going to be what killed her.

But, suddenly, there was a hand on her shoulder. There were eyes in the dark. *Sawyer*, a part of her screamed. Sawyer was there, reaching for the delicate neckline of the beautiful nightie.

And ripping it right off her body.

So the good news was that she was free. The bad news was that she was also very cold and very tired and (aside from a pair of panties) very, very naked.

For a moment, they stayed there, staring into each other's eyes, treading water in the darkness, a silent conversation taking place between them.

Well, those are my boobs.

I'm not looking.

How can you not look? They're right there.

Nope. Not gonna look.

I mean if someone tore your pants off—

Pants don't work that way.

But then the Russian was reaching for her again, clawing and desperate. And Sawyer gave her one last look.

Give me a minute.

She'd never seen anyone move like that. He was a blur in the night, lunging between them, arms clamping around the big man's neck. While Zoe struggled to keep swimming, to keep breathing, Sawyer wrapped that piece of satin around the assassin's throat and pulled. And pulled.

And pulled.

Until the man wasn't kicking anymore.

"Zoe?" Sawyer's hands were reaching for her as they surfaced, pulling her close. "Are you okay? Tell me you're—"

"I'm . . . okay. I'm okay. I'm . . ." She remembered. "Cold . . . I'm so cold."

"I know."

They turned in unison to watch the *Shimmering Sea* growing smaller in the distance.

"I don't suppose . . . they'll . . . stop . . ."

His laugh was short and sharp. "No."

And Zoe forced more air into her lungs. As long as she kept breathing . . . As long as she kept moving . . . As long as Sawyer was with her, she'd be okay.

"So the good news is I can swim and he's dead." She wondered how worried she should be that her breath was no longer white in the cold air.

They both turned to watch the body float away on the current. Then something seemed to occur to Sawyer. "What's the bad news?"

"I'm real naked."

He choked out a laugh and looked toward the shore, eyes scanning the terrain as if someone else might rise from the bottom of the river and try to kill them.

"Come on."

chapter thirty-one

Zoe had glass in her feet and water in her lungs, but the scariest thing was the look in her eyes when she said, "Put me down."

"No."

"I can walk."

"You can't walk."

"I'm fine."

"You're not fine."

"I'm . . ." she started again but couldn't finish because her lips were blue and her whole body was shaking. Her hands gripped his neck so tightly that she could have strangled the life out of him and he wouldn't have minded at all because that infuriating woman was still alive and Sawyer would never forgive himself if he didn't keep her that way.

"I can walk," she tried again, but he doubted she could even stand because she'd been in the water longer than he had. If he lived a hundred years, he'd never forget the terror of standing on the balcony for what felt like ages, trying to find them in the darkness before he dove.

What Sawyer didn't admit—even to himself—was that he had to keep walking because the cold was sinking into his bones, too, and he knew the clock was ticking. Adrenaline was pounding now, keeping him moving, keeping him warm, but he was going to crash soon and if they hadn't found shelter by then, well . . . there was more than one way to die in a freezing river.

Zoe wasn't just shivering in his arms by that point, she was shaking—her whole body convulsing as it tried to warm itself from the inside out.

"Your coat . . . isn't very . . . warm." He heard her voice quake and knew she was trying to tease, but something in the sound broke him.

"My coat is wet and the only thing keeping you from being buck-ass naked."

"You . . . don't . . . happen . . . to have . . . a . . . dry . . . one?"

In spite of everything, he wanted to smile. "No. Fresh out of dry coats. If I had one, I wouldn't share with you."

"That . . . figures . . . And I'm not . . . totally naked. I have . . . panties."

"Oh. I stand corrected." She put her head on his shoulder then, and he shook her. "No. Stay awake. Zoe. Stay—"

"I'm too cold to sleep."

"Good."

Sawyer stopped. The good news was that they were out of the river; but the bad news was that they were in the path of the wind. They had to find shelter, build a fire. Get dry. Get warm. Stay alive. And it had to happen in exactly that order. So he stopped and shifted her weight in his arms as he searched the darkness for a light, for a building. For a larger-than-average hole in the ground. He wasn't exactly in a position to be picky.

"Let me down. I'm heavy."

"You're annoying. Stay right there."

"You just want me to block the wind," she joked, but her words were getting softer—slower. They were running out of time. So he scanned the bank of the river and the dim outline of the trees and tried to think of all the ways it could be worse.

It could have been raining. Or snowing. Kozlov could have sent someone who didn't work alone. Sawyer could have jumped overboard without the Go Bag strapped to his back. So at least he had three guns, six thousand euros, four passports, two knives, and one half-dead and mostly naked amnesiac twin shivering in his arms.

"Are we not walking because I'm too heavy or because you've been slacking off on arm day? And leg day? And cardio?"

"Do you want me to take my coat back?" he chided.

"I don't know. Can I think about it?"

"The river is right there. I can put you back where I found you," he said, but she shivered in response. In less than a minute he'd be shaking too.

"Okay." She laid her head against his shoulder. "I was only wondering why we're just standing here?"

"We've got to get out of the wind," he said. "We need shelter."

"I know." She sounded annoyed, like the next time she got dragged out of a river she hoped it might be by someone a little more competent. "That's why I was wondering . . . why . . ." *shiver, shiver, shiver* ". . . we aren't going . . ." *shiver, shiver* ". . . there?"

The strange thing about nighttime in winter—especially when there's snow on the ground and a clear sky overhead—is that nothing is ever fully black. It's more a mix of grays and blues and glistening silver. So he couldn't believe he'd missed the very small, very decrepit, very real castle that stood near the water, like it had grown out of the banks a thousand years ago and now the river was trying to drag it back, stone by stone.

"Will that do?" she asked, sounding far too smug for someone who was half dead and mostly naked.

"Yeah." His smile was warm, at least, as he brushed a kiss to the top of her head. "That'll do."

chapter thirty-two

HER

Two minutes later, Sawyer was kicking open the door of a building that was only three rooms, but they were dry, and sheltered, and empty.

"Well, it's not much. But it's home."

"Thanks for carrying me over the threshold."

"You're welcome, Mrs. Michaelson," he said softly.

The largest of the rooms had a table and chairs and, best of all, a fireplace. A few pieces of old wood were stacked in the corner, and there were waterproof matches in the Go Bag, so it was less than a minute before Sawyer was striking the match and holding it to the wood. When he leaned over and blew on the flame, Zoe felt herself shiver in a way that had very little to do with the cold.

"You okay?" he asked.

She would have answered but she was too busy trying to keep her teeth from rattling together because even though they were out of the wind, it was still very cold and she was still very wet and Sawyer was looking at her in a way that would have made her tremble under the best of circumstances.

"We have to get you dry."

"I'm drying as fast as I can!" she said, inching closer to the tiny orange flame that was licking at the wood.

"Take off the coat."

"I'm naked under this coat."

"I thought you were wearing panties?"

"Panties are naked!" she shot back but he gave her a look. "They

125

are, at the very least, semi-naked and . . ." Something on the shelves caught her eye. "Are those blankets?"

She sprang to her feet, but pain sliced through her body, vicious and hot, and she crashed back to the floor. "Darn it!"

"Language," Sawyer teased, but he was already reaching for her bare foot and pulling it into his lap. "I said you couldn't walk," he reminded her, then carefully pulled something from between her toes. "Glass, remember?"

She had honestly forgotten.

"I guess it slipped my mind . . . what with the strangling and the drowning and the freezing—"

"And the shooting," he offered helpfully.

"Right! Totally forgot about the shooting. So, yeah . . . glass."

He was studying her foot in the faint light of the fire. "I don't think you need stitches, but we'll need to look you over in the morning. River probably washed most of the glass out which is a good thing."

"Yay?" she tried.

"That's the spirit!" Then he got up and grabbed the blankets. They were moth-eaten and filthy and Zoe almost wept with the sight of them. "Wet coat off. Dry blanket on."

He dropped one in her lap but she just glared at him even though her lips were blue and her teeth were rattling.

"Well . . ."

"Well what?" He was already stripping out of his tuxedo. Which . . . a hot guy stripping out of a wet tuxedo raised her body temp a little but not nearly enough.

"Are you going to turn around?"

"You know I've seen . . ." He didn't finish but gestured to what lay under Mr. Michaelson's wool coat.

"You mean when you literally ripped my nightgown off?"

"One. *Nightgown*"—he did the ironic finger quotes again—"isn't exactly the word I would use. And, two—I am, in fact, referring to the time I saved your life."

But she didn't speak. Didn't scold. Didn't laugh. And she absolutely did not move.

"Fine!" He spun to face the other direction and Zoe slipped an aching arm out of the wet wool. Instantly, the heat of the small fire washed over her skin and she sighed into the warmth.

Sawyer made a different kind of sound. "Can I turn around now or are you gonna just sit there, moaning?"

She wrapped the nasty blanket around herself. "You may turn," she said and he joined her on the floor in front of the fire.

They spread his clothes out to dry and Zoe waited for the warmth to seep into her bones, for the fear to fade. Or, at the very least, for the ability to fake it, but that must have failed her, too, because after a few minutes, he said, "Are you shaking from the shock or from the cold?"

"I don't know."

"Are you hurt?"

"I don't know." And for some reason, she just shook harder.

"Your teeth are going to break off." He sounded almost angry as he pulled her to rest between his spread thighs, back to front, his arms wrapped around her. And maybe it was the warmth of his body or the pressure of his arms, but, somehow, Zoe stopped shaking. And for some reason that was almost worse. Because as her body slowed down, her mind sped up and she didn't like where it went. At all.

"Talk to me, Zoe. Are you—"

"How do you do this?" Her voice cracked, and her nose ran but she couldn't bring herself to care. "How does Alex? How is this your life?"

But Sawyer only squeezed her tighter. She felt his fingers in her hair, combing through the tangled strands. "Well, to be fair, this is the first time I've ever done this. Exactly. Usually, there's a lot more blood and mud. And vodka."

Something about the smooth cadence of his voice made her tuck her head and smile into the soft skin of his hard bicep. "Don't make me laugh, you jerkface."

"Okay," he said, but he didn't let her go. Instead, he tossed another piece of wood onto the fire and guided her down to the hard floor, spooning around her, a wall of muscle and bone to keep in the heat.

"You take it one day at a time," he said slowly. "And if that's too much, one hour. One minute. One breath. You inhale. Exhale. Repeat." His finger brushed a strand of wet hair away from her neck, exposing the skin to the fire. "Inhale, Zoe."

She knew it was an order, so she let the warm air fill her lungs, swearing she'd never take breathing for granted again.

"Now let it out, lady. Let it all out."

And when she did, she wasn't shaking anymore. But it was like a lead blanket had settled over her body, pushing her into the floor—into him—and every ounce of energy drained away.

Her eyes were already closed and her mind was already drifting when she felt something soft and warm touch her temple. "Go to sleep, sweetheart. Go to sleep. I've got you."

chapter thirty-three

HER

The first thing Zoe thought when she heard the screaming was, *Oh no. Not again.* She was almost disappointed to stir awake and realize that the enemy Sawyer was fighting was himself.

"No!" He tossed on the cold, hard floor. "No!"

"Sawyer." She reached for his arm.

"No!"

"Saw—"

He grabbed her and slammed her to the ground, so close to the flames that sparks flew up like fireflies.

"Sawyer!" She saw the knife. She felt his rage, and she knew—she just knew—that he wasn't her Mr. Michaelson then.

"Sawyer, wake up!" she shouted, and the fire crackled and something in him started to fracture—reality seeping through—like they were back in that river and he was slowly floating toward the surface, looking for some air.

"Hey," she tried softly. "Hey, you're okay."

"Zoe." It wasn't a question. It was a reminder.

"Yeah." She hated the look in his eyes. "You're okay."

"I know." He pushed away a little too hard. "Fire's going out. I'll get more wood."

"That's not why I woke you, and I think you know that." He looked at her over his shoulder as he pulled on his dry tuxedo pants. "Sawyer. Talk to me."

But he was busting apart an old chair and tossing the legs on the fire. "That ought to keep us until morning."

"Sawyer, tell me."

He hunched low, bare feet on the cold ground, like he might bolt outside and take off through the snow—like anything would be better than being there.

"Sawyer—"

He wheeled on her. "There's a reason I don't sleep, Zoe. But you should. Go back to bed." He reached for the tuxedo shirt and tried to pull it on, but he fumbled with the studs.

"Here." She pushed his hands away and let her delicate fingers dance over the buttons. "At least you got a nice tuxedo out of the deal."

He huffed out a cold, dry laugh. "Lot of good it'll do me."

She must have looked confused because he turned to stare into the fire.

"It's not like the movies. My job . . . it's not parachuting onto embassies or playing high-stakes poker . . . My job is *using people*." He said the last words very slowly, like they were so heavy it was a miracle he ever managed to climb out of that river. "I lie, and I deceive, but, most of all, I get people to trust me. Steal for me. Tell me things they shouldn't. I use people, Zoe. And, sometimes, they get hurt."

Zoe felt brave for some reason—or maybe just stupid—but she had to know. "People like Helena?" He kept quiet but shuddered at the name. "You do sleep, you know. And you talk while you do it. Was she your girlfriend?" she asked slowly. "Your wife?"

"She was nothing. No one. She was"—he drew in a ragged breath—"*expendable*. And now she's dead." He wrapped the extra blanket around Zoe's shoulders and turned her toward the fire. "Go to sleep, Zoe. Nothing else is going to hurt you tonight."

Zoe wanted to argue—to fight—but her eyelids were too heavy and her limbs were too weak, so she just lay in the glow of the fire, trying not to think about the man who had the power to hurt her most of all.

chapter thirty-four

HER

Zoe woke up to the feel of a cold fire and a bare back and the over-whelming sense that Sawyer wasn't where he was supposed to be. She pushed up a little too quickly, and the room spun as she heard a deep voice say, "Good morning."

He was sitting on the one chair they hadn't burned—had it propped against the nearly rotten door, as if he could keep the rest of the world at bay through force of will alone.

He must have found some clothes somewhere because he was dressed in jeans and a cable-knit sweater. Mr. Michaelson's coat—dry now—was draped over her layers of blankets. The designer tux-edo jacket was balled on the dusty floor beneath her head.

"You went shopping?" she asked, still groggy.

"I got you something." He pointed to a pile by the fire. Jeans. A shirt and sweater. A pair of old boots. "The sizes are probably wrong, but . . ." He ran a hand through his wavy hair. "Hope you're not picky."

"I wouldn't know if I were." She gave a reluctant grin.

He didn't smile back, but he got those deep creases around his eyes—the kind that made men look distinguished and women look old and proved that the universe is unequivocally unfair. But they sure looked good on him in any case.

"No, I guess you wouldn't."

That time she didn't ask him to turn around. He just did it, pull-ing out two steaming cups of coffee and some food from a small sack as she tugged on the hodgepodge of clothes. The shoes were too big but he'd bought two pairs of socks and a big stack of bandages for her injured feet so she really wasn't going to complain.

131

"Okay." She tugged on the heavy sweater. "I'm decent." She sat back by the fire and took a sip of the too-strong coffee, grateful for the warmth. "So did you conjure all this by magic or . . ."

He shook his head. "There's a town about a half mile upriver. I figure we can walk there, catch a train. Maybe get a car."

It was a solid plan, a perfectly viable option, but the fact remained that she didn't know where they were going or what they were going to do when they got there. And there was something else, too—something she hadn't had the nerve to think—much less say—until that very moment.

"Why'd she do it?" Zoe blurted while Sawyer examined the bottom of her feet. For the most part, the cuts were small and shallow, but he carefully layered antiseptic on each one before wrapping her foot in a thick bandage and helping her into the first pair of socks.

"What?" He looked up from his position on the floor.

"Alex. I get why she stole the drive from Kozlov, but why didn't she take it to the CIA?"

He shook his head. "I don't know."

But there was something in his tone—in the way he wouldn't quite meet her gaze—that made her say, "You have a theory, though." She was right, but he looked like he'd rather fight another assassin than tell her. "Sawyer? *Why would Alex run?*"

He put a glob of antiseptic on the biggest of the gashes and Zoe jerked when she felt the sting, but he kept her ankle in his hand, not letting her go anywhere.

"I don't know." His voice was hard, but his hands were gentle as he held her aching foot and, oh so softly, blew against the place where she was hurt. Which might have made her squirm for different reasons, but she couldn't get distracted. She had to know.

"Why would Alex—"

"Because she went bad, okay? Because she got greedy? Because that drive is worth a small fortune to the right buyer and Alex has expensive taste? Because eventually . . ." He'd thrown the last of the wood on the fire and the flames were growing hotter, brighter, but somehow the room was a whole lot colder than it had been moments before.

"Because, eventually, this life breaks you. And you wake up one day and realize all you have to show for it is a body full of scars and a head full of ghosts and you start looking for a way out. Maybe . . . maybe it's not a drive to Alex. Maybe it's a parachute."

Zoe didn't know what scared her more: that Sawyer was talking about her sister or that, on some level, he was talking about himself. So she just said, "You're wrong. I know my sister." He huffed out a laugh that was more like a breath, soundless and borderline cruel. "I do! Alex and I are twins. *Identical twins.* We'll be connected for the rest of our lives. We're—"

"You're not her!" He probably hadn't meant to yell because, when he spoke again, his voice was softer. "You have the same DNA, but you're not her. You walk into a room and everybody smiles. You hum and the world wants to sing. Yesterday I literally heard you use the term *oopsie daisy.* You're good, Zoe. You're *good.* People like Alex . . . People like me . . ." He looked away. "We can only do this job because we're a little bit bad."

She didn't know what to say. *You're good too* would have gotten her laughed at. *You're good to me* would have made her sound desperate and lonely and all the things she didn't want to be (but probably was anyway). Because at some point Sawyer had stopped being *Mr. Spy Guy* and started feeling like *Her Guy*, and that was just another lie. Just another cover. They weren't really the Michaelsons, and they never, ever would be. Which was when she realized that she trusted Sawyer with her life. But she wasn't strong enough to trust him with her heart.

So she cocked her head. She tried to tease. "Don't you know? Sometimes villains make the best heroes."

The smirk he gave her was warm and sweet and wrapped around her like a blanket. "Then, lady, I'm the hero of your dreams."

She didn't say what she was thinking: *That's what I'm afraid of.*

"Come on. We need to get out of here before Kozlov sends someone to finish the job." He stood and she started putting on her shoes. "Can you walk? I can go get a car."

"I can walk." Her feet didn't hurt that much as she put pressure on them and slipped her arms into Mr. Michaelson's coat and her hands into Mr. Michaelson's pockets and—

"Wait," Sawyer called. "I'll take that coat and you can . . ."

But he trailed off as her fingers brushed against something and she pulled out a piece of plastic. It took her a moment to register what it was because that black card with the little golden C didn't belong in such a dusty, ancient room.

"What's . . ." And then she remembered. She laughed. "Oh. Well, we probably don't need the key to my Paris hotel room."

She started to toss it on the fire, but Sawyer was already lunging for her, shouting, "No!" There was panic in his voice she hadn't heard before—like he'd rather lose every gun and knife and safe house he owned than part with that thin piece of plastic.

"What is it?" She stared at the face she no longer recognized because, in that moment, he was a stranger—a trained operative trying to pick the perfect lie. "Sawyer . . . Why do you have the key to a room we can never use?" But Sawyer just kept staring at the card—at her—as if he wasn't sure which one was really worth saving. Which was how Zoe knew—"It's not a hotel key, is it?"

She studied the card. Solid black with that little golden C. No chip or strip on the back, so it probably wasn't a credit card. But it mattered. One look at him was enough to tell her that it mattered a lot.

"What kind of card is it, Sawyer?" She dangled it over the fire, and he cocked his head like *we both know you won't drop it*—which she wouldn't have, but she didn't pull it back either. "What—"

"It's a kind of . . . *membership* . . . card."

"Membership to what?" she snapped, and Sawyer thought a long time about the answer.

He could have killed her, knocked her to the ground and taken it, left her there with her wanted face and her blank memory, but instead he told her, "A bank."

"What kind of bank?"

"The Swiss kind."

The card hadn't touched the fire, but it felt hot in her hand anyway. "Ooh! Do I have a Swiss bank account?" She felt suddenly excited. "Whoa. Am I superrich? Is that why I'm in Europe? Do I . . ."

He shook his head, and for the first time since she woke up, he looked tired, like this whole thing was a river and he was swimming against a current that was just a little too strong. He ran a hand through his hair; it had dried by the fire and was sticking up and wavy and wild. It made him look younger, but his eyes . . . his eyes looked like he was a million years old. It was like they'd both lived a dozen lives since Paris.

Then a chill that had nothing to do with the cold went down her spine.

Paris.

She remembered falling snow and ice-covered streets, the way she'd stood with all her worldly possessions in her cupped hands and watched him change before her very eyes. He'd said something about the lip balm—about Alex. But the card had been right there—that little golden C glowing beneath the streetlights.

"This was why." She saw that moment differently. She saw *everything* differently. "This was why you chased me."

"Zoe—"

"You were willing to let me swim across an ocean until you saw this! Why?" And she knew. "You don't think this is mine, do you? You think this is Alex's."

"It's the kind of thing . . . It fits. From what I know about Alex, that fits."

He nodded toward the card, and Zoe gripped it a little tighter then slid it back into the pocket of the coat . . .

Of Sawyer's coat.

And, suddenly, the whole world went cold again.

"Why did you have it?" She was practically breathing fire, but he just looked at her like she hadn't been paying attention.

"Because it's not trash." His voice was calm and matter-of-fact, but he couldn't meet her gaze.

She limped closer and he inched back, like she was the one who could kill him with her bare hands, and in that moment, maybe she was.

"I left this card on the dresser when I emptied my pockets after Paris. So why was it *in your pocket last night*?" She asked like she didn't know, like she wasn't already begging, pleading, praying she was wrong.

And in his defense, he didn't answer.

But in her defense, he didn't have to.

She knew. She knew. And it broke her. "Because you were leaving me."

"No." Sawyer reached for her but Zoe pulled back.

"You were. You were going to ditch me. Abandon me."

More than knowing he'd only offered to save her to get his hands on that card . . . More than being lied to and led on . . . More than being strangled and shot at and drowned . . . The thing that hurt her most was simple.

"You were going to leave me . . . *on our honeymoon*!"

"*We aren't actually married!*"

He might have yelled.

She might have gasped.

And the whole world might have tilted on its axis as he shook his head, a softness in his voice she didn't like at all. "You would have been better off without me."

Is that what he thought? That she wasn't in danger? That she didn't need him? Want him? Did he really not remember . . .

"*You killed a man with a negligee!*" Zoe shouted, then headed for the door.

Outside, sunlight bounced over the icy landscape, and she had to squint against the glare.

"Zoe, wait!"

She didn't dare slow down, but she risked a glance over her shoulder. Sawyer was pulling on the backpack and pushing a gun into his waistband at the small of his back, but he was looking at her like she was the most dangerous thing around.

"What's in the bank box?" she called.

"I don't know." He caught up with her, lunging to block her path. "Nothing. Probably."

And all Zoe could do was stand in the morning light, breathing hard, listening for all the things he wouldn't say.

Like whether or not he meant it when he called her sweetheart . . . Like why he'd bought the ring . . . Like what was he thinking all those times she'd caught him looking, smirking, smiling at her . . . Like how had she been foolish enough to think she knew him when she didn't even know herself . . .

"Zoe . . ."

"You know, for a good spy, you're a bad liar." She pushed past him, heading toward town.

"Zoe!"

"Actually," she called back, "you probably aren't even a very good spy!"

He threw his arms out wide. "*I killed a man with a negligee!*"

Zoe didn't give him the satisfaction of a response. She had to get to town. She had to get to Switzerland. She had to find that bank.

And then she had to find her sister.

"Zoe . . ." Sawyer was beside her again, his stupid long legs with their stupid long stride. "Can we talk about this, please? Can we . . . Where are you even going?"

"Oh, me? I'm leaving you. Because I don't need you, remember?"

"Zoe, wait."

And for some reason she stopped. She looked up at him. It hurt, but she did it anyway.

"Can we . . ." he started, but she reached for him, arms sliding beneath his jacket and wrapping around his waist, her head against his heart. For just one second, she wanted to savor this—remember this—so she closed her eyes and sank into all his strength and warmth because he was the best thing she had, but, turned out, she'd never had him at all.

"Hey." His hands were warm on her cold skin as he tilted her face up to his. "I'm—"

She jerked the gun from his waistband—tossed it into the woods and stormed away.

"That's my second favorite gun!" he called after her.

"Then go get it!" she shouted.

But she didn't turn around.

She didn't look back.

And she didn't even think about slowing down.

chapter thirty-five

Sawyer found the gun, but he didn't see his sanity anywhere.

She knew. She knew and he didn't have a time machine, so where did that leave him besides cold and hungry and way more terrified than he wanted to admit?

He should have thrown that card overboard, tossed it into the fire. Because the moment she realized what it was, he knew it would change everything. Either she was going to hate him for lying about the card and the bank; or, worse, she was going to insist on going there herself. And now, Sawyer was pretty sure, it was both.

Oh, how he prayed it wasn't about to be both.

The plan had seemed so simple in Paris: get her someplace safe, take the card. Come back for her if he needed her. But the part he hadn't counted on was Zoe herself. And at some point, he'd made the cardinal mistake: he'd started to care. He wasn't supposed to like her, trust her, need her. Want her.

To make matters worse, he'd lied when he should have told the truth and told the truth when he should have lied, and that's how he ended up freezing and alone and scared out of his mind.

Because right then, Sawyer wasn't worried about his mission. Not the drive or the card or even Alex. Sawyer was worried about Zoe and what he was going to say when he found her.

Or, worse, what he was going to do if he didn't.

HER

By "town" Sawyer clearly had meant "living postcard" or "artisanal reenactment." It wouldn't have surprised Zoe to learn that the whole place was fake. It was just too perfect with its cute little shops and frozen waterfalls. Smiling people and delicious-smelling food. But this place wasn't a dream; it was reality. And Zoe couldn't help but feel just a wee bit bitter about it.

Because Zoe's reality was an aching head and aching feet and being shot at and strangled and nearly drowned on a regular basis. Plus, she really needed to find a bathroom. Again.

So Zoe walked on, fueled by half a cup of coffee and the knowledge that, for the first time since she woke up in that snowbank, she knew where she had to go and what she was going to do when she got there.

So she headed across the quaint little street toward the quaint little train station. "When's the next train?" she asked, but the woman in the quaint little ticket booth looked at her oddly, and Zoe tried to find the words. "Uh . . . Wann fährt der nächste Zug?"

The woman nodded and pointed at the sign. Five minutes. And Zoe held up a finger in the universal sign for *one please*. But when the woman told Zoe the price, she remembered.

Zoe didn't have any money. Zoe didn't have any ID. Zoe didn't have anything or anyone or . . .

"Willst du auf deinen Mann warten?" She was aware, faintly, of the woman saying something—of the line behind her starting to grow.

"What?" Zoe asked even as her tired brain tried to translate the words: *Do you want to wait for your husband?*

Zoe started to correct her—should have corrected her. She was already drawing a breath and trying to remember how to say *I don't have a husband* in German . . . when she followed the woman's gaze to the ring on Zoe's finger, and she realized she was wrong. Of course she was wrong.

She did have something, after all.

HIM

Sawyer didn't have to worry about finding her, he tried to tell himself. If he'd learned anything since Paris it was that he simply had to follow the path of death and destruction she'd inevitably leave in her wake. But as he reached the little town with its quaint shops and charming buildings, he didn't see any bleeding corpses or active fires and he couldn't shake the feeling that maybe he'd missed her.

Which was fine, he told himself. He should let her go.

He should run faster.

He should be worried, he thought.

He should be relieved.

Then he heard a sound on the cold, thin air and he knew what he was going to see even before he turned: a train waiting at the station, and a woman in a hodgepodge of clothes running across the platform.

For a moment, Sawyer imagined what it would be like to walk away.

Zoe was neither his mission nor his problem, and the guy he'd been two days before might have turned up his collar and disappeared on the wind. He would have called in some favors and receded back into the shadows—the only place he ever felt at home.

But now when he thought of home he didn't see shadows. He saw light and he heard laughter and he knew that it wasn't a place, it was a feeling. And he was terrified that if she got on that train without him, he'd probably never feel it again.

chapter thirty-six

HER

Zoe wanted to look out the window and watch the little town slip away as the train pulled out of the station and headed into the Alps, but she knew to keep her head down and the collar of Mr. Michaelson's coat turned up. She didn't want to be seen. But she didn't want to admit who she was hiding from, either—not until a figure appeared in the corner of her eye and a deep voice said, "Can we talk about this?"

When Sawyer dropped into the seat beside her, she wished it came with an ejector feature. All she wanted to do was kick him out—of that seat . . . of the train . . . of her life. She had no choice but to reach for the safety information pamphlet in the seatback in front of her. It was riveting stuff. Plus, knowing her luck, she was probably going to need the emergency protocols sooner or later.

"Zoe . . ."

"I'm reading."

"Zo."

"Don't call me Zo. My friends call me Zo. Or they would if I could remember having friends. Which I don't."

"And that's not my fault!"

But she just huffed and turned the page of her safety card so that she could read it again. In German this time. Because safety was important.

He looked up and down the nearly empty train car. "Where are we going? Please tell me you didn't ask for a train to Zurich? Please tell me . . ."

"Of course not. I bought a ticket for the first train out of town. I didn't even ask where it was heading."

He blew out a relieved breath. "Good. I guess that's . . ." But then he trailed off. He seemed to remember. "How'd you buy a ticket?"

She was still holding up her safety card. (It was just as riveting in French.) Her left hand was right there, practically at eye level, and she heard it in his voice the moment he realized . . . "You sold your wedding ring."

There was real heartbreak on her fake husband's face, and it shouldn't have given her such satisfaction, the wave of shock and disappointment that filled his eyes. But it did. And she didn't try to hide her self-satisfied grin. She was tired of hiding, period.

"We aren't actually married, remember?" Did she sound childish? Yup. Did she care? Not even a little.

He gave a long-suffering sigh. "Where are you even going? What are you going to do when you get there?"

"I'm going to save my sister."

"Alex can save herself," he said and she scoffed. "*She can*. All she has to do is come in from the cold. Pick up the phone. Walk into any embassy. Get on a plane to Langley. Sure, she'd have to answer some questions from some extremely unpleasant people, but *Alex can save herself*."

The train was at full speed then, the trees nothing but a snowy blur outside the window as Zoe turned to face the glass. But what she saw was him, a reflection on the window, a ghost behind her back.

"I get it. I do. You think I don't know Alex because I can't remember my address or Social Security number or the name of my second-grade teacher. But I know how to breathe and tie my shoes. I know the words to at least thirty Taylor Swift songs and that if I sit in that backward-facing seat over there I'll want to throw up in fifteen minutes. I may not remember Alex. But that doesn't mean that I don't know her. And I'm telling you, she's not a traitor. And I'm going to prove it."

For a moment, Sawyer just stared at her like maybe he should have left her at the bottom of the river, tied up on the dirt floor, stuck in that snowbank in Paris, making angels out of snow and blood.

He drew a deep breath. "I know I'm going to regret asking this, but how, exactly, are you planning on saving your sister?"

Zoe had been under the impression that Sawyer was smart. Zoe was evidently mistaken. "With this!" She held up the bank card. "You think the drive is there, don't you?"

"I don't know that—"

"Well, I'm going to get it." She felt so proud of herself with her train ticket and her plan and her mission. But then he had to go and paste a smug look on his smug face.

"Really? What's the plan? Walk in and pretend like you're your own twin sister?"

"Why not? *The Parent Trap* is a classic—"

"No!"

"No what?"

"No, I'm not going to let you risk your life because of some movie you can't even remember."

"I remember *The Parent Trap*."

"How—"

"I don't know! Okay? Maybe that's stored in a part of my brain that isn't broken." She hated how her voice cracked, how her eyes burned. "Maybe there's a part of *me* that isn't broken, believe it or not."

It was either the best thing to say or the worst—Zoe couldn't tell because everything about Sawyer changed in that moment. "I believe it," he said. "I do. But, Zoe, it won't work."

"How do you—"

"Because I already thought of it! I've thought about it a million times and . . ." Oh, he was regretting those words. She could see it in his eyes. And she knew.

"It wasn't just about the card, was it? You needed . . . me?"

"Zoe . . ."

"You were going to *steal* me? *Use* me? That was why you helped me. That was why . . ."

It was all a lie. A lie and a fraud and a con. In that moment, she felt like just another knife or Go Bag or gun. She could imagine him telling someone *Oh, that's Zoe. She's my second favorite sister* . . .

"No, Zoe, listen. Please—"

But Zoe was already up and climbing over him. She was already walking away.

chapter thirty-seven

HIM

He was an asshole. He knew the words in a half-dozen languages, but in every one it was absolutely true. He should let her walk away, cool down. Have her space. Only an asshole would bolt out of his seat and dart down the center aisle, saying, "It's not what you think."

"So it's *my* fault"—Zoe spun on him—"that I heard the words that you said in the order that you said them? It's *my* fault that you're regretting the words that *you* used. That's *my* fault?"

"No," Sawyer said, but her face seemed to get a little more murder-y, so he tried, "Yes? Yes. And no. Maybe. What's the right answer here?"

Then she groaned, whipped back around, and kept walking, out of that car and into the next. And Sawyer did the only thing that he could: he followed.

Sooner or later, she was going to have to listen to him. After all, sooner or later she was going to run out of train. But as she stepped into the small vestibule at the end of the car she stopped and turned.

"Why are you even here? I thought you were leaving me. Isn't that why you took the . . ." But she trailed off, pieces coming together in her mind. "Oh. Of course. You're following me so you can get this back." She pulled the bank card out of her pocket, holding it like a magician who was getting ready to make it disappear. "Come to steal it from me? Again? Or did you come to steal *me*?"

The fact that she was willing to flash that card around showed just how little she understood the danger she was in, so he gently eased it back into her pocket and closed the door behind them.

But that meant they were closer than they had been, and she looked up at him, fire in her eyes.

"Get. Off."

He took a step back, giving her space, but she didn't move. "*Get off the train*," she clarified before wheeling and heading toward the narrow door in the corner of the alcove. "I appreciate your assistance, but I can make it the rest of the way on my own."

The words were strong and her eyes were cold, but there was an uncharacteristic lilt to her voice, a more-defiant-than-usual set to her chin as she said it, like she was bracing for a laugh, for a mock, for some kind of cruelty to be determined later.

"Go ahead," she even told him. "Laugh. I can take it."

He had to make her see—make her know—"I'm not laughing."

It must have been the speeding train, why he felt unsteady on his feet. When Zoe pulled open the tiny door and stepped inside the even tinier compartment, it must have been temporary insanity that made Sawyer push in after her.

"Get out!"

"Not until you listen." He slammed the door. He hadn't even registered that it was the lavatory until she had to back up against the sink to make room for his big body.

"If you think I'm joining whatever the train version of the mile-high club is with you— Ouch!"

She banged her head against a small cabinet, so he used one hand to cup her head and the other to circle her waist and lift, setting her atop the counter and stepping in between her spread thighs.

"You were right," he admitted. "I thought about using you. And then I thought about leaving you."

"Uh . . . *I know!*"

"Because I don't want you to get hurt."

He let his eyes take her in, from her wild hair to the bruise to the—*damn, was she bleeding again?* It proved his point, though. He cursed silently to himself then grabbed a tissue and pressed it against her temple. He hated the way her eyes closed when he touched her—was it because her head hurt? Or something else?

Because touching her hurt him, too, but he wasn't anywhere near brave enough to say it.

"I thought about leaving last night because I thought you were safe there. I thought you'd *stay* safe there. I thought . . ." Sawyer had been trained in interrogation tactics and at least twenty different ways to spot a lie, but for the life of him he didn't know how to say—"I learned a long time ago that everyone is safer far away from me."

It was almost peaceful there, in the small, dim room on the gently rocking train. And Zoe was so close—warm and safe and alive. He had to keep her alive.

"Is this about Helena?"

He balled up the tissue and threw it in the bin. "It's about a life-time of collateral damage. I thought you'd be safer if I left, Zoe. That's all." He cupped her face and pulled her close. "I was wrong. So . . ." He drew a deep breath; he was going to need it. "I'm sorry I almost left last night. And I'm sorry I didn't tell you the truth about the card in Paris. And I'm sorry I thought about using you to access the vault. And I'm sorry that I've lost track of all the things I'm supposed to be sorry for. But, mostly, I'm sorry this is happening to you." He tucked a piece of hair behind her ear. "I'm sorry I can't keep you safe."

"It's not your fault," she whispered.

His thumb ran over the smooth skin of her cheek in the world's tiniest caress. "Of course it is."

Zoe looked over her shoulder, into the mirror—at the face the world was looking for. "As long as the world is after Alex, I'll never be safe."

"I know. I—"

"That's why I have to clear Alex's name."

It sounded so simple—so obvious and so easy. But she was also so wrong he could cry. "These people are dangerous, Zoe. They're monsters."

"I know! There's a price on my sister's head, remember? On *my* head."

"That doesn't mean you have to pay it!" Then he pressed against her, body against body, foreheads touching because he didn't trust his hands. He'd spent too much time training them to act on instinct, and if he let them near her, then he didn't trust what they might do.

So he breathed in her scent and he matched her breath for breath, and he wished he were the kind of man who could save her. And he wished she were the kind of woman who would let him.

"Let me get you someplace safe."

"You want me safe?" She seemed to take it like a dare. "And out of your hair?"

"Yes, please." He couldn't help but laugh. "Both would be great."

"Then take me to the bank." Oh, she was good. He hadn't even seen it coming. And he really, really should have.

"Just so we're clear, when I think *hey, maybe Zoe could pretend to be Alex so we can access the bank box*, it's evil, but when it's your idea, it's genius?"

"It's evil when it's a secret," she said simply, and Sawyer knew she was right. He also knew—

"It's too dangerous." He was shaking his head. "No. I'm not letting you—"

"I'm going with or without you, so unless you plan on kidnapping—"

He pulled back as much as he could in the tiny room. "Don't tempt me."

"Help me." It was the tone of her voice that did it, pleading and desperate, but just proud enough to show that asking hadn't been easy. "Help me end it."

Sawyer never thought about the end. He didn't plan for his retirement. The fact that she still thought she could get a happy ending . . . he didn't want to be the one to tell her that was the biggest lie of all.

So he made her a deal. "We can go to the bank and check it out, and if Alex is there and shows herself, great. But we're not going in, and we're not taking any risks."

"Okay." She nodded. "Yes."

And, asshole move or not, he pressed even closer. He wanted her to remember he was bigger and stronger and forget that she could break him with a look.

"But, Zoe . . . so help me. If I so much as smell Kozlov on the wind, we put Zurich to our backs and we don't stop running until we hit water."

"Okay," she said.

"I swear to—"

"Okay. Yes. Deal!"

"I need . . ." Sawyer started. "I need you to trust me. Can you do that? After last night? After this morning, if you can't trust me, then this won't work."

She was a little too quiet for a little too long, biting her lip in the way that almost killed him.

"Okay," she said slowly. "Now leave."

"No! I just said I'm not going to—"

"No. I mean get out. Please." She might have blushed. She couldn't meet his gaze. "I came in here for a reason . . ."

He suddenly remembered where they were. "Oh."

"Yeah."

"I'll just wait . . ." He tried to point over his shoulder but banged his thumb on the door. "Ow. Yeah." But the door wouldn't open. "I'll just . . ."

He pushed. He leaned. And then the door opened a little too quickly and Sawyer, a man who earned his first black belt at the age of fourteen, almost fell on his face.

"I'll be right here." He pointed to his feet and once the door closed, he was pretty sure he heard laughing.

And, worse, he was pretty sure he liked it.

Maybe that's why he missed the footsteps—didn't hear a thing until the gun cocked and cold metal pressed against the back of his neck and a deep voice said, "Move and I'll blow your fucking head off."

And all Sawyer could think was *Not again*.

chapter thirty-eight

HER

Zoe was a liar. And a fraud. And someone who should have her feminist card revoked because as soon as the hot guy with the big gun came crawling back, she let him. Worse, a part of her rejoiced at the sight of him. Because he was way better at strangling people with lingerie than she was. And he knew Alex. And spy stuff. And she was in the middle of an extremely spylike situation. So she needed someone who knew the ropes. And the guy on the other side of the door . . . well . . . he tied her in all kinds of knots. The question was, were they the kind that would hold her together or the kind that would hold her back?

He pounded on the door and she sighed, because ninety seconds of solitude was evidently way too much to ask.

"Okay! I hear you!"

But all she got was another bang or two, and Zoe knew she should open the door. She also knew she really didn't want to. Because opening that door meant looking at broad shoulders and blue eyes and feeling things she really didn't want to feel. Opening that door meant going back to pretending she was strong, pretending she was fine, pretending she had everything under control when the truth of the matter was, she spent most of her energy in any given moment trying to keep the rest of the world from seeing how very not fine she really was.

But what if she didn't have to pretend with Sawyer? What if there was more than one way for him to keep her safe?

"Sawyer . . ." She had to say it while the door was closed. She didn't think she could face him. "Don't say anything, okay? But I just . . . You have to know . . ."

Then she caught sight of her reflection in the mirror, and what she saw was a woman with bad fashion sense and no hairbrush— someone who had been through hell. And lived. But that little voice inside of Zoe couldn't keep from adding *So far*.

So she leaned against the door and said, "I'm scared, okay? Of what happens if we don't find Alex . . ." She gave a small, sad laugh. "And maybe what happens if we do. But most of all, I'm scared that I'll never find . . . myself. I'm scared that I can't trust myself. So I get that you're *Mr. I Can Kill a Man with Sleepwear Guy* but right now the only thing I care about is whether or not I can trust you? So . . . I guess that's what I'm asking. Can I trust you?"

She stayed silent for the space of five whole heartbeats, waiting, worrying. Wondering.

Had he gotten bored? Walked away? Left her? Or was the answer simply no?

"Sawyer?"

When Zoe pushed open the door, the first thing she noticed was the wind, gushing ninety miles an hour through the train's side exit and blowing all around her. She tried to pull her hair out of her face, but the strands were stiff and curly and . . .

The second thing she noticed was the banging.

And the cursing.

And the rough timbre of Sawyer's voice as he yelled, *"Run!"*

But Zoe was frozen to the spot, watching as a strange man pushed Sawyer toward the open door. He had one hand on Sawyer's throat and another on his wrist, banging Sawyer's hand against the wall over and over until Sawyer lost his grip on his gun and it flew through the doorway, disappearing into the blur of snow and trees.

A look of shock and pain and grief passed over Sawyer's face, and then it quickly turned to fury. In the next moment, he was spinning, shifting their positions in one fluid motion and knocking the man out the open door. For a long time, he just stood there, breathing hard, hands on knees, staring longingly. "That was my third favorite gun," he whined.

Zoe didn't know whether to laugh or console him, but before she could do a thing, the door to the next car slid open. A gun cocked, and a rich voice said, "Well, hello there."

It would have been so much easier if the man had growled or sneered. But, no. His voice was downright chipper—a *fancy meeting you here* tone. And something about it made Zoe's whole body shake as the stranger stared at her—a lascivious gleam in his eye.

"It's so good to see you again." He closed the door that led into the next car and stepped toward her.

He was slicker than the others, Zoe couldn't help but notice. Expensive suit and hair that didn't even blow in the wind. One look was enough to tell her he was the kind of man who liked precision and perfection in all things, and there wasn't a doubt in Zoe's mind he was more dangerous than all the goons combined.

"Get away from her, Collins." There was an edge to Sawyer's voice as he shifted, ready to pounce.

"Oh, now, Mr. Sawyer. She's quite the catch. Surely we can . . ." Collins looked her up and down. He all but licked his lips. ". . . *share her.*"

Zoe's whole body shook. Dots grew at the corner of her vision, and she thought she was going to be sick. She was going to die. She was going to—

"Touch her, and I'll kill you."

Sawyer's voice was dark and deep and Zoe finally understood all those times he'd said he was a bad guy. A villain. A threat. Because, in that moment, he was the most dangerous, beautiful, terrible, wonderful thing she'd ever laid eyes on. He looked like someone who would follow his enemies to the ends of the earth; he was a specter in the shadows, a sound on the wind. He was the thing that went bump in the night and there was no place you could run, nowhere you could hide, nothing you could ever do to keep you safe from him.

And it was all Zoe could do not to fall head over heels in love with him. The jerkface.

But that didn't change the fact that Sawyer was unarmed, and Collins was already raising his gun and aiming it right at Zoe.

"I've been so looking forward to this," the man said and Sawyer growled and started to lunge, but, for some reason, all Zoe could think about was Paris—how it had felt to lie on the cold ground watching snowflakes fall in slow motion. Like she wasn't even a part of her own body. That was how she felt right then. Outside herself. Detached.

She was aware, faintly, of the man shifting his aim as Sawyer launched himself across the car, but something was rising up inside of Zoe, and it made her kick—hard. The blow knocked the man back a step. Shock filled his face as he grabbed for a door handle that wasn't there, a wall that couldn't stop him. And Zoe didn't think—didn't wait. She just stepped closer and shoved.

The last thing she saw was the look on the stranger's face as he fell.

The last thing she felt was relief.

And the last thing she heard was Sawyer saying, "What came over you?"

"I don't know." Zoe slammed the door. "But I liked it."

The slow smile on his face was enough to tell her that she wasn't the only one.

chapter thirty-nine

There were times to celebrate life's little victories—really cherish a job well-done. This wasn't one of those times. Because Collins didn't work alone. Which meant the clock was ticking and running down fast, so Sawyer pushed Zoe toward the next car but stopped suddenly.

"Sawyer!" she cried.

"I'm down a gun." He leaned over and picked up the weapon that he'd knocked out of the first man's hand. "And now I'm not!"

Then he pushed her into the next car, ignoring the strange stares they were getting from the other passengers. Did they look like they'd just been in a fight? Probably. But he didn't have time to do anything about it, so he didn't take time to worry about it. That was one of his rules for life and covert operations and, really, it had been a long time since Sawyer had been able to tell the difference.

They were pushing out of one car and into the next vestibule when Zoe looked at him. "So I guess Kozlov found us."

Oh, how he wished she hadn't said that. Because he didn't want to lie to her, but he also really didn't want to tell her the truth.

"What?" She stopped. Because the truth was going to make her do that. "What's wrong?"

"Uh . . . more walking, less freaking out, please."

"What aren't you telling me?"

He pushed her toward the next car. "Do you want the good news or the bad news?"

For a second, she looked confused. "There's good news?"

They'd reached the back of the train by then, the end of the line.

It was as good a place as any to tell her, "Kozlov doesn't know where we are."

She was positively glowing. "Really?"

"But the CIA does."

It took a moment for her face to dim as she slowly realized . . . "I killed a CIA agent?"

He reached for the door. "Who? Collins? No! You didn't kill him. Probably. Maybe. There's only like a twenty percent chance you—"

"Not helping!" But that wasn't even the bad part, and he saw the moment she caught on. "Is there any chance he didn't tell anyone where we were before . . ."

"You threw him off a moving train? No. They know we're on this train. Which means they're going to be waiting on us."

"Is this your way of telling me we're not going to the bank now?"

He pulled open the door and peeked outside. There were houses around the bend, a highway visible through the trees. Civilization was coming up fast, so he closed the door and went to the other side of the train—of the mountain. Nothing but hills and rocks and trees and snow.

Snow was good. The more snow the better, he thought as he threw open the door and yelled over the roar of the wind. "No! It's my way of telling you . . ."

"Oh! We're slowing—"

"Try to protect your head when you fall!"

And then he pushed her.

Two seconds later, Sawyer followed.

chapter forty

HER

Zoe tried to protect her head as she fell. Really, she did. Because (1) she considered herself the kind of person who always followed instructions and (2) it seemed like a good idea at the time.

But there's only so much you can do when you hit deep snow at fifty miles an hour and the mountain is so steep that you become a human pinball, rolling down the side of a literal Alp.

She could hear tree limbs breaking. She could see the world spinning. And yet in her mind she was a cartoon character rolling over and over and over until she was the juicy human center of a giant snowball, only her feet and hands sticking out.

But when she finally stopped rolling, amazingly, she appeared to be mostly avalanche-free. Alive. She hoped Sawyer was, too. That way, she could kill him.

Then she heard a groan behind her. She saw white breath fogging in the air. And a figure pushed out of a snowdrift, breathing hard and saying, "I told you there was only a twenty percent chance of dying."

So Zoe hit him with a snowball because, really, what else was she supposed to do?

"I can't believe you pushed me off a train."

"It was barely moving."

They were walking through the deep snow, slipping and sliding and *please-don't-start-an-avalanching* their way down the mountain. And yet, she had to spin on him.

"A barely *moving train!*"

"See . . . I feel like you're emphasizing the wrong part of that sentence."

Zoe huffed and pushed aside a snowy limb.

Sawyer had to laugh. "Did you want to wait around for Collins's buddies from the CIA to find us? Brownnosing asshole," he added under his breath. "I really do hate that guy."

"We could have just waited for it to stop!"

"In a town crawling with even more CIA agents? And no doubt MI6. And"—he looked pensive— "you know, Mossad's got to be here by now. Do you want to go see your new friends in Mossad or do you want to—"

"Oops." She let the limb she was holding spring back and clobber him. But the sound he made was less *I just got a big face full of snow* and more *that actually hurt* and, instantly, she turned back. "What's wrong?"

"Nothing," he said. "I hit something on the way down and got a scratch. That's all."

"Let me see." She was reaching for the zipper of his coat.

"I'm fine." He pried her fingers free.

"You don't sound fine. Let me—"

But he just pulled her closer—tighter—until her arms were pinned in his and his breath fogged with hers. "Zoe, I am fine. It's just a scratch. And we need to keep moving."

But she couldn't shake the feeling . . . "Are you lying?"

"Constantly." He turned her around and nudged her forward, but she glanced back over her shoulder.

"You promised you wouldn't die on me, remember?"

He gave her his hot guy smirk. "Why? Would you miss me?"

Oh, she hated that cocky edge to his voice—absolutely loathed how much she liked it. "No. I just need you, that's all. For my cover."

"Of course."

"I don't have time to find another fake husband, is all."

"Naturally." They walked on for a while, sunlight filtering through the pines. She thought for a moment he wasn't going to say anything else, but there was a weight to the silence. She could almost hear him thinking . . . "I do have to wonder . . . am I still your fake husband if you sold your ring?"

She didn't mean to blush, but the blood was already rushing to her cheeks in a way that had nothing to do with the cold. She tried to look away, but he took her hand and tugged gently.

"What?" he prompted.

"Well . . ."

"Well *what*?" He sounded almost playful—teasing—until the expression turned to worry. "Zoe, what . . ."

"It was an economics thing. You see, it was worth too much. A train ticket is more an earrings-level purchase. So . . ."

She didn't know why, but the ring felt almost hot in her hand as she pulled it from her pocket. The silver caught the sunlight as it lay in her palm, looking like something forged by fairies a thousand years ago—precious and rare and full of magic.

"You didn't sell it."

His voice was soft, but his gaze was hot, like he couldn't decide whether to kiss her or spank her or maybe a little bit of both and Zoe felt her cheeks go even redder. When he slid the ring back on her finger, her hand felt funny. Tingly. Alive with possibilities.

"Okay, Mrs. Michaelson. Let's go find a ride."

chapter forty-one

HIM

The village at the base of the mountain was even smaller than the one by the river, so quaint and untouched by tourists that it wasn't just off the beaten path, it was far from any paths of any kind. It was exactly the kind of place where two strangers wouldn't exactly go unnoticed. Much less two people who looked like they had jumped off a boat, slept on a dirt floor, and toppled down a mountain.

Zoe must have sensed it, too, because she nervously tucked a piece of hair behind her ear.

"Yeah. That fixed it," Sawyer said and she smacked him on the arm. He couldn't keep from smiling.

With any luck they could slip into town, get a car, and get out without anyone being any the wiser. But as they walked down the too-empty street he saw a reflection in a window, and he realized . . . "Don't freak out, but I think we have a tail. Take the next right and I'll engage. You—"

"Oh, shut up, Mr. Michaelson." She slipped her hand into his and laughed a little too loudly.

"What are you . . ." He was turning to her. He was staring at her. But somehow he didn't see the kiss coming—not when she put her hand on the back of his neck and went up on her toes. Not when her lips brushed against his—subtle pressure and teasing touches that made Sawyer want to melt.

He'd always been good at situational awareness, but right then he couldn't plan their best escape route because there was no place else he wanted to be. He just knew that Zoe was pressed against him and her fingers were in his hair and it was way too much and not enough. Steadier. Hotter until . . .

Zoe inched back as the two police officers walked right past them without even a glance in their direction.

"See?" Her breath was warm against his lips. "I'm an excellent spy."

"That's not . . . uh . . . actual tradecraft."

"Don't be mad."

"I'm not mad," he said a little too quickly. And, in truth, he didn't sound mad, but he didn't sound normal, either. "I just wasn't expecting that . . . uh . . . maneuver."

"I know! I'm so good at undercovering!"

"That's not a verb."

"And coverting. I covert so well!"

"That's . . ." But he trailed off as he looked at her and, suddenly, he knew that there was absolutely no one with whom he'd rather undercover. "Yeah. You do."

It wasn't until they'd been walking for three blocks that he realized he was still holding her hand.

It wasn't until they'd been walking for four that he realized he had no intention of stopping.

They found the car right where the lady at the store had said it would be. All it had taken was three hundred euros and a sob story about being on the run from Zoe's ex-husband, and now they were the proud owners of a fifteen-year-old SUV that may or may not start.

But it wouldn't be reported stolen. And it was a way out of town. Because they needed a way out of town. Desperately. Sawyer hadn't seen them yet, but, soon, those streets were going to be crawling with every acronym in the business—maybe Kozlov's guys, too. They didn't have a moment to lose.

"This must be it." The SUV was big and boxy and covered bumper to bumper with at least six inches of snow. It would be slow and lumbering and the most unimpressive car on the road. In other words, it was perfect.

He leaned down and winced in pain and cursed the rocky hillside as Zoe asked, "What are you doing?"

He brushed the snow away from the driver's-side wheel well. "Your new best friend, Emmy—"

"Emiline," she corrected. "And don't make fun! She was very concerned about us being able to outrun my tortured past. You know she knocked fifty euro off the price."

"Because you told her you were pregnant!"

"What?" She looked so innocent, so proud. So beautiful. It was incredibly annoying. "I had to sell the inciting incident."

"*The what?*"

"Why are we running *now*? What drove me to leave Edward—"

"Edward?"

"The terrible man my family made me marry on my nineteenth birthday even though he's old enough to be my father . . ." Zoe explained like she couldn't believe Sawyer had forgotten the very best part.

"Damn it!" The key wasn't behind the front wheel, so he went to try the back.

"What are you . . ."

"She said the key was here. Maybe it fell . . ."

He was hunkered down on the ground, searching the snow, when he heard it. Or maybe he didn't hear it at all. Maybe he felt it, like someone walking over his grave. But before he'd even turned around, he knew what he would see passing on the street: Range Rovers. He knew what he would hear: the hum of motorcycles and the low, guttural sound of Russian curse words on the wind. Because Kozlov's guys were there.

How had those fuckers found them so quickly? He didn't know. Didn't care. Because, ultimately, it didn't matter. They were there. And soon every agency in the world would follow.

"Zoe, I want you to listen to me very, very, carefully." He slowly stood then turned up the collar of her coat and handed her the backpack.

"No." She was already going pale and shaking her head because Zoe was no fool.

"I'm going to walk back to the street and take care of some things, and I need you to get on the other side of the car and wait three minutes—one hundred and eighty seconds. Count them. Then get up and walk the other direction. Don't run."

"No!"

"Walk. And don't look back."

"Sawyer—" There were tears in her eyes and her voice cracked. Her voice cracked and that broke him.

"I put a piece of paper in your pocket. There's a phone number on it—a service I use. I want you to go back to Emiline's and tell her your ex is after us. Hide. If I don't come for you in forty-five minutes, get out of town. Tomorrow morning, call that number. If there's not a message from me, then you start running, sweetheart. You run and you don't look back."

"Sawyer." She grabbed his hand as if she could keep him there, like she wasn't just afraid to let him go—she was afraid to lose him. Like she needed him, wanted him, cared for him. Not Sawyer the spy but Sawyer the man. And in that moment, Zoe made him wish he could have more—be more. She made him believe in happy endings. She made him wish there could be one for him.

"You promised." He heard the swooping, pulsing sounds of a helicopter flying overhead and knew the agencies were coming—the agencies were there. They were all out of time. In so many ways.

"You're gonna do great, sweetheart. Go. I'll be fine." He forced a smile and turned toward the street—he started to walk away. He *should* have walked away. But he stopped. And said, "Fuck it."

"Langu—" she started, but he was already pulling her into his arms and pressing her up against the snowy car. Lips touching, tongues seeking, skin caught between fire and ice.

When he pulled back, her eyes were dazed and her lips were

parted and he had no idea if she even heard him when he pressed his forehead to hers and whispered, "I'll find you."

And then he went to buy her some time because it was all he had left to give.

HER

The asshole was going to make her a widow before she'd ever been married, and that alone made her want to kill him.

Tears she didn't remember crying streaked down Zoe's face as she watched Sawyer walk toward the end of the alley, drawing the guns from the waistband of his jeans.

Darn, the man could wear a pair of jeans.

But Zoe had to shake the thought out of her head; she had to think! When he glanced over his shoulder and gave her an irritated glance, she remembered.

"Oh. Right!" Then she scampered to the other side of the SUV and hunkered down and started counting.

One. Two.

The idiot was going to get himself killed.

Three. Four.

What kind of man can give a girl a kiss like that and then just walk away?

Five. Six.

She hated him. But most of all she hated this, kneeling, hiding, being sheltered and protected.

Seven.

She hated it so freaking much.

Eight. Nine.

A part of her had to wonder if that was the first time she'd sat alone, crying, hoping that a guy would call.

Ten.

She really, really hoped it would be the last.

Eleventwelvethirteenfourteen.

She had to do something! Help. Distract. Covert. She needed to covert her butt off, but she could hear the helicopters circling overhead so she pressed closer to the SUV, hiding. Waiting.

When a big chunk of snow fell off the vehicle's window, Zoe risked a peek through the frosty glass, hoping to get a glimpse of Sawyer, but what she saw instead was an unlocked door. Then Zoe stopped thinking. She just threw open the door and crawled inside.

The keys had to be there somewhere! *They had to*, she thought, climbing into the driver's seat, searching.

"Come on come on come on."

He would be almost to the street by that point, to the Range Rovers and the goons and the guns. So many guns. She opened the backpack and started digging. There had to be something she could use to . . . what?

That's when she saw the knife. And looked at the steering wheel. And something in her mind went *click*.

It wasn't a flashback. And it definitely wasn't a memory. But for one split second it happened—the feeling of someone else being in control of her body, of autopilot kicking on and conscious thought going dormant as her hands flew, popping open the dashboard and grabbing for the wires and the knife.

She had just enough time to think, *I'm probably going to electrocute myself* when the car started. *Did I do that? Did I dream that?* But exhaust was fogging up the chilly air and a radio was blasting, and when she tapped on the windshield wipers they pushed aside a layer of heavy snow.

And Zoe knew exactly what she had to do.

If there had been a little more time Sawyer might have made a list of the hardest things he'd ever done.

There was the drinking contest with the Turkish arms dealer who was a lot tougher than she looked. The week he'd spent in a livestock car on a train through Argentina. The mission Alex simply called Operation Mustache. But nothing in his whole life had ever been as hard as walking away from Zoe. Still, if he bought her enough time to get out . . . then, well, it was worth it.

So Sawyer cocked his guns and took a breath and . . . spun. Ready to shoot because something was coming down the alley toward him—fast. He took aim but didn't fire because he wasn't sure what he was seeing.

It looked like a tank covered with snow. No. An SUV. No. *Their* SUV. And it was flying in reverse. He actually had to dive out of the way before it slammed to a stop and the passenger door flew open; and there was Zoe, leaning over the seat. Eyes bright. Skin glowing. The single-most gorgeous sight he'd ever seen as she yelled, "I know how to hot-wire cars!"

For a moment he just stood, heart pounding, skin sweating, not sure whether he should laugh or cry or kiss that sly smile right off her face. So he just dove in and shouted, "Drive."

chapter forty-two

HER

Sawyer didn't actually let her drive. The jerkface. But Zoe couldn't be too mad because the SUV was warm and the seat was big and she could lean back, feet on the dash, gazing out at the mountains and valleys that were frosted with snow and filtered through twilight.

They'd made it out of town, and he kept the speedometer at exactly three kilometers over the speed limit because, according to Sawyer, anything slower looks suspicious and anything faster gets you stopped.

Most of the snow had blown off the hood, but some of the windows were still covered in frost, giving the light an icy blue haze that made it look like something from a dream. And maybe it was? She had a head injury, after all.

But Zoe wanted to at least pretend the man behind the wheel was real—the way one big, rough hand gripped the steering wheel and his eyes scanned the road, looking for anything that could possibly hurt her.

"What?" he asked after a while.

"What *what*?"

"I can feel you staring," he said, but he never even glanced her way.

"I was just thinking . . . you know . . . I could be a car thief."

He didn't laugh, but she saw his lips tip up. She'd started to learn that, from Sawyer, that was the same thing. "You aren't a car thief."

She took her feet from the dash and turned to him. "The *Fast and Furious* franchise had to have been inspired by someone—"

"You are neither fast nor furious."

"You're right," she said. "I'm probably more of a regular thief.

You know, the kind that steals diamond necklaces while wearing ball gowns."

The lips moved again, and she hated how warm that gesture made her. "I'd hardly call that a regular thief."

"I probably strap them to my thigh with a garter belt . . ."

The big hand gripped and regripped the steering wheel and he swallowed like he had something in his throat. "Yeah." Sawyer coughed. "That could be . . . uh . . . it."

Zoe didn't even try not to smile.

When they passed a road sign she tried to see how many kilometers it was until Zurich, but it wasn't listed. In fact, she hadn't seen it on any of the signs, which made her ask, "How far are we from Zurich?"

She thought he was probably doing the calculations in his head because it took him a long time to say, "We can't exactly take a direct route."

"I know, but we've been driving for hours . . ." She sounded like a grouchy child who really needed a juice box and some cheesy crackers. Which, come to think of it, Zoe really wanted some juice and cheesy crackers.

"Then take a nap."

"I will. As soon as you tell me when we'll get to Zurich." But there was something in the set of his jaw, the look in his eyes.

"We're not going to Zurich—"

"You promised!"

"—*yet*, okay. We're not going to Zurich yet."

"Maybe it's the half-dozen intelligence agencies after us, but it feels like we're in a time-sensitive situation here."

"We are! It is!"

"Then—"

"We slept on a floor last night," he reminded her. "We're wearing clothes I stole from a laundromat. And I'm pretty sure we both smell like river water. So, no. We're not going to one of the most secure banks in the world . . ." He looked at her. ". . . *yet*. We're going to take hot showers and get a good night's sleep, and then we're going to think this through before we do anything. Okay?"

He was saying all the right things for all the right reasons, but Zoe couldn't shake the feeling that there was way more to the story.

So she twisted in her seat and took off the heavy sweater. It was too hot and she was too frustrated. She didn't realize her shirt was gaping open until she felt his gaze on her—on the scars that covered her chest.

"It's not what you think," he told her.

"Oh?"

"I was staring at your boobs," he said, and she couldn't help herself—she smiled.

"See. That was a well-delivered lie. Good job."

"Thank you."

She could go hours without thinking of the scars and wondering exactly what had tried to kill her and was it ever going to come back and finish the job? But it was out there now and Zoe couldn't help it.

"You know, I keep thinking, I should probably get another low-cut dress? Maybe a halter top?"

"Well, you won't get any complaints from me but you might get cold."

"True." She gave a sad smile. "But maybe then people would stop trying to kill me. No one would mistake me for Alex then, would they?" She gave a sad laugh, honestly not sure whether or not she was joking.

Zoe didn't realize she was rubbing the scar until she caught him staring, and she pulled her hand away like it had burned her. "I don't know why I keep doing that. I guess my muscle memory isn't the butt-kicking kind?" And she couldn't help but feel incredibly disappointed.

The smile Sawyer gave her was slow and dark and mildly indulgent. "Oh, I don't know. You threw a CIA operative off a moving train and hot-wired a car."

She couldn't help herself. She beamed. "I did!"

"And you're not a terrible dancer."

"Especially considering I had to lead."

When Sawyer's lip quirk turned into a full smirk it felt like the greatest compliment in the world. She turned to look at the black ribbon of highway snaking through the valleys and over the mountains.

"So if we aren't going to the bank, where are you taking me?"

The smirk faded, the hand on the wheel tensed, and she could have sworn the windows frosted over when he said, "Someplace safe."

"Like a safe house?"

He was silent for so long that she thought he hadn't heard her.

"More like a house . . . that's safe," he said, and it was like the sun had finally slipped behind the Alps and plunged the whole world into darkness. Zoe hated it, the feeling that Sawyer would have rather been back in that alley than on the way to wherever they were going. But they were going anyway.

So she tried to brighten her voice, tease him—to bring his smile back. "Are you going to blow it up with a snowball?"

"You do realize that the snowball didn't actually . . ." He let out a frustrated sigh and shook his head and it felt, to Zoe, like victory. "No. This one won't explode. No one knows about this one."

"That's what you said about the first one," she teased but Sawyer kept his gaze on the highway.

"Even I forget about this one." The sun slipped behind the mountains and the whole world turned gray. It wasn't until Zoe's eyes were closed that he whispered, "Or I try to."

HIM

He should have missed the driveway. The snow was deep and the night was dark, and the trees had grown, unhindered, for a decade. So it was mostly instinct that made him slow and turn through the tiny gap in the brush, grateful for the tall tires of the SUV as they churned through the deep snow, headlights slicing through the trees as they headed up the mountain.

Everything had changed. And yet it was exactly the same, or so it felt twenty minutes later as forest gave way to clearing and the headlights shone back at him, reflected in a wall of darkened windows.

The cabin looked even smaller than he remembered, its pitched roof holding up under the weight of a foot of snow.

He never thought he'd be glad to be back, but for the last thirty miles, his hands had been shaking and his brow had been sweating and the dark road had started to swirl before his eyes. When he moved to take off his seat belt, he was hit by a wave of pain so deep he thought he might pass out. He'd been sitting for too long, and now the adrenaline was gone.

All that remained was a deep, throbbing ache and a sticky shirt, and the relief that they'd made it, even if it was the last place on earth he wanted to be.

"What . . ." Zoe stirred awake then grinned at him, like a little girl who had been having the most wonderful dream. Her hair was a halo in the moonlight, and she looked so pure and innocent that he hated his own hands for how badly they wanted to touch her. "Where are we?"

It was harder than it should have been to tell her, "Home."

chapter forty-three

HER

The snow was up to Zoe's knees as she crawled from the SUV and trudged toward the cabin. She could see her breath in the air and smell the pines, and every cell in her body felt alive for the first time. She didn't know there were that many stars—millions of them glistening overhead. She wanted to make a wish because surely, somewhere out there, one of them had to be falling.

"Coming?" Sawyer called from the porch.

She couldn't believe it when the key was under the mat. Weren't safe houses supposed to come with retinal scanners and voice-activated attack dogs and keypads that shoot acid if you type in the wrong code? Evidently not, and Zoe couldn't help but feel a tiny bit disappointed as she followed Sawyer inside.

She reached for the switch by the door, but nothing happened when she flipped it.

"No power," he said. "We're off the grid. I'll see if I can get the generator going in the morning. In the meantime, there should be some candles around here somewhere."

It didn't take long for her eyes to adjust to the darkness. One whole wall was windows, after all, and moonlight filtered through, reflecting off the snow outside—too bright for the middle of the night. The whole place was covered in dust and smelled like it hadn't known fresh air in ages, and if it hadn't been for the tall stone fireplace and old furniture, she might have wondered if they'd just unlocked a tomb.

"We should have gas for hot water and wood for fires, and . . .

Shit," Sawyer mumbled and she heard something hit the floor just as he struck a match.

Light flickered, the tiny orange glow washing over the dusty floor as Zoe bent down to retrieve the candle that was rolling toward her.

"Looking for . . ." she started but trailed off as she came eye to eye with the dark stain on Sawyer's shirt.

Her first thought was that he'd spilled something—that she should give him a hard time for being clumsy. But the stain was wet. And the stain was very, very red. And his face was very, very white. And in the flickering glow of the matchlight she saw it in his eyes—she knew.

So she looked up at him and said, "I'm going to kill you."

"You're a real jerk, you know that, right?"

Sawyer did know, but that wasn't the time to recount all his lies and betrayals and crimes both large and small. He was reclining on the couch, surrounded by at least a dozen candles and one very large bottle of vodka. He just hoped it was large enough.

"Don't drink all that. I need it." She grabbed the bottle back.

"Need it for— Son of a bitch!" he shouted as she poured liquid fire into the gash in his side.

"This is from the mountain, isn't it? You said it was just a scratch."

"It *is* a scratch," he said and she gave him another splash. "It's— fucking—"

"Language!" she scolded as she set the bottle aside and brought a candle closer to the scratch that . . . okay . . . was a little longer and a little deeper than he might have initially led her to believe.

"You were going to fight ten of Kozlov's guys—"

"I only saw four. Five. Shit—" Another splash. "Well, now you're just wasting it to be mean." He grabbed the bottle back and took a swig. Something told him he was going to need it.

"Walk away, Zoe," she said in a too-deep voice. "I don't need your help, Zoe. You're just a girl, Zoe."

"Hey, I never said—"

"And then you gave me a Certifiable Movie Kiss and went to take on twenty guys way bigger and stronger and tougher—"

"Hey!" Now the thing that really hurt was his pride.

"*You could have died.*" He so wanted her to be teasing, but the tears in her eyes were real and so was the tremble in her voice. "You could have bled to death. You could have—"

He sat upright even though it hurt like hell, even though he'd just stopped bleeding, even though she wasn't really his to comfort, his to console and touch and soothe.

She wasn't really his.

So why did it feel like he had every right in the world to cup her face and feel her warm cheek in his cold palm? Why did it feel like there was a safe deep inside of him and the tumblers had finally clicked into place—the deep satisfaction of knowing that he'd cracked it.

"Hey," he whispered, even though she wasn't really his. And she never, ever would be.

She turned her head—lips brushing against his cupped hand—and it was all he could do to choke out, "I didn't die. I'm okay."

He watched Zoe bite back screams and tears and at least a million words that neither of them had the strength to say. Then he let her push him back onto the sofa. He felt the brush of her hair as it glided over his bare chest, the touch of her fingers as she traced every scratch and bruise—like she wanted to make sure he was safe—he was whole.

Sawyer had been in danger pretty much every moment of every day for a decade but that felt like the very first time anyone would actually care if he got hurt.

"Zoe . . ." His voice was rough in a way that had nothing to do with blood loss or vodka. "Baby, I . . ."

"Sawyer . . ." Her fingers traced over his skin, burning like the flames.

And then she pulled a piece of wood out of his side and Sawyer saw stars as he screamed and she leaned closer.

"Don't ever do that again. I have no intention of becoming your fake widow."

She threw the bloody stick onto the fire then got up and stormed away—left Sawyer lying there, wondering which part of the last three minutes was more painful.

chapter forty-four

HER

Zoe didn't know why she wasn't sleepy. Maybe it was the long nap she'd had in the car or the chill that still clung to the stuffy air of the cabin, but she strongly suspected it had more to do with the man who refused to lie still even though she had only just finished sealing the wound in his side with superglue (yes . . . *superglue*).

The jerkface.

She could hear him down below, locking doors and drawing shades, stoking the fire, letting all the heat rise to the loft overhead.

The place should have come with bearskin rugs and lots of mounted antlers, but there were only a few pictures on the walls—black-and-white photos of trees and snow and the still, summertime waters of a lake. Zoe walked down the stairs, examining every one, silent as a thief, no idea what she was going to steal but certain that something precious lived hidden in those walls, swearing she wouldn't stop until she'd found it.

"Are you hungry?" he called from down below.

There was really just one room. A few cabinets and appliances that could loosely be called a kitchen, a rickety table and chairs, and the big stone fireplace and old, dusty sofa. But somehow when she glanced over the railing, he seemed small for the first time since she'd known him.

"This place is always stocked with canned goods and first aid." Well, at least that explained the superglue.

"And vodka," she helped out.

"And vodka." He took a deep swig from the bottle she hadn't even noticed he was holding. "I can heat up some soup or—"

"I'm fine."

"It's no trouble."

"I'm not hungry." She was walking down the stairs when the light of her candle landed just right on one of the photographs and she realized that it wasn't just a picture of a lake. There was a child in it, too—a little boy—doing a cannonball off a long dock in the distance.

She took another step and brought the light closer to another picture: pine trees drooping under the weight of heavy snow—and, almost obscured by the branches—a tiny set of footprints leading to a snowman.

But it was the next photo that made her stop—made her stare. Because she recognized the fireplace and soft rug, but in the dark, she hadn't noticed the little boy who was lying on his stomach, setting up dominoes, one after the other. There was a mischievous smirk on the child's face, and even though the photo was black and white, somehow she knew that his eyes were a clear, bright blue.

"No!" She leaned on the railing. "Nooooooo!"

"What?" Sawyer shouted, panic in his voice.

"No way. No *way*! No *freaking* way!"

"What?" This time he sounded leery.

"Is that . . ." She trailed off as she pointed to the photo and he slowly brought the vodka to his lips again. His throat worked as he gulped it down. *One. Two. Two and a half.* Then he set the bottle on the counter and wiped his lips with the back of his hand.

His shirt was still off and, for a moment, she wondered if maybe she was developing a fever because why else would the sight make her so hot and swoony? Maybe she'd been hurt in the fall? Maybe . . .

"I can neither confirm nor deny . . ."

Zoe looked back at the little boy in the photo. "It's you! Gasp!"

Sawyer let out a weary, put-upon sigh. "You know, most people don't actually *say* 'gasp'; they just—"

"You were *a child*!" She took a step closer to him. And he took a step closer to her. "You were *cute*!" she said, like that was the most vicious accusation in the world. Then she cocked her hip. "What happened?"

She'd meant it to tease, to joke. Because her favorite thing in the world was teasing this grumpy, growly man who never let her drive and was really good at building fires and pulling glass out of toes and drinking vodka while shirtless.

It wasn't supposed to make him grimace and growl in the not-fun way. But something shifted in that moment. She knew it the moment he said, "That's classified," and walked away.

She found him on the porch, staring out over the snow that glistened like a sea of crystals. "We should be safe here." He grabbed an armload of firewood, then ushered her back inside and locked the door.

"Sawyer . . ."

"This place isn't in my name." He walked to the fireplace and dropped the wood. "The bills are paid out of a numbered bank account, and I haven't been here personally in twenty years, so—"

"Sawyer."

"—no one can tie this place to me. Not the agencies and definitely not Kozlov. You take the loft. I'm used to the couch. And I don't sleep—"

"You might sleep if you tried it in a bed for once!"

"No, Zoe. I wouldn't. So take the fucking loft." She'd seen him frustrated and tired and hungry and annoyed and excited and terrified. But she'd never seen him mad before—not at her.

Then he started blowing out candles, leaving nothing but little whisps of smoke swirling like ribbons in the moonlight.

"Why do I get the feeling you'd rather let me stab you in the other side than tell me what this place is?"

"It's nothing. Really. Just someplace I used to come when I was a kid. That's all."

He started to push past her, but she reached for him. She wasn't sure why. It's not like she could stop him—take him—beat him in a fight. But as soon as her fingers grazed his skin he froze.

"Get some rest, lady." His lips twitched at the name he used to call her, but it sounded different now, and for the life of her, Zoe couldn't pinpoint how or why.

He opened his mouth as if to say one more thing, but the words didn't come—just a quick breath. And then the last candle went out.

chapter forty-five

HER

The light from the fireplace danced across the steepled pitch of the ceiling. It was like some kind of puppet show the fire was putting on just for her, but Zoe was too tired to pay attention to the story. So she stayed in the big bed in the big loft, worrying. Thinking. Listening to the sounds from down below—the scrape of a chair against the floor, a curtain being drawn, sparks shooting out from the fire and catching on the screen.

How many times did she start to get up? To call for him? She lost count. And before she knew it, she was sleeping. Right up until the moment when she wasn't.

At what point does a person become immune to the sound of screaming? Zoe wondered an instant before she bolted awake to the sound of, "No!"

"Sawyer," she said as she threw the covers off. He'd found an old T-shirt for her to sleep in, but the air was cold on her bare legs as she ran from the toasty loft to the man who was lying on the sofa, sweat pouring off him even though it was colder there closer to the fire.

"Sawyer?" She expected him to bolt awake and act like nothing had happened, but he was drenched in sweat and had turned the color of paper.

"Run!" he shouted, but Zoe only moved closer. He'd kicked off a blanket and the gash in his side was angry and red but it wasn't bleeding—yet. He tossed again. His leg kicked the vodka bottle and it fell to the floor but didn't shatter.

"Sawyer . . ."

"Zoe!" he shouted, still fighting ghosts in the darkness. He was going to open his wound again. No glue was that super.

"Sawyer!" She tried to pin his arms down, but even injured— even asleep—his body knew what to do and in the next moment she was flying through the air and landing on the soft rug in front of the fire. Sawyer was on top of her. His hands were on her throat.

"Saw . . ." All Zoe could think was that she was getting really tired of almost being strangled. But this time Sawyer wasn't going to show up to save her.

"Saw—"

She tried to pry his fingers free, but he was too strong. She tried to do *The Move*—the one that had flipped a Russian assassin on his butt—but Sawyer was too heavy.

She tried to say his name, but the word wouldn't come. Maybe it was the late hour and dying fire but Zoe was pretty sure the room wasn't supposed to be that dark—the stars weren't supposed to be *inside*, swirling and growing at the edges of her vision.

So she let go of his arms and reached out, searching, looking for the vodka bottle. For something. Anything. When her fingers found the pillow, she didn't think twice. She just grabbed it and swung.

She couldn't have hit him very hard, but still, it jarred him. He stumbled back, even though, technically, he was sitting down, legs on either side of her hips as he leaned over, looking . . . stunned. Blinking slowly. Eyes coming into focus as he took in her ragged hair and old T-shirt, wild eyes and . . .

She knew the moment he saw the red rings around her neck because his gaze turned dark and vicious, but the person he wanted to hurt was himself. Hands that had been like steel around her throat were soft as they cupped her face. "I'm so sorry. I'm so sorry. I'm so . . ."

He tried to push away, but Zoe wrapped her hands around his wrists, holding him there. "I'm okay."

"I'm so sorry. I'm—"

"I'm okay." She made him look at her. "Sawyer, I'm fine."

Suddenly, his body went slack, like a wire that had just been cut, and he slumped against her. "You were dead." He pulled her closer, held her tighter—like he needed to feel her heart to know it was still beating. "You were dead. You were . . ."

He looked like he wanted to get up, to leave—to run—so Zoe moved, rolling on top of him, her legs straddling his this time, settling more and more of her weight atop him. "I'm okay," she said, but his hands were still touching her face as if trying to memorize every pore and eyelash and freckle.

"You died. You were dead. I couldn't save you," he said so low she almost didn't hear it over the pounding of her heart.

"You did save me." She couldn't hold back her laugh. "You saved me plenty."

"I can never save Helena. But this time . . ." He screwed his eyes closed and pulled her tight against his chest, arms around her like a vise. And Zoe understood.

"It was me? This time? In your dream?"

She felt his nod, but he didn't even try to speak.

It was too hot, all of a sudden, with the heat from his body radiating through her too-thin shirt.

"I couldn't save you."

"Shh." She ran her fingers through his thick hair and the subtle scrape of nails against scalp made him shiver. "You save me. And I save you. We're a mutual saving society," she told him, but he didn't say a thing.

They lay there for a long time in the flickering light, breathing in time like a dance. Had it really just been three days since he'd found her—since he'd been a stranger? She felt like she knew all his smirks and his huffs—what it meant when his jaw ticked or his hands flexed. She felt like she knew *him*. She just didn't know . . .

"Who was she? Who was Helena?"

"I told you. She's no one." He tried to push her away again, but Zoe had the leverage and the willpower and she wasn't going to let it go that easily.

"Tell me. Please."

He stared up at her, waiting, thinking. Then he pushed a strand of hair out of her eyes and tucked it behind her ear. "I was new and young and cocky. I thought I had to make a name for myself, so when we learned that Kozlov was moving large sums of money through a German bank . . . Well . . . That was my first big mission. Find someone with access—someone who could help us trace the money. That's who Helena was, Zoe. Just a nice woman who had access to a server and was willing to stretch the rules to stop the bad guys. She was . . . *expendable*."

His gaze found hers in the darkness. "The moment I heard she was compromised, I drove like hell, but . . . I didn't get there in time." He turned to face the fire. "I never get there in time."

It was like the key piece of a puzzle falling into place, a quiet, satisfying click that only she could hear. "That's the dream? The reason you can't sleep?"

He bit his lip and nodded slowly, but when he turned back to her it felt like the whole world got very slow and very still and even the flames in the fireplace stopped dancing. "It used to be."

She swallowed hard. And knew—"Now it's me?"

"And now it's a million times worse."

She felt his hands on her legs, a slow, steady motion as his palms slid up and down her thighs, over and over, holding her atop him in a gentle rocking sway.

"They didn't catch me." Zoe pressed down, wanting him to feel her weight. "I'm here." She cupped his cheek and he turned to kiss her palm. "I'm real. I'm alive. They haven't caught me. They haven't killed me."

That was supposed to be the end. Period. But she watched him pull back, retreat into whatever shell they hand out at Spy Guy School as he said, "*Yet.*"

Then he rolled and flipped her onto her back, but didn't linger. He just stood and walked away.

A moment later, she saw a candle flicker to life; she heard the shower start, and all Zoe could do was lie there, waiting for her heart to stop pounding.

HIM

Sawyer stood in the bathroom for a long time, watching steam collect on the mirror, building from the outside in until all that remained was a small speck of clear glass, but even that was too much because Sawyer hated what he saw. He hated how he felt. And, most of all, he hated what he'd almost done.

He'd almost killed her.

And then he'd almost kissed her. Maybe more. And, oh, how he had wanted more.

He remembered the feel of her smooth legs under his palms, the weight of her body as she straddled him. Had she noticed what she did to him or was she too busy almost dying? He hoped like hell she never knew.

He felt the room go cooler—clearer—as the steam escaped, and he turned to see her standing in the open doorway, tentative, like she might be trespassing where she wasn't wanted; totally, blissfully unaware of the fact that he wanted her way too much.

"It's not your fault." She inched toward him.

He studied the last bit of his reflection in the mirror. "You don't know what you're talking about."

"It's not your fault," she said again, like maybe he hadn't heard her, like those words wouldn't haunt him for the rest of his life. "I'm here. And I'm okay. See?"

Then she brought his hand to her chest and pressed his palm against the thin cotton of the T-shirt so that he could feel her beating heart.

"See? It's beating. It's . . ." But she trailed off and he watched her face change as if that fact surprised even her. "It's beating. It's okay."

But the T-shirt was so old and so worn and the steam was so heavy that the cotton clung to her and he could actually see the outline of the scars he couldn't stop his fingers from tracing. He felt her start to pull back, but he wouldn't let her—couldn't let her go.

"Stay where you are." He was turning, pressing her against the counter while his finger carried on its path. "I don't care how you got them. I just know they made you who you are and you're beautiful. They're beautiful. You're the most beautiful thing I've ever seen . . ." His finger followed the rough line between her breasts, and he felt the moment her breath changed to something deeper.

"I'm not ashamed that I have scars. Or embarrassed—"

"Good."

"But they scare me." Her voice was so soft he wasn't sure if she was admitting something to him or to herself. "I don't know what happened. I don't know what tried to kill me or how I survived it. So they scare me. Because . . . what if it tries again?"

And something about the words—the frailty of her voice and the subtle tremble of her lip made him snap. "Nothing's going to hurt you. Do you hear me? I won't let it. Lady, nothing's going to hurt you ever again. Never. I will die before I let that happen."

There were tears in her eyes, but she nodded and bit her lip, and it broke him—his will and his resolve. So he gripped her tighter—pulled her closer. Even though he knew he should stop. He had to stop. But no one told his hands that because the left one snaked around her waist and was changing the angle, tilting her hips toward him, while the right followed the lines of her scars.

His feet had found their way between hers as she leaned against the counter, and he was spreading her legs—not much—just enough to feel the moment her body shifted. The shower was still running, the pounding of the water matching the pounding of his blood.

"Do you remember the train?" he asked, and she seemed startled by the question.

"I . . . I remember the train," she stammered.

"Do you remember the bathroom?"

"Yes." Her voice was small and yet, somehow, it echoed.

"Do you remember how I sat you on that counter and spread these pretty legs? How I stepped right in between them?"

185

Her lips parted and, so help him, if she said one of those innocent little comments about knees and sucking he was going to explode.

"I . . . I remember."

"This won't be like that. Because I'm betting you've got nothing but a pair of skimpy panties on underneath that T-shirt, don't you? Something made for a honeymoon. Something made to rip right off a woman's body, and I'll do it. I'll drop to my knees and do it right now and I won't get up until I'm good and ready."

Her chest rose and fell, and he couldn't help himself, he let his gaze linger on the sweet little peaks that were protruding out of that damp shirt.

"So I'm going to tell you one thing, Zoe, and I need you to listen to me, baby. Can you do that?"

Numbly, she nodded.

"Good girl." He put both hands on her hips, the better to either lift her or push her away. He didn't know which one would haunt him for the rest of his life but he was absolutely certain that one would.

"Now you have two options. I can put you on this counter and do all the things that I just said plus a hell of a lot more. Or you can go back to bed and get a good night's sleep, and in the morning we can both act—" He couldn't help himself; he leaned closer and brushed his lips over hers once. Twice. And when her tongue peeked out the third time he almost lost it. It took every bit of his training and every ounce of his will to pull back. "In the morning we'll both act like this was a dream. Okay?"

His hands were kneading and her hips were moving and neither of them were even really aware of it by that point. Muscle memory. It's a powerful thing.

"So what do you say, lady?" Hands drifted lower, pulling her tight against the weight of his arousal. "What do you say?"

She closed her eyes and whispered, "Close the door."

chapter forty-six

HER

Zoe didn't know how long she laid there, looking at the fire, feeling the rise and fall of Sawyer's chest beneath her cheek and marveling at how soft his skin was. Because, seriously, his skin was really, really soft, which made no sense whatsoever for such a hard man who had probably never owned a skincare product in his life.

But she couldn't keep her fingers from running through the light dusting of hair on his chest, over the ridges of the muscles.

Exhaustion wrapped around her, pressing her down. But she also felt like she might float away. Both. At the same time. She didn't try to understand it. She just wanted it to last. Because, for the first time since she woke up on the snowy ground, Zoe didn't care about her past or her memories. She didn't want to know who she'd been or what she'd done or all the ways she'd almost died.

She just wanted this. She just wanted now. She just wanted him.

So she laid there, trying not to fall asleep because she wanted the night to last as long as possible. She wanted it to last forever.

She was just starting to calculate how much soup and vodka they'd need to never leave the mountain when she heard—

"My mother was a genius." Sawyer's voice was barely louder than the crackling of the fire and somehow Zoe knew not to ask any questions. "If she'd been a man, she probably would have been recruited by NASA, Harvard, MIT . . . But she ended up at this tiny university no one cared about, researching the electromagnetic spectrum. She was so far ahead of her time—so far out of their league—that the men in her department tried to deny her tenure because they couldn't even comprehend what she was doing. Cell towers. Satellites. *Signal Intelligence . . .*" He spat out the last two words like they were bitter.

"Her work changed everything. But the men around her never understood that. Until, one day, she met a man who did. He was handsome and charming and he told her she was beautiful . . . He showed an interest in her work and told her she was brilliant . . . He told her all the right things. Because my mother was a genius . . ." He drew a haggard breath. "And my father was a spy."

Zoe's first instinct was to bolt upright and ask a million questions, but Sawyer pressed a kiss to the top of her head and traced circles on her back and, somehow, she knew the story wasn't over.

"I saw him once a year. *Here.*" He gestured to the dark and dusty cabin. "He won this place playing cards in Monte Carlo, so it was never on any records. Which meant it was safe. For him. For me." His fingers were in her hair then, a soft and gentle sweep that made her eyelids heavy. "It was the only place he ever let me call him Dad."

"I'm sorry," she said softly. "I didn't mean to make you go someplace you hate."

He shifted until they were lying face-to-face, his hand a warm weight on her hip.

"That's the worst part. When I was a kid, I *loved* it. I couldn't wait to come back. I used to think that, someday, I'd stay forever and never have to leave. Someday Mom would come too. Someday we'd be a family, but . . ."

She heard the words he didn't say: *spies don't get a happy ending.* And a little voice in the back of her mind whispered, *but maybe they could?*

"As I got older, I figured he was just some jerk who used my mother and threw her away. But I was wrong, I found out later. He used her for sex, sure. But, mostly, he used her for secrets." He looked into the fire, unable to face her as he finished, "And what she got was me."

Zoe wanted to tell him there were worse things to end up with. She wanted to say his story wasn't over yet. She wanted to crawl through time and tell that little boy he wasn't just some spy's collateral damage—he was hers now. And she wasn't giving him up without a fight.

"Mom died when I was nineteen. Car accident," he added numbly. "I was so fucking alone. But a few months later I got a call. Evidently, my test scores impressed certain people and I fit a certain profile—had a certain set of skills. Turns out there was a reason my deadbeat dad paid for me to take martial arts and learn archery and do summer exchange programs abroad. By the time I found out what he was, it was too late to change what I am."

"I like who you are."

His fingers made a slow sweep across her skin. "I swore I'd never be like him, sweetheart. That I wouldn't use women. Leave them damaged or broken. I swore . . . But then I met Helena."

"That wasn't your fault."

"Was tonight my fault?" Zoe saw it then—the ocean of pain and doubt Sawyer was swimming through, and she knew why he'd shared more in the last five minutes than he had in the entire time she'd known him.

"Is that what you think?" She didn't know whether to be hurt or very, very angry.

"I followed in my father's footsteps, but I don't want to be like him."

"You're nothing like him." She had to make him see, but all he did was push her hair away when it fell like a curtain around her face.

"That's sweet, lady. But you don't know him. Hell. You don't even know me."

"I know I wanted this. I know I wanted you. I know . . . I know you'd never hurt me."

"I'll kill any man who hurts you." She felt his lips brush against her hairline, tracing over her fading bruise like he could heal it with a touch. "Even if that man is me."

And then Sawyer closed his eyes. And slept.

chapter forty-seven

HIM

The first thing Sawyer thought when he opened his eyes was that he must be dead. It was far more likely than the alternative: that he had slept. That he had slept but hadn't dreamed.

"Good morning."

At the sound of the voice, he rolled and reached for his gun—was just starting to aim it when he felt cold air on his bare chest and remembered the room and the night and the woman who was dancing around the cabin's kitchen, humming over the sound of frying food.

Zoe. Kitchen. Zoe. Humming. Zoe. *Bathroom*. Zoe. Bacon?

He uncocked his gun and rubbed his tired eyes. "What time is it?"

"Almost ten." She glanced over her shoulder. "I must have made you sleepy."

She looked sheepish. She might have blushed. But all Sawyer could think was *no, you made me forget*. And then he almost said exactly that because, evidently, sleep didn't make him sharper. It made him sluggish and slow and sentimental—the three *S*'s that would probably get him killed.

When she cracked an egg in the pan, he heard the sizzle and his mouth began to water. "Breakfast is almost ready," she called, so Sawyer pulled on his jeans and padded toward her in his bare feet, synapses starting to fire . . . slowly.

Something was wrong with that picture. His father's cabin smelled like bacon and fresh coffee, and there was a woman dancing, humming . . . *caring* for him there. No one had cared for Sawyer in so long that it took his sleep-addled brain a little too long to realize—

Zoe. The cabin. Fresh food.

"Where did you get all this?" he asked, already terrified the answer would be—

"There's a town."

He was going to kill her. Strangle her. Tie her up and . . . tickle her? Or something. Possibly a whole lot of something depending on how the first part went. "Damn it, Zoe. You can't just go off on your own, looking like—"

"A rogue spy on the run?" She gave a long-suffering look over her shoulder and shrugged—actually shrugged! Like he was overreacting. Him. The man who (not to belabor the point) *had killed an assassin with a negligee!*

She slid two eggs onto a plate then added bacon and licked her fingers and, so help him, his anger faded into a much more dangerous emotion as thoughts of last night drifted through his head.

Zoe appearing at the edge of the steam-filled room.

Zoe perched on the bathroom counter.

Zoe crying out his name.

Zoe.

Zoe.

Zoe.

But the little vixen had the audacity to say, "Trust me, no one was looking at my face."

"You can't possibly know . . ." he started but trailed off as she turned.

At first, he wasn't sure what he was seeing because she was still Zoe in the morning light. Same honey-colored hair. Same mischievous smile. Same green eyes. But then his gaze slid down her body to her very large, very round, very . . . *pregnant* belly?

"See? No one was looking at me and thinking *Ooh! There goes the most lethal woman in Europe!*"

It was true, he would have admitted if his brain hadn't been full of other, far more primitive thoughts. Like *yes*. And *this*. And *mine*.

And Sawyer actually felt his world tilt. He might have staggered. Because the sight of Zoe in the cabin. The thought of Zoe and his child. The very idea . . . It was ludicrous and dangerous and vicious—the way it bore right into his gut. It was salt in a wound he didn't even know he had as he stood there, inches away from all the things he never knew he wanted and just realized he couldn't have.

But what if he could?

No. Sawyer needed his sharpest knife. He had to cut that thought out before it spread.

"Go ahead. Say it." She took a bite of bacon and pulled the pillow out from beneath her shirt. "I'm so good at undercovering!"

But Sawyer didn't say a single thing. He just ate his breakfast and ignored the feelings that were pinging around inside of him because who needs feelings anyway?

Three minutes later he was on his second egg and contemplating another when something occurred to him. "Hey, maybe you're a chef."

He waited for her to say that she was no doubt the heiress to a bacon empire, that maybe she had invented toaster strudel—that she was obviously the next Julia Child and spent her days encrypting classified messages into recipes for pound cake, but Zoe stayed quiet. And if Sawyer had learned anything, it was that a quiet Zoe was very, very scary.

"What's wrong?"

She looked almost nervous as she glanced at him over the rim of her coffee cup. "I was thinking about our trip to the bank today."

"No. *I'm* going to the bank today," he said emphatically but the look in her eyes told him he was in for a fight. He was going to need both knives and at least one gun and maybe another negligee.

"No. *We're* going to the bank."

"I'm not putting you in danger." He grabbed the last of the bacon just for spite, but she snatched it back and crammed it in her mouth all at once.

"I'm always in danger!"

"Of choking."

She swallowed hard and looked like she didn't know whether to argue or kiss him—to scream or to cry. So she looked down at her hands instead. "I'll always be in danger until we get that drive."

Her eyes were so big and her voice was so fragile that he thought the words might break him. So he tugged until she was perched on his knee, until she was back in his arms, and he didn't let himself think about how right she felt there.

"Hey. Listen to me, you've done great. Really. Even . . . this"—he pointed to her massive T-shirt and the pillow—"is genius. But you can't just break into one of the most secure banks in the world with a pillow up your shirt."

Sawyer expected her to argue or complain, stamp her foot or maybe even kiss him again as a distraction, but Zoe just sat there, looking at him like maybe he'd lost twenty IQ points overnight—and maybe he had—because he was in no way prepared to hear her say, "Who said anything about breaking in?"

"Zoe—"

"I mean . . . I already got the stuff."

Sawyer felt his blood go cold. "What . . ." That's when he noticed the pile: scissors and makeup and clothes. A platinum blonde wig. And cherry-flavored Kool-Aid.

"Kool-Aid?"

"We're gonna have to dye the wig."

"Well, I like the idea of a disguise, but that will just make you look even more like . . ." And then he remembered . . . "No!" But she was giving him that jaunty look, the one that said this was all a game and she was winning. She was wrong. She didn't even know how wrong she was.

"Of course I look like Alex no matter what, but Kozlov's guys knew she was on the run, so they were probably expecting her to change her appearance. The people at the bank won't be, so it's probably better for me to match her style as closely as—"

"No! I thought we agreed—"

"We can't go to the bank and not check out the box, and the easiest way into that box is for me to *be* Alex. You know that."

He had known that—back before he'd known her. Back before he'd cared for her. Back before—

"No! I'm telling you . . . Kozlov is going to have men all over that bank, and if Kozlov is there, the CIA will be there. And Interpol. And MI6."

"And Mossad," she added helpfully. "Don't forget about Mossad."

"Oh." He huffed out a dry laugh. "Lady, I never forget about Mossad. And that's why the answer is no."

"But . . ." She trailed off, something in her eyes as she looked at him, calculating. Worrying. Wondering. "This is about last night, isn't it?" He hated how small her voice sounded, how fragile and frail she seemed.

"No," he said at the same time his gut screamed *Yes*.

"Because it doesn't change anything," she said, and he felt his heart change rhythms.

"It doesn't?"

"Of course not." She bristled and crawled from his lap, and all Sawyer wanted to do was pull her back. "I know what last night was."

"What was it?" Suddenly, it wasn't a hypothetical or a theoretical. It wasn't any kind of . . . ethical. He needed to know . . . Except he really, really didn't. Because putting it into words—making it black and white—was absolutely terrifying for someone whose life had always been gray.

"It was a danger bang."

At first, he was certain he'd misheard her. "A *what?*"

"A danger bang. In the immortal words of Keanu Reeves, relationships that begin under extreme stress—"

"Are you quoting *Speed* right now?"

"—are doomed to fail. Last night was a whole bunch of adrenaline and dopamine and about a million other chemicals in our bodies getting all mixed up and going *bang*. That's what last night was." But she couldn't face him when she said, "Right?"

He wanted to tell her she was wrong. He wanted to set her up on that table and prove it to her again. He briefly revisited the tying-her-up option because that seemed pretty useful on a number of levels, but she was looking at him like it was just that simple.

Like that was all it had been . . . for her.

Sawyer knew how to protect himself. What to guard and where to shield and all the little ways to keep from bleeding out. But right then . . . He'd never felt more vulnerable in his life.

"Okay." He stood. "Fine. But you're still not going to the bank."

"You said—"

"I said we'd check it out. That means recon, maybe a good old-fashioned stakeout."

"But—"

"They want to kill you!" The words were already echoing off the high ceiling and frosty glass. "What about that do you not get? They want you dead. They want Alex dead. If anything happened to you . . . If you think I'm letting you walk into a place they are absolutely watching, then—"

"How do you know they'll be watching the bank?" she shot back. "Did *you* know Alex had a box there? Heck, do *we* know Alex has a box there? For all we know, that could be where I store my first edition *Pride and Prejudice* or my collection of autographed baseball cards or the top secret potion I've been making in my lab because I'm the world's foremost love scientist."

"Love scientist?" He really hated how much he wanted to laugh.

"How do you know? Tell me."

It shouldn't have been so hard to say, "I didn't know Alex had a box there. No. But—"

"Then they probably don't know either!"

Sawyer couldn't look at her smirking mouth without wanting to kiss it. "I can't believe we're having this conversation." He glanced down at the clothes on the table. "Where did you get black leather pants? Correction. *Why* did you get black leather—"

"I'm trying to look like a spy."

"Spies don't actually . . ." But he trailed off and shook his head. "You know what, never mind."

He dropped into a chair. Sure, he'd had more consecutive hours of sleep in the past day than he'd had in the past year, but he was the kind of tired that sleep itself wouldn't fix. And Zoe was too. He could see it in her eyes and the set of her shoulders, in the way she had picked at her fingernail until it was red and sore.

"I *have* to do this. Don't you see? If the world is trying to kill me because they think I'm Alex, then, narratively speaking—"

"That's not a real thing—"

"—the only way out is for me to *be Alex*."

She couldn't have been more serious. And, worse, a part of him was terrified she was also right. "How are you supposed to be a sister you don't even remember?"

"Easy. You're going to teach me."

chapter forty-eight

HER

HOW TO BE YOUR OWN TWIN SISTER

A List by Zoe Whatsername

- Don't smile unless you're flirting.
- Don't flirt unless you're desperate.
- Don't enter any room you don't have three different ways to exit.
- Don't walk too quickly.
- Don't walk too slowly.
- Always know what's behind you.
- Never, ever check your tail.
- If you have to shoot, it's probably already too late.
- So, whatever you do, don't miss.

As Zoe drew a deep breath and looked at herself in the bathroom mirror, she couldn't help but think about Paris. She remembered staring through that darkened window, watching Alex on TV—the way their faces had overlapped and all she'd seen were the ways they were alike. But three days later, she was acutely, terribly, overwhelmingly aware of how much they were different.

So she was more than a little nervous as she tucked a strand of too-red hair behind her ear and opened the door.

"Hey!" Sawyer called from the kitchen. "I was thinking, since we don't know what kind of cover Alex was using, we should . . ."

He trailed off.

He looked.

He stared.

He seemed at risk of maybe—possibly—swallowing his own tongue.

Or at least that was how it felt to Zoe as she stood in those skin-tight clothes, wondering, *Is he dumbfounded in the good way or is he dumbfounded in the bad way and how will I ever know and does it even matter and—*

"That's . . . um . . . you're . . ." Eventually, he crossed his arms and made a noise she hadn't heard since she'd come out in Mrs. Michaelson's unzipped dress. "Yeah. No one is going to think you're pregnant in that."

He had a point. Tight black leather. A top that barely reached her waistband so she really wanted to slouch but #38 on the HOW TO BE LIKE ALEX list was "be inferior to no one" so that kind of seemed posture-specific and Zoe didn't want to risk it.

So she threw her shoulders back. She tried to walk, but her pants were ridiculously tight. And her boots were ridiculously tall. And she felt . . . well . . . ridiculous.

"How does Alex walk in these things?" She looked down at her new boots. "And does she always wear her pants this tight?"

He tensed. "Why do I feel like this is a trick question?" he asked but Zoe was already stretching and bending and . . .

"I have a feeling they're too tight? Does Alex really fight like . . ." She tried to kick but almost fell as she twisted, looking. "Did my pants split open? How does Alex do this? How does she fight and walk and stay alive in pants that are constantly on the verge of splitting . . ."

Zoe stuck her butt out and tried to touch her toes and Sawyer turned a deeper shade of crimson.

"Please don't bend . . ."

"Seriously. Are my pants splitting open?" She craned her neck and looked over her shoulder as her heart started pounding. "I feel like I'm . . ."

I'm not strong enough. I'm not brave enough. I'm not Alex enough and the whole world is going to see it and you're going to see it and how am I supposed to be someone else when I can't even be me and—

The pressure seemed to break then—not in her pants—but in Zoe herself. She felt like she might split right down the middle. Her hand reached up and traced the scar that ran between her breasts. She didn't know why. She had forgotten it was there until she felt it through the fabric of her shirt. It was like the real her was trying to claw to the surface—take the wheel—remind her of the thing she should never forget: *I'm not as good as Alex. I'm not as strong as Alex. I'm not as brave as Alex.*

It wasn't something that she thought. It was something that she *knew*. Like the alphabet or the names of the states or the fact that she didn't have the skin tone to wear yellow. She knew that she was less than Alex in the same way she knew that ten was less than twenty. In the way she knew—

"Hey." His hands were on her arms and his gaze was like an anchor, the only thing that could keep her from floating away on that vicious current of self-doubt.

"Hey, where'd you go, lady?" Sawyer pulled Zoe closer, and she breathed in the clean, fresh smell of him and wanted to curl up and sleep for a thousand years. She wanted to pretend they were the only two people in the world, but she couldn't do that—she had to pretend to be Alex.

"What's wrong?" His voice was gentle.

It had seemed so easy. *In theory.* So basic and sensible. *In theory.* She could walk in, be her sister, grab the drive, and ride into the sunset with the really hot, really broody, really deceptively kind man. *In theory!*

But in practice, her pants were too tight and her palms were too wet and her heart was pounding way too hard in her chest. The whole world was full of shadows, and she had no idea what was going to jump out at her.

"I'm not like Alex," Zoe said, finally looking up at Sawyer. "I thought I could do this. It sounded like such a good idea—like shampoo with conditioner but what you get is hair that's not really shampooed and also not really conditioned and *I don't know how I know that*! I just know that I'm in these ridiculous clothes, trying to pull off this ridiculous plan, and . . . No one is ever going to believe I'm Alex!"

"I know. You're nothing like her." She might have been insulted if it weren't for the kindness in his eyes—the wicked gleam as he said, "You're better."

"But these pants . . ."

"And hotter. Did I mention hotter?"

"But—"

"And kinder. And smarter. And funnier. And . . . Who jumped off the bridge, Zoe? Who got us out of Paris? Who hot-wired the car?"

For a moment, she actually thought it might be a trick question, but she couldn't help looking up at him, admitting, "I don't know how I did those things. I wasn't even thinking when I did them. But I'm thinking about this, and what I know is no one will ever believe that I am—"

He stopped her with a kiss. It was quick and soft and gentle, and for a moment Zoe forgot about her pants and her sister and the bank. Zoe forgot about everything except that man and that moment and that feeling. But, too soon, he was pulling back and tipping her face up.

"I worked with Alex for five years. Now guess how many times I wanted to kiss her."

She really didn't want to guess, though. And she really, really didn't want to know. "You don't have to—"

"Never, Zoe. Not once." She opened her mouth to protest, but he cut her off. "I thought she was beautiful and smart and cunning. I thought she was a great operative. And I was glad she was on my side, but I never wanted to kiss her."

"You probably say that to all your danger bangs." It was a joke. It was. But he wasn't laughing and neither was she and when he pressed against her, looked into her eyes, she knew—she knew even before he said—

"It wasn't a danger bang."

And then she wanted to cry—emotion springing out through her eyes because she was just so full she couldn't hold it in as she shook her head and her voice got all wobbly and her cheeks got all wet. "It wasn't a danger bang."

His hands cradled her face, pushing the too-red strands of the wig away from her eyes—like he couldn't take the chance she might not see. "And that's why I'm telling you, you don't have to do this."

"No." She kissed him quickly. And she knew it—in her gut and in her bones and in her soul. "That's why I do."

chapter forty-nine

HER

Zoe didn't remember Zurich. But, then again, Zoe didn't remember anything. Her own face had been a surprise, so she didn't know why she was expecting her memory to come surging back as they circled the streets around the bank.

"Any of this look familiar?" Sawyer asked with a gentleness that almost broke her.

"No. But that doesn't mean I've never been here, considering . . ." She pointed toward her empty head. Her stupid, worthless, fallow brain.

"Hey. It's okay. We always knew this was a long shot." They were stopped at a red light and he was staring at her. It was like he knew what she was thinking—like he could read her mind. Oh, how she wished he could read her mind. Maybe then he could tell her all the things she didn't know.

They'd been circling the bank for an hour, and the sun was getting lower—the sky darker. Streetlights were starting to glow in the twilight, and Zoe could feel the sands in the hourglass—a drip-drip-drip that told her they were running out of time.

So she wasn't surprised when Sawyer parked the SUV and looked at her. "Are you sure about this?"

"No?" she said without thinking. "I mean yes. I mean . . ." She looked at him again but didn't say another word. She just reached for the door.

"Zo—" he started, but she was already walking away.

He caught up with her in the small park across from the even smaller bank, staring at the building on the opposite corner. With its old stone walls and stained-glass windows, it didn't look like a business—more like the kind of house that belonged to someone with roman numerals after their name.

"Are you sure that's a bank?" she had to ask him.

"Yes."

"Because it looks like a club. You know, the kind that has tufted leather chairs and everything smells like cigar smoke."

"It's not."

"Maybe a really high-end brothel?"

He coughed and shook his head and mumbled something that sounded a lot like *what am I going to do with you?* but he said, "It's a bank."

"But—"

"I promise. It's a bank. A Swiss bank. So I guess it *is* a club, of a sort. Very exclusive. Very private." He was quiet for a moment before adding, "This one has a reputation for being a little . . . intense. I'm not surprised Alex picked it. Now, you've got your card?"

She pulled the thin black card out of the pocket of her too-tight pants. "Got it!"

"Okay." Sawyer's voice turned harder, colder. In that moment, he wasn't the man who had kissed her, held her, teased her. He was the man with a dozen different safe houses and fifty Go Bags on three continents. "Walk me through it."

"I go in. Give them Alex's name—"

"No names," he reminded her.

"Right. Swiss bank."

"They'll either scan your card or ask for your number. The most important thing is the number," he told her, even though they'd already been through this a dozen times.

They'd found a black light among Sawyer's father's arsenal at the cabin, and as soon as they held the card beneath it, a twelve-digit number had appeared. Sawyer had made Zoe memorize it, drilling it into her over and over. She didn't know her address or her Social

Security number or if she had a cat or whether or not someone was, hopefully, feeding her possibly nonexistent cat . . . But she was going to remember that number for the rest of her life.

"They'll confirm you're Alex and take you to your box. Don't bother going through the contents in there. Just bring everything back here. We'll go over it later. What matters now is getting in and getting out. Alive." He gripped her arms as he finished. "Don't talk to anyone you don't have to talk to. Don't look directly into any cameras. Walk like you own the place. Just, remember, you belong there. And you're a badass."

"Right. Because I'm Alex."

"No." He was looking at her strangely, cocking his head like *isn't it obvious?* "Because you're you."

His hand was in her hair then. She wanted to lean into his warmth, but he surprised her by tucking something in her ear. "Comms unit. We can communicate through these. Don't try talking to me, but I can talk to you—try to walk you through it."

"Wait." Something occurred to her. "Why aren't you going with me? Just go with me."

But he was shaking his head. "I wouldn't go with Alex . . ."

Her voice cracked a little when she said, "And I'm Alex. Maybe." Then she couldn't help but laugh. "It's gonna be hilarious if that really is my box."

He flashed a crooked grin. "Yeah. Maybe you'll find all the diamond necklaces you stole."

She should have smiled or laughed. It was her turn to tease, but instead she found herself blurting out the words she'd spent all day trying not to say. "What happens if they know it's not my box? If they know I'm an imposter? If—"

"You'll be detained and arrested," he said calmly. "But that's not going to happen. Hey. Listen to me. The first thing they teach at spy school is to let people's assumptions do the heavy lifting. The bank is small and people will recognize you. That's why you're wearing that crazy wig. We *want* them to recognize you and immediately associate you with Alex. But their business was built on anonymity, so you're gonna walk in there and they're gonna see what they want to see, and then they're gonna leave you alone."

"Okay." She took a deep breath and looked up at him, a mischievous glint in her eye. "So what you're saying is . . . there *is* a spy school?" It was supposed to be a joke, so why did Zoe feel like crying? And, worse, why did Sawyer have to see it? Stupid Elite Spy School—

"Hey, it's okay." His hands were warm and gentle as they cupped her face. She felt his thumbs brushing across her cheeks, wiping away the tears that were seeping out of the corner of her eyes. Stupid, stupid eyes. She had to make them stop, but Sawyer was just right there, so tall and strong and—

Something snapped inside him. She saw the moment it happened because he reached for her hand. "Get back in the car. We're leaving."

"No."

"You don't have to do this."

Of course I have to do this.

"We can find another way."

There is no other way.

"We have other options."

We're all out of other options.

She thought the words but couldn't say them—she couldn't say anything, so she threw her arms around his neck and kissed him a little too hard for a little too long, and when she pulled back, his breath was a whisper on her lips.

"Don't go," he said. "We can run. We can hide. Put Zurich and Kozlov in our rearview mirror and never look back."

It was so tempting, to run, to pretend. She'd woken up in Paris, a woman with no past, but as she stood in that dark square in Zurich, all she wanted to be was a woman with a future. And there was only one way that could happen.

"I have to know why I had that card. I have to help Alex. I have to figure out who I am," she said, but she saw something in Sawyer's eyes, pain and fear and heartbreak.

"Zoe." He pulled her closer and she felt his breath on her skin. "You don't have to do this for her."

"I'm not." She kissed him again, soft and quick. "I'm doing this for us."

Then she walked away. High heels. Tight leather. A sway that didn't really go with her particular body but she kept it anyway, words like a mantra in the chilly air.

"I'm Alex. I'm a spy. I'm a badass. I'm—" She slipped on some ice and fell. "I'm okay!"

chapter fifty

HER

"Welcome back . . . madame." The man in the alcove on the other side of the doors looked polished and professional and . . . scared. Yup. Very, extremely frightened. Wide eyes and pale skin and a voice that cracked every so often. "I'm afraid . . . That is to say, the time is . . ." He gulped. And the next part came out all at once. *"We will be closing soon but whatever madame needs we will accommodate."*

"Oh, I know you're closing soon. I won't be long!"

"Don't forget, you're Alex." Sawyer's voice was a warning in her ear, so Zoe stood a little straighter but she couldn't decide what to do with her hands because they were always there, hanging off the ends of her arms. And speaking of arms . . . where were they supposed to go? Maybe—

"If madame would follow me . . ."

The man was looking at her pointedly, gesturing for her to follow him through a metal detector. He held out a basket.

"What's this for?"

He seemed surprised by the question. "It is for your . . . uh . . . metal items, madame."

"I don't have any . . ."

"Your knives, madame." The man lowered his gaze and his voice. "You will need to leave your knives."

"Ohhhhh. My knives!" Zoe said as if it had somehow slipped her mind that she was a dangerous spy who was always armed to the teeth. "I . . . uh . . . left them in the car. You know how it is. These pants don't have very good pockets. Which is what's wrong with pants. I'm more of an A-line dress kind of—"

"Okay, *Alex*," Sawyer whispered in her ear and she stopped talking.

"No knives today! So should I just . . ." She motioned to the metal detector. "I'll just hop on through—"

"No hopping," Sawyer warned. "*Do not*—"

She hopped. She couldn't help it.

The attendant looked surprised when not a single alarm was triggered, but he quickly collected himself and led her to another room. This one was larger, grander. But it still didn't look like a bank. More like the lobby of a hotel where a sitting US senator would take an extremely high-end prostitute, or so Zoe thought as the greeter handed her off to a woman in a burgundy blazer.

"Welcome back, ma'am." The woman had a crisp British accent and sounded like someone who had once worked at Buckingham Palace but left for this place because it was more exclusive. "Your number, please?" She slid a pen and piece of paper across the marble counter.

Zoe hadn't been expecting that and, for a second, it threw her. She picked up the pen and started to write but it felt off somehow, like she was in a play and had missed her cue so she blurted out the line that no one was waiting for.

"I'd like to see my box. My safe-deposit box. Which I have in this establishment—"

"Easy," Sawyer soothed. "You belong there and you're doing great. Just take a deep breath."

So that's exactly what she did. Then she handed over the card and the paper and watched the woman examine both like she was checking Zoe's answers on a pop quiz, and all Zoe could do was stand there, praying that she'd passed.

"We'll just need to verify your identity." The woman gave a smile but Zoe's blood turned cold because the woman was reaching beneath the counter and pulling out a small metal box with a slightly curved indentation perfect for . . .

"Your finger, ma'am." The woman only sounded a little bit impatient, and Zoe smiled like, *Oh, this ol' thing. I do this all the time and I know exactly what is happening and—*

"Ow!" She jerked back and looked down at the tiny drop of blood beading on the end of her finger.

"So sorry, ma'am." The woman chuckled. "I keep telling them we should use a less painful way to check your DNA but security is paramount."

"I eat pain for breakfast," Zoe said.

"You what?" Sawyer choked.

But the woman in the burgundy blazer simply smiled. The little box glowed green. And when a pair of elevator doors slid open the woman ushered Zoe inside. But as the doors closed, Sawyer's voice faded from her ears and she was left with nothing but a bloody finger. And static.

Sawyer should have relaxed. They wouldn't have put her in the elevator if they hadn't bought the ruse, but he couldn't wrap his mind around how anyone could ever confuse Zoe and Alex. But, more importantly, how had he?

Alex was all sharp edges and straight lines. Zoe was softness and sweetness and sass. She was quirky comebacks and knowing winks. And yet there wasn't a doubt in his mind that Zoe was the more dangerous sister.

Because she made him hope.

She made him want.

She made him wonder if maybe there might be more to life than covers and legends and lies. Zoe made him long for something real. Maybe if they found the drive . . . Maybe if they took Kozlov off the board . . . Maybe if the powers that be would let him walk away . . . Then maybe . . .

He glanced down at his watch: eight minutes until closing.

The sun was down, and darkness had fallen over Zurich. Pedestrians cut across the park. Buses started and stopped on the busy street. But Sawyer stood perfectly still in the square, his gaze never leaving the doorway.

And that was his first mistake.

chapter fifty-one

HER

Well, at least I'm not claustrophobic, Zoe thought as she stood beside the woman in the burgundy blazer, riding the tiny elevator deep underground. She had no idea how long it took. She didn't think about how far they went. All she knew was that when the doors finally opened, they were in a room that was all stainless steel and glass and . . . wait. Were those lasers?

The woman swiped an ID badge through a reader and the red lines flickered.

Yup. Definitely lasers.

Suddenly, her leather pants seemed even tighter and Zoe couldn't get a deep breath. She wanted Sawyer's hand in hers, his voice in her ear. She wanted to go back to being Mrs. Michaelson or at least the person she'd been at the cabin—the woman who slept in old T-shirts and Sawyer's arms. Yeah, Zoe thought wistfully, she'd liked being her a lot. And maybe she'd get to be her again. Just as soon as she stopped being Alex.

She followed the woman to a large alcove behind a velvet curtain. It looked like a dressing room at the world's stuffiest department store.

"I'll only be a moment," the woman said then pulled the curtain behind her, leaving Zoe alone.

"I'm in," she whispered, but all she heard back was static. "I don't know if you can hear me, but . . . I miss you. Darn it. Now I hope you can't hear me. That was—"

"Here we go!" the woman said a little too cheerfully as she slid aside the velvet curtain and placed a box on a narrow table. She pulled the curtain. She walked away. But Zoe didn't move. She didn't even breathe. She just stared down at the box like it held the secrets of the universe and she wasn't even sure if she wanted to know them anymore. Somehow, she knew that her life would be divided into two sections: before that moment and after. And she couldn't help but worry about what was waiting on the other side.

She might have stood there forever—staring—but the clock on the wall was ticking way too loudly, echoing off the stone and steel. So Zoe took a deep breath and threw open the lid and looked down at a handful of passports, some cash, a handgun.

And there—right on top—a flash drive.

A spotlight didn't shine and angels didn't sing, but they could have; because it was there. That was it. She'd been right and she wanted to high-five the world—and maybe she would—just as soon as she changed clothes. She grabbed the drive and slipped it into her cleavage because, really, where else was she supposed to put it? She filled her jacket pockets with cash and was already reaching for the curtain when it slid aside again.

She half expected the woman to ask if she could get Zoe something in another size, but her arms were already full.

"Oh. I'm sorry." The woman looked surprised. "Did you not wish to see your second box?"

Your second box.

Zoe heard the words. She saw the box. It was right there—in the woman's arms. But she was sure she must have misunderstood. The same nerves that had been doing a dance a moment before were suddenly frozen, midkick. Like someone had hit pause on the world.

"My second box?"

The woman put the box on the table and held up the piece of paper—the one Zoe had nervously filled out while she rambled. Sure enough, the last three digits were different from the number on the little black card. So Zoe stood there for a long time, looking between her *two* boxes. And she couldn't help but whisper, "*Muscle memory.*"

She hadn't remembered that box existed, but her hand had known to write the number.

"Ma'am?" The woman was starting to sound confused—concerned. Leery.

"Oh, I forgot about that! Yes. I need something out of this one, too. I was so worried about getting out of your hair before closing time that I . . . I won't be long. I promise. Say, do you know someplace good for dinner near here?" She tried to sound casual—she tried to look casual. She was pretty sure she was failing but the woman forced a smile.

"Why don't I write down some suggestions while I give you some privacy, yes?"

"Yes. That would be . . ." She looked down at the boxes. "Oh yes."

Zoe wasn't sure why she held her breath—why her hands trembled. The first box had held exactly what she'd been looking for, but somehow it was this second box that scared her. So she was careful as she released the latch and pulled off the lid and looked down at—*herself.* Or who she had been, once upon a time.

There were photos of two little girls who needed braces, of twins who seemed nothing alike. One strong and fierce and one small and pale.

Zoe wanted to look at every single picture, take in every single detail and mine them for memories, but the clock was ticking louder. Time was running out. She had to get back to Sawyer, give him the drive, end it. She had to end it once and for all, but then her gaze caught on something: an envelope marked FOR ZOE, and Zoe didn't think twice, she grabbed it and shoved it in her pocket.

She'd read it later, she told herself. When she had time and tea and maybe a nice cookie. *Yeah, I could go for a cookie,* Zoe thought as she headed for the door.

It was later, darker, and so much colder when Zoe exited the bank, but she didn't even feel the chill. She had a thumb drive in her boobs and an envelope in her pants, so she was obviously doing an excellent job of undercovering.

Sawyer was going to be so proud. The CIA was going to want to recruit her. She'd be parachuting into North Korea before she knew it. Clearly it was time for her to join the family business, she thought as she waited for a lull in the traffic and crossed the busy street.

She was wrapped in a warm coat of satisfaction, giddy on the rush of being someone else and getting away with it as she jumped the icy curb, expecting Sawyer to be there, waiting. But she had to stop and scan the little park, searching the darkness until she saw him on the other side of the square.

She didn't even try to hold back her smile. She was the least covert person in the world as she raised her hand and waved.

"Oh my gosh! You're never going to believe . . ." But she trailed off as she realized . . .

He wasn't smiling. He wasn't laughing. He wasn't racing to pick her up and swing her around and, really, it was a very *pick someone up and swing them around* kind of moment! Instead, he stood too still, and he looked too serious.

When the first little red dot appeared on his black sweater, Zoe thought it was a mistake, a piece of thread or lint. But then there was another. And another. And Sawyer shouted, "Run!"

chapter fifty-two

HER

Zoe heard the first squeal of the tires just as she saw the first swarm of men. And suddenly she was back in Paris, standing on a bridge, listening to Sawyer tell her to put her head down and keep moving. She was on the deck of the *Shimmering Sea*, promising that she would shoot to kill and not give it a second thought. She was standing on a snowy square in Zurich, knowing Sawyer could save himself—get out alive—but only if he didn't have to save her, too.

Only if she saved herself.

So Zoe didn't think, didn't plan. She didn't have time to worry. She just took off, running as fast as she could in high heels and leather pants. She didn't care about the snow. She wasn't thinking about the ice. And when the bus came barreling down the street, she darted out in front of it—heard the blaring of the horn and the screech of the tires—but Zoe didn't even think about looking back. She just kept running, arms pumping, skidding around corners and down sidewalks.

She had to find cover.

She had to keep moving.

She had to be smart.

She couldn't stop to think.

His voice wasn't in her ear anymore, but Sawyer would be okay. Sawyer would find her—she'd find him. They'd find each other. A part of her had to think—had to believe—that they would always find each other. Everything would be okay—it had to be. But only if she got away.

Sirens were blaring in the distance but coming closer. Faster.

Two cars were on her heels and bearing down. One jumped onto the sidewalk, sending pedestrians screaming and diving out of the way, so Zoe darted into a narrow alley. She heard the cars slam on the brakes when they couldn't follow, but she kept running. Zoe had to keep running . . .

To the end of the alley and onto the next street. But when she glanced over her shoulder and saw she was alone she slowed to a walk. She jerked off the red wig and tossed it in a garbage can—fanned out her blonde hair and tried to blend into the tide of pedestrians walking home from work.

She could do this. She could disappear. And then she'd find Sawyer. And then everything would be okay again.

Except nothing was ever going to be okay again—she knew it as soon as she saw the line of SUVs slamming to a stop in front of her. Doors flying open. People shouting, "Freeze!"

She spun and tried to run in the opposite direction, but more police cars and SUVs filled the street behind her. She was officially surrounded. But still Zoe turned, looking, trying to find a way of getting back to Sawyer. And the cabin. And the life she'd had—for a little while. Because, at the moment, her life was nothing more than sore feet and chaffed thighs and too-bright headlights slicing through the night. She actually had to raise her hands to block the glare.

"Put your hands up, Alex. It's over."

My hands are up, she wanted to yell because . . . hello . . . *glare blocking!* Why wasn't this dude paying attention?

But the man kept walking toward her slowly, like she was a lethal weapon, like any sane person would be scared but he was approaching her anyway because he was scarier.

"It's time to come in, Alex," the voice said, and something about the silhouette in that too-bright light made her start to sweat.

"We're on the same side, remember?" He chuckled softly. "It's okay, Alex. It's over."

"See?" Zoe tried. "About that . . . would you believe I'm not the spy you're looking for?"

The man was close enough that she could see his eyes then. The cuts and bruises on his face—and something inside of Zoe went sideways. She actually felt the world tilt.

"I know you," she said before she even realized it was true. Before she remembered . . . "You were on the train."

His laugh was a cold, dry sound. "For a while."

And she realized . . . "Ooh! I didn't kill you!"

His smirk turned sinister as he reached behind him and pulled out a pair of handcuffs. "Forgive me if, this time, I'm not taking any chances. You've already done enough damage."

Zoe tried to take some comfort in the fact that it was her—*not Alex*—who had knocked him down that mountain. It was Zoe who had hurt him. The last time the two of them had faced off, Zoe had won.

But it was hard to feel victorious when the headlights were so bright, and she was so scared. And Train Guy was so close, shouting "On your knees, Alex!" way too loudly—like he wanted all of Zurich to hear how tough he was.

But when Train Guy—no, *Collins*, she reminded herself; Sawyer had called him Collins—spoke again the words were softer, like they were in on a secret. "I was hoping I'd see you again."

It was the tone of his voice that did it. Suddenly, her head began to pound and the world began to spin—way too fast and far off center. She felt like she was on a merry-go-round that was out of control. Images flying by way too quickly—

Footprints on white sidewalks.

The Eiffel Tower, hazy behind a curtain of snow.

Collins flying from the train.

Sawyer smiling at her.

Sawyer reaching for her.

Sawyer.

Sawyer. He was the one fixed point in her whole world, the only thing keeping her from tipping over. She had to find Sawyer, save Sawyer. She had to—

"We have unfinished business, don't we?"

She felt the man's breath on her ear and his hands on her skin.

He was so close. How had he gotten so close? And Zoe knew she was going to be sick. Really, truly sick. Because the pictures in her brain were a blur now, and she was so dizzy she thought she might fall down.

"No." She was shaking her head. "I'm not Alex. I don't know you. I don't . . ."

A dark shadow sliced through the too-bright wall of light. Someone shouted, "Shit!," as an engine roared. Tires squealed. And Zoe wondered if her brain was on fire—that would explain why there was suddenly so much smoke in the air.

The lights were spinning faster, and a loud screeching sound was making her ears bleed. All she wanted to do was push that man down another mountain, but how could she do that when she couldn't even see him for the smoke—when she could barely breathe? When her head was splitting open and her eyes were seeing double because . . . wait.

Zoe really was seeing double, she realized. She must have been. Because there was suddenly *another* Zoe. This one was sitting on the motorcycle that had leapt over the line of SUVs and was currently spinning around and around, tires screeching and sending up a cloud of black smoke before slamming to a stop and looking at Zoe like she was a moron. Which she was.

Because one of them really was a badass spy. One of them really was a lethal and highly trained weapon. One of them was oh so obviously Alex. And she was staring at Zoe, disgust and annoyance on her face, as she shouted, "Get on!"

Part of Zoe wanted to lecture about helmets and brain trauma and the dangers of motorcycles in winter, but she was already throwing a leg over the bike and wrapping her arms around the other woman's waist—her sister's waist.

And Alex was already hitting the throttle and zooming off into the night.

chapter fifty-three

HER

Zoe was pretty sure she never lost consciousness—she probably couldn't have stayed on the bike if she had. But that didn't stop her from making a vow that she would never get on another motorcycle ever again.

Ever.

She was torn between squeezing Alex's waist so tightly she was afraid she might pop her sister right in two and worrying that if she held on too loosely she would fly off the bike and hurtle through the sky and maybe never come down. Or come down really, really hard. Zoe knew it was the second one she had to worry about, but she managed to be afraid of both, somehow. Zoe managed to be afraid of everything.

"For crying out loud, hold on!" Alex shouted back and Zoe squeezed—her eyes. Her arms. Her legs. Zoe squeezed everything.

"When I move, you move!" Alex shouted and Zoe tried to mimic her sister's motions, the subtle sways and sharp jerks that saw them zooming through the streets of Zurich, down alleys and over bridges, under overpasses and through—

Yup, at one point they drove through the lobby of a five-star hotel, shooting out onto a narrow street until they were going the wrong way down a one-way and, impossibly, no one followed.

Eventually, the city streets faded away and Alex revved the motorcycle faster. The frigid wind blew against Zoe's face; her hands felt like ice as they held on to Alex. And through it all, Zoe tried to find her balance. Literally. Figuratively. Because when she closed her eyes, she saw the man from the train and knew she was surrounded.

But when she opened her eyes, she saw the white lines of the highway zooming by way too quickly.

So Zoe kept her eyes on the back of Alex's neck and wondered if that was what the back of her own neck looked like. It was a stupid thing to wonder but it felt like the only safe thought in her head—like any other thought could literally kill her.

She didn't know how long they drove or how far they went. If Alex was as paranoid as Sawyer (and something told Zoe that her sister was probably far, far worse), she knew they must have looped and crisscrossed and backtracked a dozen times. But, eventually, even Alex seemed to relax. Zoe literally felt her posture change and her muscles loosen. The motorcycle slowed, blending in with the sparse traffic on the winding highway.

Still, Zoe was surprised when Alex steered the bike off the road and onto a scenic overlook a few minutes later. Tires on snowy gravel. Moonlight on mountain peaks. And one lone, yellow pole light shining overhead.

Her cheeks were so cold they burned, and her hands were starting to shake. Her legs were so numb that when she finally climbed off the motorcycle, she thought she might collapse before she could stumble to the low rock wall that skirted around the edge. She wasn't going to look over into the abyss, though. She couldn't take the risk of getting dizzy. Besides, she was afraid of what might look back.

So instead, she looked at . . . herself.

For a long time, Zoe tried to understand what she was feeling because it wasn't exactly déjà vu. She'd known she had a twin, of course, but it was still surreal to stare into a face like hers—eyes like hers—and feel like she was looking at a stranger.

Everything about Alex was harder, tougher, stronger. She actually seemed comfortable in those leather pants. Even the red hair seemed natural.

Zoe looked like a little girl playing dress-up, but Alex looked like she had spent her whole life becoming the woman on that mountain.

For days, all Zoe had wanted was to find Alex—save Alex—but she finally understood what Sawyer hadn't been willing to say: that maybe Alex wasn't just hiding—wasn't just missing. That maybe the version of Alex who'd had anything to do with Zoe was already dead. That maybe that had been the case for a very long time and Zoe hadn't just forgotten her sister. Maybe she'd never really known her at all.

"What the hell are you wearing?"

As questions went, it wasn't the most obvious place to start, but Zoe couldn't fault her sister's directness.

"Clothes?" Zoe tried because, evidently, Alex got the brains as well as the toughness and the coordination and the ability to wear leather unironically. Besides, Zoe had other, more important things on her mind, like—"What . . . How . . . What just happened?"

"You went to the bank!" Alex shouted. "That's what happened! What were you thinking, Zo? *Were* you thinking? Please tell me someone put a gun to your head or a bomb in your bra and made you walk in there? Because, otherwise, you might be a moron and I really hope you're not because that shit's genetic."

Alex was staring at her. White breath in the dark air. Skin flushed with sweat in spite of the freezing wind. She looked like someone who knew things—like someone who knew *herself*—and Zoe had never been more envious of anyone in her life.

"Zoe!" Alex shouted.

"No . . . no one was watching the bank. The bank was clear. No one was watching—"

"Of course someone was watching the bank!" Alex threw up her hands and walked back toward the motorcycle and for a split second Zoe wondered if she was going to leave, just get on and drive away. For a moment, Zoe wondered if she wanted her to.

But Alex turned, voice as cold as the wind as she asked, "What are you doing in Europe? Why were you at the bank? Why . . ." They must have gone full circle because she came back to, "What the hell are you wearing?"

It was so surreal, like looking at a mirror in a fun house. Or a fairy tale. And for a moment Zoe wasn't sure if she was blessed or cursed as she stood there, seeing down the road not taken at what her life might have been—who *she* might have been—if things had gone a different way.

"We-we're . . ." She didn't want to stammer but she couldn't help herself. "We're identical. I went to the bank because we're identical."

"I gave you that box number in case I died! Which, news flash, *not dead yet*! So I don't know what the hell you're doing here, but you're going home. Now."

Zoe felt small in the presence of someone who was exactly her same height. She felt small and weak and fragile, and she hated it. It was way more fun being the woman Sawyer thought she was. But Sawyer was a stranger and Alex had obviously known Zoe since the womb, so clearly Alex was the expert. And Zoe hated that, too.

"You're on the first flight home, so help me—"

"Fine!" Zoe didn't realize she was shouting until she saw the shock in her sister's eyes. "Great. I'd *love* to go home. Where is home, exactly? Just point me in the right direction and I'll get out of your hair."

"What are you talking about?" Alex seemed leery then. Like maybe a black ops division of the CIA had perfected body-swapping technology. Maybe some next-gen cloning or . . . Maybe Zoe was an enemy agent who had been given extensive plastic surgery and a little light brainwashing? Alex looked like she didn't know what was happening but she wasn't going to trust this weird chick with the knockoff version of her designer face. There could only be one Alex and she had no patience for any cut-rate imposter, even her own sister.

"The first thing I remember is waking up in Paris three days ago," Zoe said softly. She was far too tired for shouting.

"What?" Alex asked. Then, worse, Alex laughed. "You mean . . . You think you have amnesia?"

"No. I *know* I have amnesia! Because I woke up in a snowbank with a bruise on my temple and nothing in my pocket except some lip balm and a few euros and a half-used tissue . . ." She took a deep breath. "And something that looked like a hotel key but was really a membership card for a fancy-pants bank in Zurich." She threw her arms out wide. "And now we're here."

Alex stepped closer, fire in her eyes. "Where did you get the card?"

"That's the part of that story that interests you? Not the bloody snow or the—"

"Where did you get the card?"

Now Zoe really was confused. "You gave it to me."

"Of course I didn't. Now where did you get it?"

"*I. Have. Amnesia!*" Maybe Zoe wasn't in a nightmare. Maybe she was in a time loop, because no matter how many times she said the words they never got any less crazy.

"This is crazy," Alex said, proving her point.

"I know!" Zoe snapped. "My entire memory is nothing but head wounds and bloody knees. Uncomfortable shoes and people shooting at me. But that doesn't mean it isn't—"

"This is real life." Alex rolled her eyes and something in the gesture hit Zoe like a punch; an avalanche of déjà vu was starting in the mountains and barreling her way fast. "*This isn't one of your books, Zoe!*"

The avalanche was there, sweeping over her and carrying her away.

Her life didn't come back to her. Nothing flashed before her eyes. There was no dream sequence or montage set to a remixed-but-timeless pop ballad. It was more like Zoe was a magnet that had just felt metal for the very first time. Something was close. Something was right there, rising to the surface of her consciousness until . . .

"I like books." As profound epiphanies go, that one was, admittedly, lackluster, but something was still growing inside of her and, suddenly, Zoe knew. "*I write books.*"

And Alex . . . Alex just gave her a dry, quizzical look, so over Zoe and so bored. She was probably grateful none of her cool spy friends could see them then. She would have acted like she didn't even know Zoe, loser that she was. But Zoe wasn't a loser. Zoe was . . .

"I'm not a high-end jewel thief . . ."

"A *what*?"

"I'm an author!" Yes! That was it! That was—

"I think we need to go back to the part about the head wound." Alex finally looked concerned.

But Zoe felt lighter than she had in days. "I have to tell . . ." She trailed off as she remembered the sight of Sawyer in that little park, covered with lasers. Sawyer surrounded by agents. She thought about screeching tires and the distant sound of gunfire and she lunged for Alex, desperate.

"Do you have a phone?"

"What?"

"I need a phone! If we get separated, I'm supposed to call and leave a message for him. I need to get to a phone."

But Alex was going stiff again. "Call who?"

Suddenly, Zoe remembered that Alex didn't know she and Sawyer were . . . well . . . whatever Zoe and Sawyer were. Allies? Friends? More? There were times when she caught him looking at her, when his lip quirked and he put his hand on the small of her back. . . . When he was kissing her and holding her and telling her that it hadn't been a danger bang . . . When she let herself hope they might be more.

"Zoe!" Alex shouted. "Call who?"

But before Zoe could speak, a voice came floating on the wind, saying, "Me."

He was a shadow in the darkness, but he was there. He was there and he was alive and he appeared to have most if not all his original parts. There were a few new bruises, maybe a little dried blood. But he was there. And Zoe forgot all the things that, moments before, she'd been desperate to tell him. She just ran and threw herself into his arms, felt her feet go off the ground as he held her so tightly that she could actually feel his heart beating against hers.

"You found us."

"I found you."

She kissed him once on the lips but that wasn't nearly good enough, so she peppered more kisses on his cheeks and on his chin and that's how she knew that he was smiling—because she kissed that smile right off his face.

"You found me," she said on a sigh then pulled back. "Wait. How did you—"

"Your comms unit has GPS."

"Oh! Fancy!"

"Zoe." Alex's voice was a warning, and Zoe felt her sister moving through the shadows, but she couldn't take her eyes off Sawyer.

"Are you okay?" she asked. "I saw all those laser guns—"

"That's not what they're called."

"—pointed at you, and I wanted to help, but you told me to run, so I—"

He held her face in his hands—not like she was fragile: like she was precious. And Zoe had never been so achingly aware of the difference. "You did the right thing. Now, did you get it?"

"Zoe!" Alex shouted, but Sawyer's face was just right there—so close. Kissing close. So she kissed him again because she could.

"Yes." The word was a whisper against his lips. "I got it." Then she stuck a hand down her shirt and watched him try not to grin.

"Need some help looking around down there?"

"No," she chided then pulled the thumb drive free and handed it to him. His eyes went wide at the same time something else changed. Maybe the wind. Maybe the clouds drifting back over the moon.

But she felt Alex at her back, heard her low command. "Zoe, come over here. Now."

And Zoe realized that they were still in the shadows—too far from the yellow ring of light to really see—so she took Sawyer's hand and called back, "It's okay, Alex. It's just Sawyer."

"Zoe." Alex didn't sound okay. "Walk to me. Now."

"Alex." Zoe tried to tease. "Sawyer's on our side, remember? He's CIA, too."

Then Alex inched into the light and Zoe noticed two things: the gun in her sister's hand and the look on her face as she said, "No. He's not."

chapter fifty-four

HER

Zoe wanted to laugh—would have laughed—if it hadn't been for the look on Alex's face—dark and cold. And the way she held the gun—like it was just another part of her, and it wasn't going anywhere. Ever.

"Step away from him, Zoe." Alex's voice was low and even. "Do it. Now."

And still Zoe was the moron who asked, "Why?"

Alex looked annoyed. "*So I can kill him!*"

But Alex was wrong. Alex had to be wrong. "No. Sawyer's on our side. He's CIA. He's . . ." She trailed off as she looked up at the man who wasn't looking at her because his gaze was locked on Alex, mirroring her every move, like boxers in a ring. Circling. "He's one of the good guys?"

And, so help her, it sounded like a question. Because he didn't look like a good guy, not with every part of him on high alert. Muscles tensing, jaw clenching. She shouldn't have even been able to see it in the moonlight, but Zoe knew him so well by that point. She knew him in the dark. But it was different this time, and it gave her a new kind of tingle, way down in her gut, and one word echoed in her mind: *dangerous*. Sawyer was dangerous.

"I told you, sweetheart, I'm not all good." That little boy grin was back on his hot guy face, but his voice was lower and darker, and Zoe thought she was going to be sick.

"Zoe!" Alex was shouting and Zoe was shifting—away from Sawyer and the line of fire and the lies. Mostly, she wanted away from the lies. But her sister just sounded annoyed. "Get out of the way so I can kill him!"

"Come on, Alex," he called. "Why don't you put the gun down—"

"No. I need this gun because *I'm going to kill you with it.*" She sounded like she really wished everyone would pay attention.

"Alex," Sawyer said with exaggerated patience, "I don't know what the hell is going on with you, but . . ."

"What's going on with *me*?" Alex actually laughed. "He's a traitor, Zoe. Kozlov turned him. He works for Kozlov. He—"

"Alex! Will you . . ." But Sawyer trailed off as, suddenly, everything changed. The grin slid off his face and his gaze shifted to the highway that snaked through the mountains, a black ribbon rising and falling with the Alps. "Shit!" He swung back to Alex. "Listen, we've got about two minutes before all hell breaks loose, and you both need to—"

And then all hell broke loose.

The dark night was suddenly too bright—full of headlights and dome lights springing to life as people charged out of cars. There was shooting and screaming and a lot of (probably Russian) cursing as Alex dove behind the motorcycle and opened fire. Something slammed into Zoe, trapping her between the icy ground and the rock wall and—

Sawyer. His face blocked out the moon, and his weight pressed against her, keeping her down or keeping her safe and, right then, she wasn't sure of the difference.

"You're a liar." She tried to push him off, but his big stupid body was too big and stupid and full of muscles.

"Of course I am. But you have to listen to me. I—"

Alex screamed and fell to the ground. Zoe saw her grip her shoulder and try to shift the gun to her other hand—she tried to keep shooting, but the gun didn't fire anymore. She was out of ammo. And they were out of time.

"Zoe!" Sawyer shouted, and she stopped fighting. She just looked up into those blue eyes that were now the color of ice. "No matter what happens . . . No matter what, just know . . ."

He traced her cold cheek, staring at her like he was memorizing the curves of her face. It was the same way he'd looked at her in the light of the fire—like he couldn't believe she was real. Like he couldn't believe she was there. Like he couldn't believe she was his. Because she had been his—she had. And, worse, she'd been happy.

And, suddenly, Zoe didn't know who to trust—the sister she didn't really remember or the man she didn't really know.

But she *did* know Sawyer. Didn't she? She knew his quirks and his sighs and the ghosts that haunted him and the things that soothed him . . . She knew him. And in that moment she was *Team Sawyer*; *Team There Has to Be a Reasonable Explanation*; *Team Alex Doesn't Know What She's Talking About Because This Guy Is Clearly Amazing.* Zoe was *Team Happy Ending* and would take that foolish, reckless hope to her grave.

She was just getting ready to say so when the shooting stopped.

And Sawyer said, "I'm sorry."

Those two words . . . she felt them like a blade. They slipped between her ribs and pierced her heart, and she knew she was going to bleed out because she'd been wrong. About him. About them. About everything. And all she could do was lie on the cold ground, listening to the crunch of tires on icy gravel as a new set of headlights sliced through the night—the subtle *click* of someone opening the back door of a car that was long and black and looked like what you'd drive if you had all your clothes made out of puppies.

When an old man crawled out, Zoe knew immediately who—or what—he was.

Kozlov.

He had probably been massive once, but age had made him smaller and weaker, and now he carried himself like a wild animal who refused to live in a world where he wasn't the top of the food chain. What time took away in muscle, this man made up for in evil—Zoe could see it in the set of his jaw and the look in his eyes as he snapped, "And?"

She should have been afraid of him. She should have been terrified. But the scariest thing on that mountain was the look on Sawyer's face as he climbed to his feet. She watched as he grew taller and stronger and darker.

Posture changing. Features shifting. It was like every muscle in his body suddenly morphed into something that was genetically the same but totally different.

She watched Sawyer become his own evil twin, and all Zoe could do was lie on the icy ground, wondering if she was watching him pull on a facade or take one off? All she really knew was that her Sawyer was gone.

He pulled the drive from his pocket and handed it to Kozlov, smirked down at Zoe on the ground. "I told you I could get her to trust me."

She was wrong, Zoe realized. *She was wrong.* Her Sawyer had never existed at all.

She was aware, faintly, of Kozlov looking down at her like she was a curiosity—a sideshow. A freak. She felt naked and vulnerable and exposed, but also numb and empty and brittle as a sick smile spread across the old man's face.

"Bring the traitor," he said flatly. "Kill the blonde."

A dozen men lunged for Alex, who was shouting and screaming and fighting. She was fighting so hard that no one seemed to notice the way Sawyer was looking at Zoe, stepping toward Zoe, grabbing Zoe by the arms and pulling her to her feet.

She tried to jerk away but Sawyer was a wall of muscle, pressing forward until she felt the snow-covered ledge against the back of her legs.

"Careful," he warned. "Do you want to fall down another mountain?"

Somewhere, Alex screamed. "Run, Zoe!" But Zoe was frozen, staring at Sawyer, who had lied. Sawyer, who had schemed. Sawyer, who had broken her in ways that might never, ever mend.

"I was wrong," she told him. "You're exactly like your father."

Then Zoe turned around. And jumped.

Screams followed in her wake, Russian curses and arching searchlights, but Zoe didn't care about that. She just tried to protect her head as she fell.

chapter fifty-five

HIM

Sawyer looked into the darkness at the place where Zoe used to be. In his heart he was still reaching for her, grabbing for her, pulling her close and keeping her safe. But in his head, he was hoping she fell hard and fast and was already halfway down the mountain.

It was maybe the truest thing he'd ever told her—that everyone was safer far away from him.

The wind had picked up and snow swirled through the yellow beams of the Bentley's headlights. The whole fucking world was swirling, and he thought he was going to be sick. Because Zoe was gone, dissolved in the darkness like she'd never been there at all.

"Your woman has heart," Kozlov muttered, almost like he approved.

And Sawyer had to remember. "She's not my woman."

"If she is not dead, will she make trouble?" Kozlov asked, and Sawyer tried to keep a straight face. It was harder than it should have been because . . . *Oh yeah. Zoe would make trouble.*

He wanted to chase after her, beg with her, plead with her. He'd make her understand and—

"You fucking bitch!" Kozlov's favorite henchman shouted. Sawyer heard the sickening crunch of fist meeting face, and he remembered . . .

Alex was still here . . . The drive was still here . . . His job was still here . . . And if he jumped, Kozlov's guys would follow. Kozlov's guys would find him, and if they found him, they'd find Zoe. And the truth was Zoe was the most naturally resourceful person he'd ever undercovered with. She'd be safer without him.

If she wasn't unconscious . . .

If she wasn't bleeding . . .

If she wasn't broken . . .

If . . .

"I'll go after her. Make sure she can't cause any more trouble." He was starting to jump. He was starting to fly, when Kozlov gave a shrug.

"We have this." The old man held up the drive while his thugs threw Alex into the back seat of the Bentley. "Leave the blonde. She is nothing."

Sawyer turned back to the abyss one last time, searching for any sign—any sound.

She is everything.

chapter fifty-six

HER

Maybe she was knocked unconscious by the fall. Or maybe she just slept. Zoe didn't know—didn't exactly care. All she knew was that she dreamed. She must have. Because there were voices all around, floating through her mind like ghosts as she remembered—

Alex standing on the mountain, shouting, *This isn't one of your books, Zoe!*

A man in a surgical mask and cartoon-covered scrubs covering her mouth. *Can you count backward from one hundred for me?*

A woman with green eyes saying, *No, sweetheart, you're not strong enough to go with Alex. But look, I brought you a new book.*

Her mind was a blur of faces and places, but the words were almost always the same.

Don't run, Zoe.

Be careful, Zoe.

You're too weak.

You're too fragile.

You're too frail.

Then a deeper, colder voice was in her head, saying, *I told you I could get her to trust me.*

The words cut through the fog in Zoe's brain and pulled her from the dream, and she lay in the dark for a long time, certain of two things.

One: She had been born with a bad heart.

And two: That was the first time it had ever been broken.

The snow was cold and soft beneath her, and she waited for a surge of memory—a flash of recognition. But her whole life felt like a dream she couldn't quite hang on to—scenes and lines and memories that were floating away on the wind.

She could remember hospitals and libraries and watching other children play. She recalled kind smiles and the sound of distant laughter. But mostly she just lay there, exposed and unprotected, wishing she could forget the past few days, just wipe them from her mind completely. But she wasn't going to be that lucky ever again, it seemed. Because even though her memory was still a vast, gaping void, there were some things that she just knew—like the fact that she was lying in a snowbank . . . again. And she had no idea what she was supposed to do . . . again. And, most of all, she was alone . . . She was alone and she was going to stay that way. Again.

She'd come so far since Paris, but somehow Zoe had ended up right back where she'd started. Only worse. Because this time there would be no Sawyer. And the worst part was realizing that, in a way, there never had been.

It shouldn't have felt like such a loss, losing one person. But Sawyer had been her only person. So she laid there, looking up at the stars, thinking about how some of them were so far away they were already dead before their light even reached earth.

Sawyer was like that.

He'd been lost for days—weeks. Forever. Long before his light even reached her, it was already out. And just because he'd been standing in front of her—kissing her, holding her—a few hours before didn't mean he wasn't already gone.

WELL, I GUESS IT COULD TECHNICALLY BE WORSE
A List by Zoe Whatsername

- She hadn't broken any bones.
- She hadn't frozen to death.

- She was getting really, really good at falling down mountains at high speed.
- She'd probably never have to see Sawyer ever again.

By the time the sun finally broke over the top of the tallest mountain, Zoe had been walking for an hour. Or two. Or twenty. Who was to say at that point? But as she reached a small town teeming with tourists, she had already laid out her thoughts the best way she could, and no matter what order she put them in she always came to one conclusion: Sawyer was a liar.

Which, actually, was a good thing, she decided. Because maybe he'd been lying about *everything*. Maybe it was perfectly safe to go to the US Embassy and explain her broken brain. . . . Maybe there were a few people who were actually on her side. . . . Maybe there was someone she could trust. . . .

Really, the more Zoe thought about it, the more it made sense. After all, if Sawyer wanted to keep Zoe away from the real CIA, what better way to do that than to convince her they couldn't be trusted?

He'd had to keep her isolated. He'd needed to keep her alone. It was almost embarrassing how easy that must have been. She was so gullible and desperate.

And lonely.

It would have been so easy to blame the amnesia, but Zoe knew that wasn't it. She would have been susceptible to his charm and his smile and his muscles—to whatever gravity kept her in his orbit—no matter what, and thinking about it . . . Well, thinking about it didn't change it, so Zoe tried not to think about it at all.

Instead, she used a little of the cash she'd shoved in her pockets to buy some food and a sweatshirt that said SWITZERLAND IS CHEESY! Then she bribed a taxi driver into taking her all the way to Zurich. But, most of all, Zoe tried very, very hard not to cry.

Because even though she hadn't gotten her entire memory back yet, she'd remembered enough to know that while Alex had spent their childhood learning how to kill a man with crayons, Zoe had been busy writing fan fiction about the hot Smurf with the pencil behind his ear.

Alex was the strong one. Alex was the tough one. Alex was the one who was made to take on international villains and lying hot guys, and Zoe was . . . not.

There was no way Zoe could write her way out of this one, so she'd go to the embassy. She'd turn herself in. She'd tell her story and get some help. The CIA could get Alex back. The intelligence services of the world could deal with Kozlov.

Maybe if she was lucky, they'd let her enter the witness protection program—get a whole new life because, the truth was, she wasn't in a hurry to remember her old one.

But the closer the cab got to the embassy, the more the little voice in the back of her head began to whisper—like someone talking through your favorite movie, intent on ruining the kissy parts.

With every second, the voice got louder, asking, *Then why didn't Alex hand over the disk?* And *How did you get the bank card?* And *What were you doing in Paris?*

Zoe could see the gates on the next block, the flags. The marines. Oh, how she wanted to run toward the marines, but the voice was right there, saying, *Then why doesn't Alex trust the CIA?*

And Zoe could no longer ignore the fact that, if Sawyer being bad were the answer, then she shouldn't still have so many questions.

He'd told her not to trust him. Not to believe him. He'd called himself a liar so many times that a tiny, traitorous part of her heart had to wonder if maybe Sawyer hadn't been lying about *everything*— just the big things. Like who he was and why he was putting up with her and whether or not she could actually pull off leather pants.

"Hey, lady," the driver said from the front seat. "You have euro?"

Yes. Cash. Of course. She'd promised half up front and half when they got here, so she leaned forward and dug into her jacket pocket.

And that's when she felt the envelope.

And that's when she remembered the second box.

And that's why Zoe sat there, staring at her name in her sister's writing, feeling like maybe she was tempting fate. Alex had given her access to that box in case she died, after all. And Alex was alive.

Maybe.

Hopefully.

There was a small chance that Alex was still alive, and if Alex was alive, then Zoe had to keep her that way!

But how was she supposed to do that? Exactly?

In the next moment, she was ripping open the envelope and pulling out a note. Maybe Alex loved her. Maybe Alex missed her. Maybe Alex wanted Zoe to know that she would never be alone as long as she kept Alex in her heart. Maybe . . .

Z,

A lot of people would kill for this.

It's the only copy. Keep it safe.

—A

Well, that was anticlimactic, Zoe thought just before she tipped the envelope and something fell into her palm and she looked down at—

The flash drive.

For a moment, Zoe thought she must have hit her head again, because she distinctly remembered pulling the drive from Alex's box. She remembered handing it to Sawyer and—her stomach soured—Sawyer handing it to Kozlov.

But what if Alex made a decoy? What if Kozlov had a fake?

The drive felt like a visceral, living thing as it lay in the palm of Zoe's hand. Like it was something that could hurt her. Or save her. She wasn't exactly sure which. But one thing was certain: she wasn't alone with nothing anymore.

Now, she was alone with *everything.*

"Lady?" the driver asked as they neared the embassy gates.

There was a billboard across the street—a picture of two mountain peaks rising above the clouds, snow-covered and almost mythical as a long bridge stretched between them like something made of ice, and Zoe thought of all the ways she could fall down.

"Lady?" the man sounded impatient. They were so close to the gates that she could practically see the marines' eyes.

"Just keep driving," Zoe said. "Just keep driving."

Two hours, three taxis, and four stops later, Zoe had a cheap motel room, a large assortment of burner phones, two changes of clothes, and a plan. Because Zoe needed to be smart. Zoe needed to be patient. Zoe needed to think . . . like a spy.

But, aside from Alex, there was only one spy of Zoe's acquaintance. Luckily, she knew just how to reach him.

chapter fifty-seven

HIM

The sun was almost up by the time they reached the Kozlov compound on Lake Como. Sawyer should have slept in the car, but every time he closed his eyes he saw Zoe disappearing in the darkness. Every time he moved he felt himself reaching for her and coming back with a fistful of empty air. Every time he tried to think, he heard her voice saying *I was wrong. You're exactly like your father.*

Which was okay, Sawyer told himself. His father would know what to do.

The lake was still and the compound was silent, but Sawyer knew it wouldn't last. Kozlov's top lieutenant was flying in from Moscow with a special, highly encrypted laptop, and once it was there, Kozlov would open the drive and make a copy. And as soon as he no longer needed the drive . . . well . . . then he'd no longer need Alex.

Like all of Kozlov's compounds, this one was a veritable fortress of guards and gates and fences, but it had been a late night and a long morning, so the house felt almost empty as Sawyer walked down the long hall toward the sound of . . .

Humming.

Just like Zoe, Sawyer thought as he reached the woman tied to a chair in the middle of the empty ballroom. She had a split lip and a black eye, but she looked as regal as a queen, even as he pulled the gag from her mouth and she kept singing, "*I'm gonna kill you sloooowly. I'm gonna make it huuuuuurt.*"

She'd do it, too, Sawyer mused, but the thought just made him smile. "You ready to get out of here?" he whispered.

"Fuck you."

"Come on, Alex. Let's— Shit. These are chains, Alex. They literally chained you to this chair."

"Of course they did. If they'd used zip ties, I would have been highly offended."

Sawyer looked up from the lock. "This would be a lot easier if your sister didn't have my favorite pick . . ." He trailed off as he realized Alex was scowling at him.

"You do realize that as soon as you get me out of these chains I'm going to strangle you with them?"

And, suddenly, Sawyer wasn't smiling anymore. It had been over a week since he'd started chasing, worrying, wondering . . . "I don't know why you stopped trusting me, Alex, but we're on the same side, remember? Would I be getting you out of here if I'd turned?" She honestly had to think about the answer, and Sawyer saw that for the opening it was. "Why'd you do it, Alex? We were supposed to get the drive together. Why didn't you wait for me? Why'd you run?"

"I heard Kozlov and Sergei. They knew I was CIA."

"So"—he started to snap, then realized—"You thought I told them." Sawyer felt the words like a blow.

For the first time, Alex looked sheepish. "I didn't know if I could trust you or not," she admitted. Right before her gaze turned as sharp as a blade. "And then you showed up with my little sister and I stopped wondering."

But something about the words—the indignant look in her eyes—made him chuckle. "Little sister? You're twins!"

"I'm thirteen minutes older," Alex said with more superiority than a woman chained to a chair should ever be able to muster. "It was a decent plan, I'll give you that. Bring her to Europe. Slip her the card. Get her to be me at the bank."

"I didn't bring her here! I didn't even know she existed until I found her half dead in Paris and thought she was you."

"You used a poor, defenseless woman—"

Sawyer couldn't help himself—he laughed, far louder than he should have before dropping his voice. "Your sister is many things. But defenseless?" He raised a brow. "Really?"

"What kind of psycho pulls someone like her into something like this?"

Suddenly, Sawyer didn't feel like laughing anymore. "*Someone like her*? What does that even mean?"

He watched Alex morph from angry to confused to . . . heartbroken, the look in her eyes all but screaming *do you really not know*?

"She was two days old and weighed three pounds the first time they cut open her heart. They did it again six months later. And one more time before the age of four. Zoe can't run. Zoe can't fight. Zoe gets winded going down escalators."

He heard the words. He knew they were true, but in his mind, he was tracing those scars in the firelight. He knew what they tasted like and where they led. Except he hadn't known where they'd come from or why they were there. He kept waiting for this new information to change those old wounds in his mind somehow—to change her—but if anything, it just made him angrier.

"You have no idea what your sister is capable of."

"And you do?"

Sawyer couldn't help but think about the woman who had jumped off a bridge in Paris, shaken off a Russian assassin on the *Shimmering Sea*. She'd tossed a CIA agent off a moving train and performed minor surgery on him by firelight. Yeah, he knew Zoe. He knew Zoe. And he—

"You may think she's expendable, but—"

Sawyer saw red. "Don't call her that. Don't ever call her that!" Sawyer roared, looking down at eyes that were just like Zoe's, only harder, sadder.

"You don't know her," she told him.

Sawyer was wrong. They weren't Zoe's eyes at all. "Then neither do you."

He almost had the lock open when he heard the commotion outside. Through the ornate windows he saw a seaplane bobbing on the lake. A guard was already running toward the house, a laptop under his arm, and Kozlov was shouting in the hall.

"Shit! Sergei's here," Alex said.

Sawyer almost had the lock. He was close. He was almost finished when he heard . . . *laughter*. But not the cold, cynical kind that filled his life. No. It was the kind of laughter that was pure and good and sounded like—

Zoe.

That was Zoe's laughter, and it washed over Sawyer like music, lilting and sweet—up until the moment he remembered where they were, and panic surged inside of him. He had to get her out of there. He had to—

"You fell for her." Alex was staring up at Sawyer, confusion and wonder on her face, as if starting to realize—"*You're in love with Zoe.*"

Sawyer wanted to protest—to tell Alex she was delusional and stupid and wrong because that had to be better than admitting she was right.

"I . . ." He was aware of the laughter stopping, of shouting taking its place and filling the halls, but the inside of his head was even louder—words rattling around like *That's crazy*. And *don't be ridiculous*. Or *I barely even know her*. But what came out was, "I don't deserve her."

He risked a look at Alex, expecting her to tease or joke or for lasers to come shooting out of her eyes. But all he saw was pity. Because he was right. And she knew it. He didn't deserve someone like Zoe. And he never, ever would.

"*Where is the traitor?*"

Sawyer barely had time to leap away from Alex before Kozlov stormed into the room, laptop open. But there were no files on the screen—just a home movie of two little girls who needed braces, one of whom was doing handstands in the grass while the smaller, paler girl lay on a blanket, reading. Laughing.

"What is this?" Kozlov shouted and Alex's busted lips curved into the smile of a woman who was holding all the cards.

"Looks like you've got the wrong drive there, big guy. *Oops*."

Kozlov roared and threw the laptop. It shattered against the wall as the compound turned to bedlam. Guards shouting. People running. And through it all, Sawyer stood there, thinking. The good news was that Kozlov needed Alex alive—now more than ever.

The bad news was that Sawyer still had to get her out. They had to go. Now! But they couldn't go now. She was the center of a tornado—the eye of a storm—and she was staring at him through the chaos, a determined gleam in her eye and a subtle shake of her head as she mouthed two words.

FIND HER.

Sawyer was almost to the water before he found a place quiet enough to pull out a burner phone and try the number again. The call connected, but he wasn't actually expecting to hear—

"You have two new messages."

He was holding his breath when her voice came through the line a moment later.

"Hi. Hello. It's me. Zoe. This message is for Sawyer. Or whatever his name is. If he gets this. If this is even a real number, which . . . nothing else was real, so . . ." Her voice cracked then trailed off and he heard the muffled words, "Shoot. Delete. Delete. Dele—" *BEEP*.

When the second message began it was still Zoe's voice but everything about the tone was different, like she'd spent an hour on YouTube watching videos called *How to Be a Badass*.

"If this is Sawyer, listen up. There's an outdoor ice rink just outside of Zurich. Meet me there at noon tomorrow. Come alone or you'll be sorry." The line was silent for a long time before she added, "This is Zoe, by the way. Uh. Bye."

Sawyer noted the time and the place, but when the service asked if he wanted to delete the messages or hear them again, he deleted the second and saved the first. Kept his phone to his ear and listened to her voice again.

And again.

And again.

chapter fifty-eight

HIM

The next day, Sawyer came to the ice rink alone, and he got there early.

He'd replayed Zoe's message a dozen times, always listening for something in her voice that would tell him if she'd gotten hurt in the fall, trying to hear some noise in the background—a clue where she might be. Was she warm enough? Safe enough? Did she have money for food and shelter and slightly-more-comfortable shoes? He needed to know. He needed *her*.

Kozlov's guys were looking for her again. The agencies were no doubt still after Alex. So Sawyer had to find her before someone else did. The only question was, what was he going to do with her then? Kidnap her for real this time? Lock her up inside another cruise ship? Force her to wear even more leather pants? But would that be torturing her or torturing him? Really, it was a toss-up.

So he sipped his coffee and scanned the outdoor skating rink that was just outside the city. The scratchy sound system was playing music, and the crowd was getting thicker with people lacing up their skates, kids calling out *watch me, watch me!* But he wasn't worried that he'd miss her. No. Zoe was never going to be invisible to him ever again. The only question was had she changed her hair? Would she still be dressed like Alex? Or would she look like the woman from the snowbank? Maybe like Mrs.—

"Michaelson!" At first he thought he'd willed the name into existence—that he'd dreamed it. "Paging Mr. Michaelson to the concession area. Paging Mr.—"

"I'm Michaelson," he told the girl in the booth. "You paged—"

"Your wife left something for you." The girl scanned him up and down, as if trying to decide if he was worthy, then she held out a small padded envelope and popped a bubble with the gum he hadn't even realized she was chewing.

"Where's my wife . . ." He was looking around. "*Where is Mrs. Michaelson?*"

"Oh"—the girl's mouth curved into a curious grin, like sitting behind that desk was an interesting job all of a sudden—"she's already gone."

The words hit Sawyer so hard that he was turning—he was already walking away before he remembered the package. He ignored every bit of his training as he ripped it open and tipped it out and a small silver ring landed on the palm of his hand.

Even though he knew it couldn't still be warm from her skin, it burned him, searing into his flesh like a brand, a mark that only he could see and feel but would last for the rest of his life.

Whatever sliver of hope he'd held on to died in that instant. He was a guy who did bad things for good reasons and that was never going to change. Someday soon, he'd get Alex back and take Kozlov down. But there would always be another Kozlov and another cover and another mission until the man he'd been with Zoe faded away forever.

Good. Let him die, Sawyer thought just as a phone began to ring. He dug back into the envelope and pulled out a burner.

"Zoe!" Sawyer's pulse was in his ears as he answered. "Are you okay?"

"Is my sister alive?"

"*Are you okay?*" he asked again because how was he supposed to say anything else? That mountain she'd fallen down was eight hundred meters high. He knew. He'd looked it up. And now her voice was on the other end of the line—he could even hear her breathing. "Are you hurt?"

Someone must have fallen on the ice because an ambulance was approaching, the sirens so loud he heard them in stereo. Here. And also through the phone. Which meant that Zoe was close. Zoe was there.

It was like diving into freezing water, looking through the dark. He hadn't been able to see her that night in the river. He'd *felt* her, sensed her. Known her. So he took off at a run, following the sound of the sirens. Through the people and around the buildings then into the trees at the edge of the—

"Zoe?"

The sound must have scared her because she whirled and tried to step back but there was no place to go and she banged into a tree.

"Sweetheart?" Sawyer tried to keep his voice low as he dropped the phone and held up his hands. "I'm gonna give you something, okay?" Slowly—very slowly—he pulled out his Glock and tossed it on the ground in front of her. "That's for you."

But Zoe just stood there, staring and confused. "That's your favorite gun."

"I know." He laughed softly—something he hadn't even known he could do until he met her. "It's yours now. Shoot me with it if you need to, okay?"

She didn't stoop to pick it up, but she kept it between them, like it could protect her, there on the ground.

"Are you okay?" he asked again because nothing else mattered.

"I'm fine." She sounded tired and annoyed and he wanted to kiss the little crease between her eyes until it smoothed away. "Is my sister okay?"

"She's alive. She sent me to find you. Those were her exact words: *find her*. So I'm here. And, for the record, I don't blame you if you don't believe me."

"I don't know what to believe anymore." He heard pain in her voice. Not fear. *Fear* he could have handled. But he thought about a baby no bigger than the palm of his hand. He thought about a four-year-old in a hospital gown. She was fearless. Of course she was. She was never going to be afraid of him. He was nothing in comparison.

"Zoe, please . . ."

"Listen," she snapped. "The drive Kozlov has is a fake."

And for a second, the whole world seemed to freeze. The music went away and the crowd stopped milling. "I . . . I know. But how did you . . ."

"Alex had two boxes at the bank, and I accessed both. The real drive was in box number two. So—" She threw her shoulders back and stood a little straighter. "I've got a message for your boss."

"He's not my boss, sweetheart. He's my mission."

"Funny. Because that's not how it looked when you *gave him the flash drive.*"

"I gave up the flash drive to keep you safe!"

"You kept yourself safe. *I* had to jump off a mountain!"

"Because I gave you the idea!"

They were inching closer and closer because they always did— they always would. He couldn't stay away from her any more than a compass could stop pointing north.

"You did *not* give me the idea!" Oh, she was annoyed. And indignant. And glorious. Right up until she realized—"Wait. *Did* you give me the idea? No. You just wanted me out of the way for your mission—"

"I wanted you safe because I'm in love with you!"

Sawyer couldn't hear the sirens anymore. Not the sound of the wind or the cries of the crowd. There was nothing but those words, floating in the frigid air. He wanted to pull them back. And he wanted to shout them louder. Because Alex was right. He was in love with Zoe. *He was in love with Zoe.* Zoe, who was just standing there, gaping. Stammering. "You . . . You . . ."

"I know, sweetheart—"

"*I'm not your sweetheart!*"

He shook his head. He had to make her see. Did she really not see? "You're my everything."

A tsunami of emotion washed across her face. Anger and fatigue and hope? Fury and rage and longing. It was like she was experiencing a lifetime of feelings in those five seconds, running the gamut, the spectrum, trying every single emotion on for size before settling on—

"What gives you the right to give certifiable movie kisses and say certifiable hero lines and stand there with your certifiable hot guy smirks while telling me you just wanted to save my life? What gives you the right . . . you *absolute jerkface*!"

Sawyer gave it a second then shouted, "I don't know what that means!"

"It means I'm in love with you, too!" she shouted even louder and the wall of ice inside of Sawyer slowly began to crack. And then he was reaching for her. Because he needed to hold her and kiss her and tell her again. He was never going to stop telling her—showing her. He was never going to stop.

But Zoe stepped away. Just one step. Just a few inches. And yet it was like watching her fly down another mountain she went so far so quickly. She was instantly out of reach.

"I love you." Her voice was softer and her eyes were closed. "But I don't trust you anymore."

It was the most pain he'd ever known. Real and physical and deep until all that was left were broken bones and split skin. He was bloody and mangled and never coming clean. They were just words. And they were going to leave a scar.

"Zoe . . ." he said because it was easier than arguing. "You have to trust me."

"No." She shook her head and rubbed her eyes. "I don't."

"Then why . . . Why call me if you don't trust me?"

She looked at him like he really must be a moron—like the answer was so clear and just right there.

"Because you want the drive. That's the one thing I can count on. Ever since Paris . . . I was always looking for my sister, but you . . . You were always looking for the drive, weren't you?" Her voice cracked and her hand shook as she rubbed her runny nose, but he didn't bother to answer. "It's the one thing I can count on."

"*You can count on me,*" he told her, but she didn't say a thing. And then a new worry grew inside of him. "Do you have it now?"

He couldn't keep the fear out of his voice, and she couldn't keep the irony out of hers.

"Of course that's what you'd say."

"That drive is poison, Zoe. It's a target on your back and you need to give it to me."

"Why?" She gave a quick, cold laugh. "So you can give it to Kozlov? Maybe hand it over to the CIA or MI6. Or Mossad. Or—"

"Of course I'm going to hand it over! That drive is how we get rid of Kozlov. It's the only way we . . ." He ran a hand through his hair. He could have told her a hundred lies in a half dozen languages, but, right then, the truth was the only thing that mattered. "It's how we get free. It's how we get safe. That drive is everything."

I love you. But I don't trust you anymore.

"Listen up, *Mr. Spy Guy*, that drive might be your freedom, but it's *my sister's life*. So forgive me if I don't tell you where it is."

He didn't even try to hide how much that hurt him. "You know me, Zoe."

"Do I?" she bit back, stronger now. It was like she was still rolling down that mountain, momentum taking over and picking up speed. "Who are you, Sawyer? Really? Are you the guy who said I was just a waste of time and ammunition or the newlywed who dipped me on the dance floor or the man who held me in his arms and told me that I was beautiful? Or are you the thug who works for Kozlov? Huh? Who are you? Because I watched you turn into that guy right before my eyes, and I realized I . . . I love you." Her voice trembled but her eyes were like steel. "But I don't know the real you at all."

There were birds in the trees and children shouting in the distance, but the world was suddenly quiet and still and achingly empty.

"No, sweetheart. You're the only one who does."

Zoe closed her eyes and Sawyer couldn't stop himself from inching closer—from reaching for her—from needing her skin against his.

"I know Alex didn't trust me for a while there; and I get why you're hesitant to trust me now. But I'm not the villain here, lady. I'm just a guy who saw twelve pissed-off Russians and had to play it by ear." He blew out a frosty breath. "I get that it probably looks like I didn't choose you. But I watched you almost die a dozen times, Zoe. And I wasn't gonna do it again. I can't. I won't. So I'm going to keep you safe, sweetheart. And then I'm going to earn your trust."

She was just right there. He had to make her see . . . "There's no place I won't go and there's nothing I won't do to prove myself to you."

It was like she couldn't hold his gaze. Like it was too hot. She had to put it down. And she seemed almost nervous to admit, "I was going to go to the embassy . . ."

"Good! Okay. Let's do—"

"But then I realized that Alex didn't trust the CIA. And she didn't trust you. But you know who she did trust?" She gave a laugh that was part hiccup and part giggle and wholly, complctely lovable. "*Me.* She trusted me. So I'm going to trust myself." He watched her straighten her spine and summon her courage, and he loved her so much it hurt. "So I need you to listen very, very carefully and do exactly what I say."

HER

He said he loved her.

She said it back.

Zoe honestly didn't know if anyone had ever said those words to her before. She definitely didn't know if she'd ever hear them again. But as she sat in the back seat of a taxi fifteen minutes later, her fingers were on her lips, like the words might still be there—like she could touch them. And she was amazed to realize she was smiling.

She tried to stop. She really did. Because it wasn't the *I love you* she would have written. But, somehow, that made it better. Somehow, in spite of everything, it was really, really good and that made it really, really scary and she started freaking out for whole new reasons.

Because from the moment she woke up on that snowy street in Paris, she'd known Sawyer could hurt her. But that was the first time she realized he could break her—not her heart. *Her.* He could break her into a million pieces and then she wouldn't just lose her sister. She'd lose everything. And she realized that to save Alex . . . to get Kozlov . . . to get off this awful ride . . . She'd do *anything*.

The sun was bright through the window as the taxi turned. They were almost back to the city and her mediocre hotel room and her plans. The day was getting away.

So she pulled out a fresh burner phone and dialed the number she hadn't thought she'd ever use. When she heard a deep (and somewhat confused) voice, say, "Hello?" Zoe couldn't help herself. She became spontaneously southern.

"Hi there! I get that y'all probably have a million questions—which I am more than happy to answer—but . . ." She took a deep breath. "This is Mrs. Michaelson. And I need something of a favor."

chapter fifty-nine

"How sick is she?"

Sawyer didn't realize how much the question had been weighing on him until he'd said the words aloud. "Zoe," he clarified, as if he could have been asking about anyone else. "Her heart. Is it . . ." *Broken?* "How sick is she?"

Alex looked at him across the dim back seat of one of Kozlov's SUVs. The two thugs in front were singing along with some Russian pop star, and for a moment he wondered if she'd actually heard him.

But then Alex said, "She's not." Her voice was soft, and her face was full of shadows. "Not technically. Not anymore. She hasn't needed surgery since we were kids. Now she's just weak. Fragile. Frail. Always has been."

But Alex was wrong. She was so wrong he wanted to laugh.

"What?" she asked, but all Sawyer could do was shake his head and bite his lip. All he could do was remember—

"The woman I met in Paris didn't know that."

Sawyer felt the SUV turn as the Bentley followed them higher and higher into the Alps. Once they slowed and stopped, he crawled out and looked around a parking lot teeming with tourists and skiers, backpackers and families. But there were no guards and no metal detectors. Nothing but honor and the fear of collateral damage to keep Kozlov and his guys from killing everyone on that mountain which meant—*Shit.* Kozlov was going to kill everyone on that mountain.

Sawyer looked down at the burner phone, praying that he'd misunderstood. Surely Zoe had a different plan—a better plan. Surely—

Ding. Sawyer read the newest text.

Take the gondola to the first station.

That's when Sawyer noticed the wires that rose to the top of the peak, the line of people waiting to get onto the red cable car that was gliding toward them. "We're going up."

"If you are lying . . ." Kozlov's voice was low. It was the only thing scarier than when Kozlov shouted. "If *she* is lying . . ."

"She wants her sister back," Sawyer told him. "She'll be there."

So they joined the line and boarded the car and, five minutes later, they were flying over snow and rocks and jagged cliffs to the midpoint of the mountain.

Her instructions had been simple: he was supposed to bring Alex and Kozlov and no more than two guards, and they were supposed to follow her texts to Zoe and the flash drive. They'd make the exchange, then go on their merry way, or so Zoe thought. Because Zoe was good and kind and generous. She probably didn't realize that Kozlov was going to kill her. And her sister. And probably Sawyer for good measure.

So Sawyer just stood there, staring out at the tall peaks and sweeping vistas, trying not to think of all the ways this could go horribly wrong.

"Relax," Alex whispered as she leaned against the frosty glass. "If there's one thing my sister knows, it's how a plot comes together." A smirk teased at the corner of her lips and Sawyer wanted to ask a million questions, but the cable car was already sliding into the station.

The doors opened and, immediately, he shivered. It had to be at least ten degrees colder at this altitude, but that wasn't why his blood froze.

He looked around. There were signs for restaurants and restrooms, a small lake where people could ice-skate in winter or use paddleboats come spring. There were nature hikes and scenic outlooks—tourists eating at picnic tables and taking selfies. But there was absolutely no Zoe.

"She is not here." Kozlov scowled, and Sawyer knew there was a chance the old man was getting ready to shoot him where he stood.

"She wants her sister back. She'll be here." Sawyer sounded like a broken record, but he turned, still scanning, still searching, until he saw the poster that covered the gondola station's longest wall. It was an artist's rendering of two massive buildings carved into the sides of nearly identical peaks—a long crystal-like structure spanning between them.

COMING SOON! the sign read. THE WORLD'S LONGEST HIGH-ALTITUDE GLASS-BOTTOMED BRIDGE!

For a moment, Sawyer just stood there, thinking about perfectly cooked steaks and chocolate mousse and the way Zoe had wriggled into Mrs. Michaelson's tightest dress. And he knew. He knew, and he didn't know whether to be terrified or impressed.

"Why in the world are you smiling?" Alex whispered, but all Sawyer could do was shake his head. The phone *dinged* again. But Sawyer already knew what it was going to say.

Go to the restricted section. The cable car will take you up.

Everyone was watching, staring. "She's waiting for us."

Kozlov raised an eyebrow, as if to say *waiting where?*

So Sawyer pointed to the top of the mountain—to the place so high it was hidden in the clouds. "Up there."

chapter sixty

HER

Technically, it wasn't the tallest peak in the Alps—not even close—but Zoe couldn't deny the view was gorgeous. She probably would have appreciated it more if she hadn't started to realize that she was *definitely* afraid of heights. And sharp falls. And maybe a tiny bit prone to altitude sickness? But that could have been nerves doing weird things to her equilibrium. After all, this was her very first hostage exchange. At least as far as she could remember.

But even she had to admit it seemed to be going pretty well. She'd contacted Marc and Anthony and explained their situation. And, sure, maybe she hadn't explained *everything*, but it's amazing what people will believe if you use phrases like *National Security* and *Top Secret* and "*the Romeo and Juliet of Covert Operations.*" They'd been all too happy to oblige.

Then she'd simply had to send the texts and set the stage and think of all the ways this could go horribly, terribly wrong. Because that was her best chance of making it go right.

Or so Zoe told herself as she stood there, shivering, and trying very, very hard not to vomit.

HIM

The cable car they found in the restricted section wasn't so much a cable car as it was an open, metal cage, loaded with rebar and equipment and supplies, but there was still plenty of room for a notorious Russian mobster, two goons, one moron, and a hostage.

Sawyer could actually feel the air getting colder and the wind blowing harder as they rose, and by the time they made it to the top, the air was frigid and snow swirled around them like a tiny, non-stop blizzard. That had to explain why there were no workers milling about and the equipment all sat, abandoned and covered in ice.

Part of the peak had been blasted away and a huge building was growing up in its place, as if sprouting from the mountain itself. It was a marvel of stone and steel, but it was far from finished, so Sawyer wasn't sure what to expect as they set out, searching for Zoe.

She wasn't in the half-finished room at the top of the stairs. She wasn't on the wide platform that overlooked the sweeping vista. As they walked across the uneven ground, Sawyer fought against the bad feeling that was growing heavy in his stomach. Because, with every step, they got closer to the railing. With every step, he remembered the look on Zoe's face when she said, *You're just like your father* and hurled herself into the abyss.

Surely she wasn't going to try that again? Because, this time, they were much, much higher and Kozlov was much, much angrier, and there was no darkness now. Just a thick cover of clouds filling the air and threatening snow.

"I am out of patience." Kozlov was giving Sergei a look that said *this looks like a good place to dump a body* when a voice cut through the cold, thin air.

"Hello! Hi there! Excuse me!"

Zoe.

The clouds seemed to part as Sawyer inched closer to the railing and the voice that was saying, "Welcome to the hostage exchange!"

He couldn't believe what he was seeing. There was an iPad on an easel by the railing and Zoe's face was staring back at them. Smiling. Safe. He almost fell to his knees in relief because *Zoe was safe.* And, most of all, she was far out of Kozlov's reach. He just hoped she stayed that way.

"I hope everyone had a good trip? Didn't get too cold on the cable car? I started to tell you to wear layers, but I didn't want to overstep. This is my first hostage exchange. How am I doing?"

"You are out of time," Kozlov told her. "Where is my drive?"

Sergei pointed his gun at the back of Alex's head, then shifted a little, like he didn't want to get brains all over him by standing downwind.

"Now, now. We'll get to that," Zoe said calmly. "Fun fact: Did you know they have cameras all over that construction site for people to watch the progress and for safety protocols, and, well, I won't bore you with the details? Just . . . smile. You're on camera! Now we're not broadcasting *live*, of course. But the footage is being stored on three clouds even as we speak. Which is ironic because we're actually *in* a cloud right now—how cool is that? I thought—"

"Zoe!" This time Alex was the one who snapped.

"So here's how it's going to work." iPad Zoe put on her *serious face*. "You are currently on Mount Fratello, which, as you know, is in Switzerland. But did you know the mountain actually straddles the Italian border and there's an almost identical peak on the other side? And, well, surprise! That's where I am! See? Yoo-hoo! Over here!"

"Did my sister just say *yoo-hoo* during a hostage exchange?" Alex sounded like she wanted to die of embarrassment—like maybe she was going to turn around and beg Sergei to pull the trigger.

But Sawyer was spinning, searching the foggy sky for the familiar figure on the other side, waving from a construction site that was a mirror image of their own.

"So a very dear friend of mine is building the world's longest high-altitude glass-bottomed bridge," iPad Zoe explained. "You're going to be able to walk all the way from Switzerland to Italy through the air! Isn't that cool? And terrifying. Personally, I think that might be a little terrifying, but—"

"She rambles when she's nervous," Alex said.

"Yeah. I know." Sawyer nodded.

"Anyhoo . . ."

"Kill me now," Alex mumbled and Sergei actually cocked the gun, so Sawyer pushed his arm down just as iPad Zoe's voice wobbled and went darker.

"Let's just say, I've learned a lot in the last few days, and the big takeaway is that you never really know who to trust. And you're probably better off if you don't trust anyone. Ever."

It was like someone had shoved a knife through Sawyer's heart—that's how it felt to know that he'd hurt her, that he'd deceived her. That the one person in this world who really knew him was someone who still didn't trust him and maybe never would.

"Sooooo," Zoe drew out the word. "I can't exactly trust y'all not to kill us if you get your drive first."

"Did she just become spontaneously southern?" Alex asked.

"Yeah," Sawyer whispered, "she does that."

"And, Mr. Kozlov, you can't trust me to actually deliver your flash drive once you hand over my sister. So, as far as I can tell, the only way for everyone to get what they want is for us to do this exchange at the *exact same time*."

"How will we do that?" Kozlov actually sounded intrigued—maybe even mildly impressed.

"Oh, I'm so glad you asked." Zoe might have clapped. She definitely beamed. She was riding the rush that happens when a plan comes together—right before everything falls apart. "Do you see that big pulley system to your left? They use it to send supplies from one side to the other. I'll attach the flash drive on my side and you'll attach Alex on yours. We both have emergency stop buttons, so if either of us tries to pull a fast one . . . we hit stop and no one gets what they want."

Then she leaned closer to the camera, eyes narrowing, gaze burning. No one could accuse her of being a ditzy blonde—an imposter Alex—when she said, "I don't care about your business or your crimes, Mr. Kozlov, so I don't give one flying flip about your precious drive. I just want my sister back. Now do we have a deal?"

The wind blew and the snow swirled and there was no place on earth colder than that mountain when Kozlov said, "We do."

"Awesome." Zoe clapped again. "Alex, you'll need to hook into one of those harnesses and backpack thingies."

"*Backpack thingies?*" Alex sounded indignant. "Backpack thingies? Those are parachutes, Zoe."

"Oh, I don't know what they are. I just know they're a part of the mandated safety equipment, and safety equipment is very important. So . . ." Zoe shifted the iPad so they could watch her drop the flash drive into a bucket and hook the bucket onto the cable on her side of the border.

Sawyer didn't want to look at the screen, though. He wanted to look at Zoe—the real Zoe—but she was too far away, in another country, separated by an ocean of ice and snow and frosty air. She was gone. She was gone and he was never going to see her again, so he looked at Alex instead.

Alex who was staring back at him with eyes that weren't quite Zoe's eyes but might be the closest he'd ever see again. Alex whose hands were bound with zip ties. Alex who had been his partner and his friend—right up until the moment she stopped trusting him, but he couldn't be angry about that, Sawyer decided. Because, otherwise, he never would have found her sister.

"Well?" Kozlov barked, so Sawyer reached for one of the thick nylon straps that dangled from the cable and hooked it onto Alex's harness.

They were standing so close he could feel her shaking in a way that had nothing to do with the cold.

"Just . . . tell her . . ." *That I love her. That I need her. That I want her and respect her and will never, ever deserve her and I'll hate myself for that fact every day for the rest of my life.*

"End this," Alex whispered. "End this and tell her yourself."

He felt the pressure of her bound hands as they slipped into the pocket of his jacket. He saw the silver flash of his favorite knife as she cupped it between her palms. And when Kozlov hit the button to set the cable in motion, Sawyer hoped no one could hear his heart stop beating as he watched Zoe's sister drift over the edge.

"Tell her yourself," Alex whispered again, then disappeared into the clouds.

chapter sixty-one

HER

Zoe watched the drive fly away and congratulated herself on a hostage exchange well done. Really. Ten out of ten. Would exchange again.

She knew exactly where the emergency stop button was and if Kozlov got any ideas, she wouldn't hesitate to use it. But Kozlov wasn't a fool. Evil, yes? Stupid, no. He wanted his drive back, and there had been a look of begrudging respect in his eyes. He wasn't going to risk it.

The farther away the drive got, the better Zoe felt. She probably shouldn't have resented such a tiny thing, but knowing what that drive had meant to Sawyer . . . That it was the reason he'd helped her . . . That it was the reason he'd been with her . . . That he'd already chosen that drive—that mission—over her . . . Well, Zoe was glad to be rid of it.

But he said he loved you, that little voice in the back of her mind whispered. Just before a louder, sharper voice said, *Sawyer lies.*

Twenty feet beneath her, an unfinished walkway curved around the icy cliffs before stretching over the ancient glacier that spanned between the two tall peaks. Sawyer's life—Sawyer's world— was on the other side of the mountain, so Zoe just stood there, trying to keep her heart from breaking.

Alex was almost to the halfway point, and Zoe told herself it was almost over. As long as the cables kept pulling her sister closer and pushing the drive farther away . . . As long as Kozlov didn't get any ideas . . . As long as Zoe held herself together just a little while longer . . . Then she and Alex could take the cable car down the

Italian side of the mountain. An SUV was waiting at the bottom. They'd be finished. They'd be free. They'd be—

"Hello, Zoe."

Zoe heard the voice. And . . . clapping? A sharp, mocking sound that sliced through the thin air and struck her like a blow. But it was the sound of her name that made her stomach churn. She felt dizzy and outside herself and far too light—like she might blow away.

It was a sensation she'd felt before: once on a train in the Alps and again on the dark streets of Zurich. She'd felt that way every time she'd seen—

"Collins." She looked at the man who had creeped up behind her. And she realized . . . "You called me Alex in Zurich." She gripped the railing, terrified she might fall.

He stepped slowly forward and Zoe inched a little bit back.

"Of course I did. Couldn't let my colleagues know that you and I had . . . history."

The sun was too bright then—the world was too loud. But Zoe wasn't on the mountain anymore.

She was standing on a street in Paris.

She was looking down at a card for a bank.

She was saying, "What is this? I don't understand. You said Alex would be here, Mr. Collins. You said she needed my help?"

"Oh, I'm sorry. I should have been more clear. I don't need you to help Alex, Zoe. I need you to be Alex."

She laughed. It was insane. "Wait. Are you saying the Central Intelligence Agency needs me for a Parent Trap scenario? No one will ever believe I'm my sister. I'm nothing like her."

"Oh, obviously. But you'll forget that very soon." There was a syringe in his hand and he was coming closer. "Soon, you'll forget everything."

The needle plunged into her arm and Zoe felt her legs give out as she fell. Her head slammed against the ground and blood ran into her eyes. She had to get up. She had to run. She had to—

"You can't fight me, Zoe." The smirk on his face was nothing short of evil—like she was just too stupid to realize that he'd already won. He must have forgotten that his gun was in the holster on his ankle. He definitely

wasn't expecting Zoe to grab it. But she did, and he gave a cold, hard laugh. "Are you going to shoot me, Zoe?"

"I'm considering it." She tried to sound tough even though her head hurt and her arm hurt and her feet hurt. She should have worn better shoes, she thought as she backed away.

"Go ahead." He actually smiled. "Run. You've got thirty minutes before that shot kicks in—give or take. That little cocktail isn't exactly cleared for field use, but I've made an exception for you. Thirty minutes, Zoe, and you won't remember any of this."

"Good. It seems like the kind of thing I'm going to want to forget."

It was starting to snow. The first flakes landed on her hot cheeks, melting and blending with her tears. She was backing away. She was almost gone.

"I'll find you, Zoe. I'll find you!" he called as a bus pulled to a stop and Zoe threw the gun into a trash can and ran for it. She ran as if her life depended on it because she knew, deep down, it did.

Mountain Zoe blinked against the too-bright light and remembered. It wasn't the middle of the night. She wasn't in Paris. She wasn't looking for Alex. But the smirk on the face in front of her . . . the smirk was exactly the same.

"I thought I hit my head," she said. "But you did this to me. You did this to me *on purpose*."

He gave a callous shrug. "It would have worked, too, if the wrong spy hadn't found you."

The wrong spy . . .

Sawyer.

Sawyer had found her. He'd blown up a safe house and pulled a Go Bag from an electric box and pressed her up against a chilly window. He'd jumped off a bridge and held her beneath a tarp and tossed her a pen and given her the gift of her own name.

It was Sawyer. It had always been Sawyer.

It would always *be* Sawyer.

He'd killed a man in a freezing river and kissed her in front of a fire and looked at her as if she was the most beautiful, wonderful, terrible, amazing thing he'd ever known.

He'd told her he loved her. He'd told her. And he'd *shown* her when he handed the drive over to the worst man in the world and all but pushed her down a mountain.

Because he loved her. Because he cherished her. Because he had chosen her in a hundred different, little ways and one big way that mattered.

So she looked at the man who had drugged her and lied to her and used her. She looked at the man who could only be there for one reason: he was working for Kozlov. And if that was the case . . .

"I knew there was a reason I shouldn't trust the CIA."

"Very good," he said like the condescending asshole he was.

"I knew there was a reason I called *them* for backup instead."

"Very . . ." He hesitated. And, oh, how he worried. "Wait. Who?"

"Them." Zoe pointed over his shoulder, and the man turned and looked at the clear, blue—*and very empty*—sky behind him.

Which was when Zoe pulled a piece of rebar from a pile on the ground. And swung. He cried out and crashed to the ground. He was just lying there—far too still—when Zoe turned to the iPad and shouted, "Sawyer, run!"

Then she went to the railing and jumped because it seemed like the thing to do at the time.

chapter sixty-two

"Sawyer, run!" Did he hear Zoe's voice through the iPad or across the icy expanse? Sawyer didn't know. Didn't care. He just knew that Collins's smarmy face had been on the screen; he was too busy thinking about the way Zoe had transformed with one look at the man on the train. But, most of all, he heard the question Zoe had asked over and over: *Why didn't Alex go to the CIA?*

The moment he saw the sinister smirk on Kozlov's face, he knew.

"You have a mole at Langley." At that point it wasn't a question.

He saw the gun in Kozlov's hand, felt Oleg and Sergei on either side of him, easing closer and closer. Carefully, Oleg jerked Sawyer's gun from his waistband.

"How long?" Sawyer asked because he had to keep the old man talking.

"Just before the bitch stole the drive," Kozlov said, and Sawyer nodded because Alex had been right—of course Alex was right. Someone *did* tell Kozlov she was CIA, and for almost two weeks she'd been out in the cold. Alone.

Then a scream pierced the air.

Sawyer turned and watched in terror as Zoe sprang over the railing of the observation platform on the other side. But Kozlov wasn't looking at Zoe. He was watching Alex, who must have used the knife to cut herself free. She was almost at the midway point—getting ready to cross paths with the drive—when she leapt from one cable to the next. The wind gusts were so violent that she actually swayed, blown like a leaf, but she held on tightly as she pulled out the drive.

"Stop her!" Kozlov shouted and Sergei headed for the stairs that zigzagged down the side of the mountain and then out onto the glass-bottomed bridge.

And Sawyer . . . well, Sawyer just lunged for Oleg, grabbed his arm, and threw him at Kozlov like the world's worst bowling ball. Hey, it wasn't pretty. But it worked. They both crashed through the temporary railing and down the jagged rocks to land on a platform by the stairs, but all Sawyer could do was watch with his heart in his throat as Zoe started climbing down the icy cliff on the other side. Sawyer had to get to her. He had to save her. He had to—

And that's when he remembered the pulley system and threw the thing into high gear. He grabbed hold of the cable and flew through the frigid air that sliced between the peaks. The swirling ice and snow stung his face, but he could still hear the shouting and the shooting as Oleg opened fire down below.

Up ahead, Alex dropped onto the glass bridge and started running in the opposite direction—toward Zoe and Italy. Toward safety and home. But Sergei wasn't far behind her, gun out and closing fast. Sawyer saw it all from his place in the sky. In fact, he was probably the first to realize—

The bridge wasn't finished—it just dead-ended in midair.

"Alex!" he yelled as she slammed to a stop, staring out over the cold, empty void. The drop was at least fifteen feet, but Sergei was barreling toward her. There was no place to go. She looked up at Sawyer and, for a heartbeat, she looked like Zoe—like at any moment she was going to roll her eyes and call him a jerkface.

But before he could drop to the bridge to help, she yelled, "Go get my sister." Then she spread out her arms and jumped.

"Alex!" Zoe was running across the ancient glacier that was really just a field of ice and snow—extremely unstable ice and snow—and Sawyer died a little with every step she took.

"Zoe! Stay there!" he shouted, but she kept running. Infuriating woman. And then, worse, she stopped.

Her eyes filled with terror as she looked behind him then shouted, "Alex!"

Sawyer glanced back in time to see Sergei jump from the unfinished bridge and onto Alex. They crashed to the surface, rolling and fighting, and Sawyer watched in horror as the drive flew from Alex's hand and across the icy ground.

The drive that he'd searched for. The drive that he'd killed for. The drive that wasn't just his job—it was his future.

That drive was the end of Kozlov and the thing that was most likely to keep Zoe safe, so Sawyer stopped thinking and just . . . let . . . go . . .

He felt himself flying through the air and crashing to the top of the glacier. He heard the ice crack beneath him, felt the slide as the snow began to roll down the steep slope like a wave.

The wind blew around him, stinging his skin with icy pellets. Dusty snow was like smoke, filling his lungs. But he could see an outcropping of rocks poking up through the glacier's surface, so lunged for them, grabbing hold and stopping his fall, but the drive wasn't so lucky. It was twenty feet behind him and still sliding. Almost to the edge now. Almost gone.

"Sawyer!" Alex shouted, but he couldn't even turn; he was too busy clawing and crawling toward the drive that was slipping closer and closer to the edge. Grappling for balance. Desperate for traction. But he couldn't stop. He'd given five years of his life to stopping Kozlov. He had to get there. He had to get *it*. He was so close now. He just had to—

The moment Zoe screamed the world stopped.

The wind stopped blowing and his heart stopped beating and everything he'd ever loved or wanted or feared converged on the place where Collins was dragging Zoe to the ground. Hands on her throat. Squeezing. And everything—literally everything—changed.

The drive was nothing. Kozlov was nothing. His career . . . His father . . . They were all nothing compared to the terror of watching the woman he loved die.

"Zoe!" he yelled, charging back up the glacier, trying to climb and claw his way toward her, but the slope was too steep and the ice was too slick and she was just too far away.

She was too far away, but Sawyer had to reach her and save her and tell her . . . He had to tell her that she was the only thing on this earth that mattered. So he clawed harder, faster until—

He hadn't gotten to see her use The Move on the boat. He'd been too late to watch her free herself from that Russian assassin, but this time he saw her twist and kick and push until Collins was off her—until she was free. Kind of. Because Collins was still right there—just a foot or so away.

"You fucking bitch!" he shouted, but Zoe kicked again—not at the man. *At the ice.* Her heels pierced the snowy surface then pushed, and when he lunged again, the ice shifted. Just a little. And then it was crumbling and Collins was sliding. Falling. Washing away on a wave of ice and snow.

Zoe's cheeks were pink and her hair was wild, but when she smiled down at him, she was the most beautiful thing he'd ever seen, and for the first time in his life, Sawyer believed in happy endings.

But then the smile faded. The snow shifted. And crumbled. And in the next second, Zoe was sliding too—faster and faster toward the edge.

"No!" Sawyer roared, diving for the rocks again, anchoring himself with one hand while he stretched out with the other. Straining. Praying. Reaching—not for her hand but for his future. For his everything.

"Zoe!" he shouted over the sounds of Collins's screams—

"Fucking bitch!"

And when he felt her hand grip his . . . when he saw Collins wash over the edge while Zoe was still there—clinging to him . . . when he was finally able to breathe, to see. To smile . . .

All he could say was, "Language."

chapter sixty-three

HER

Zoe felt Sawyer pull her to the safety of the rocks. "Are you okay?"

"I'm okay."

"Are you . . ." Ice clung to her hair and tears froze on her cheeks, but he was looking at her like a man who wanted to warm her with his lips and never let her go.

But then she saw something over his shoulder. The drive. Twenty feet away and still inching, slipping—"Sawyer!"—sliding over the edge.

He didn't even turn around.

"I don't care." He traced her skin with his lips. "Let me warm you up."

But she pulled back. "You chose me." There was wonder in her voice. And love. But absolutely no surprise.

"Always." And then he kissed her. Like she was oxygen and water and life itself. Like they could survive there—on their little island of stone—for eternity as long as they had each other. They could make it. They'd be okay. She really thought it was true. Right up until the shots rang out.

Impossibly, Zoe seemed to hear them first, because she dove, dragging Sawyer to the rocky ground. She felt his body over hers, protecting her. Warming her. But she could see Kozlov and the second guard standing on the unfinished bridge. Bits of ice and stone flew up as bullets landed way too close. Maybe forever wasn't that long, after all, she thought, just before a cry pierced the air.

Alex was on the ground, pinned beneath the first guard's lifeless body. Zoe heard her sister scream then watched her roll the guard away and shift and—

Suddenly, the guard's gun was in Alex's hand and Alex was aiming at the bridge overhead—not at Kozlov. At the bridge itself. And then she fired.

One after the other, the bullets pierced the thick glass. Zoe heard it crack. She saw it break. And then the bridge began to crumble and fall. A long, elegant line of destruction sweeping its way across the glacier. A lit fuse of shattering glass racing toward Kozlov and the second guard.

And then they were falling.

They were sliding.

They were gone.

The wind kept blowing and the snow kept swirling, but the loudest thing on that mountain had to be the sound of Zoe's heart as it tried to beat its way out of her chest.

"I . . ." Zoe couldn't get a deep breath. "Is it over? Did we win?"

"Yeah. I think we won." Sawyer's hand felt warm against her frozen cheek. Her skin burned and her throat felt like fire, but Zoe was alive, and Sawyer was safe, and Alex—

"Alex!" Zoe was on her feet and heading toward her sister when she felt Sawyer tug her back.

"Stay there, Zo!" Alex ordered, but her eyes were trained on Sawyer. "The drive! Did you get it?"

But Sawyer just smiled down at Zoe. "I saved everything that mattered."

Zoe saw her sister start to argue—to roll her eyes and call them morons—but Alex's scorn morphed into the world's most reluctant smirk as she looked at Sawyer. "Hurt her and I'll kill you. Slowly."

And Sawyer said, "I know."

It should have been over. It would have felt like *The End*, but Zoe realized that Alex was still creeping down the steep incline, closer and closer to the edge.

"Stay there!" Zoe warned.

Sawyer must have read her mind because he shouted, "It's over, Alex. Kozlov's dead."

But Alex was shaking her head. "Kozlov's network is alive and well."

"It's over," Sawyer tried again. "You can come in. There's a CIA mole at the bottom of the mountain along with the man he was working for. No one will suspect you now. Come in. It's over."

She turned, wind in her hair. "It's over when I get that drive back."

Sawyer lunged and Zoe screamed, "No!" But the word was nothing but an echo as Alex ran and leapt—arms and legs spread wide. Hanging on the air—weightless on the wind—before she reached for the little loop on her vest and tugged. A parachute sprang free a moment later and all Zoe could do was watch as her sister faded, disappearing into the clouds.

Sawyer dropped to the rocks beside her, both of them breathing hard in the high altitude and thin air, both of them looking like they weren't sure whether they should laugh or cry. But Zoe knew better.

"Are you okay?" His hands were running over her face and her neck. His hands were everywhere.

"I'm fine."

"Are you hurt."

"I'm okay."

"Are you—"

"Sawyer!" She had to make him stop. She had to make him see. "I . . . I'm sorry." She read the confusion on his face. "Don't get mad. But . . . I have a confession to make. I might have . . . uh . . . lied."

Sawyer looked at her, like *why are we talking when we could be kissing*, but he managed to raise an eyebrow and say, "What kind of lie?"

"I did have Marc turn off the live feed from the cameras, but I also had him send a link to MI6."

Sawyer tensed. She couldn't read his expression, and that's what worried her. "You did?"

That time, when she pointed into the distance there really was a dark speck breaking through the clouds and coming closer. Just about ten minutes too late. But, well, better late than never, she supposed as a second dot appeared on the horizon.

"And Interpol."

Sawyer raised an eyebrow when a third helicopter rose above the blanket of clouds.

"And that would be Mossad."

He huffed out a sound that might have been a laugh—or a curse. She couldn't tell over the roar of the helicopters that were now so close she could make out the disapproving glares of hot guys in expensive suits and dark glasses. Sawyer saw them, too. She felt him bristle or maybe shiver. Every muscle in his body went tense. Everything seemed to change.

"Sawyer?" she asked, but he was already pulling her closer and kissing her deeper, even as the helicopters circled and the ice blew and figures all in black literally started rappelling down on cables.

"You chose me," she whispered again because it felt like the only thing that mattered.

He touched her forehead with his, the air thick with white breath and swirling snow. His voice was barely more than a whisper. Like an oath. "Always."

Before she could kiss him again, a man landed on the ice in front of them, shouting, "Which one of you is"—he checked his notes—"the Denominator?"

chapter sixty-four

HER

So it turns out, if you plan a hostage exchange that results in the death of a rogue CIA operative, a criminal mastermind, and two henchmen, people are going to have a lot of questions. Or so Zoe thought as her life became a blur of snow and ice and whirling blades, badges and empty rooms and truly terrible coffee. Question after question, person after person, until Zoe started to wish she'd grabbed a parachute and followed her sister off that mountain.

"You must be tired." The man on the other side of the table had probably given his name in the helicopter. She assumed he was MI6 because his accent was crisp and smart and he looked like the kind of man whose official title was *His Grace, the Duke of Hottington*— but everyone called him Hots for short—because that's where Zoe's mind went after eight cups of coffee.

"Where's Sawyer? I really need to talk to—" *Was he in trouble? Had he been arrested? Given a medal?* Zoe had no idea. She just knew she needed Sawyer and a bathroom and not necessarily in that order. "Can I please talk to Sawyer?"

"In a bit." Hots gave her the kind of self-deprecating smile they obviously taught at spy school. How else could he and Sawyer both be so good at it?

"I won't keep you long. But I do need to show you something." He laid a picture on the table. She looked down on snow and rocks and a bright blue strip of fabric discarded on the ground. "Our team found this at the base of the mountain."

The parachute was ripped.

"She's okay," he rushed to add. "Or, at least, we assume so, because . . ." Hots dropped something else onto the table. "A courier delivered this an hour ago."

The flash drive.

Hottington leaned closer, studying Zoe in the harsh overhead light. And Zoe heard it—"Courier? Why wouldn't she bring it herself? Why—"

"I don't know. But Alex is alive, Zoe. And no one is chasing her anymore. She's alive, and, eventually she'll stop running."

Zoe didn't realize how heavy that worry had been until she let herself put it down. It almost didn't seem real, but Kozlov was dead and Collins was gone, and Alex was alive. Alex was going to be okay. So why did Zoe feel so awful?

"Miss Sterling?"

It took an embarrassingly long time to realize he was talking to her.

"Wait. Is that . . ."

Hottington ran a hand through thick, wavy hair that was a little more salt than pepper, but it looked good on him because he had a Y chromosome and life was inherently unfair. He studied her confused expression and realized—"You didn't know your last name, did you?"

She shook her head because, evidently, she'd forgotten how to speak, too.

He put his elbows on the table and leaned a little closer—a posture that screamed *you didn't hear this from me*.

"Officially, our friends at Langley insist the serum Agent Collins injected you with doesn't exist. But, unofficially, they assure me it isn't fatal and, in time, could largely wear off." He toyed with the edge of the photograph. "Zoe, do you mind me asking, what do you remember?"

She thought about hospital beds and Christmas mornings and Alex pushing her on the tire swing in their backyard. She could recall the smell of new books and the sound rain makes on rooftops. But, mostly, she remembered Sawyer. Dancing on the *Shimmering Sea* and fighting for the last piece of bacon and—

"Ms. Sterling . . ."

"Right. Yes. Uh . . . Collins brought me to Paris. He said Alex was in trouble and he needed me to Parent Trap my way into the bank."

Hots choked back a laugh. "Excuse me?"

"Parent Trapping? It's a classic identical twins trope that . . ." Oh, she wished people would keep up. "Anyway, I told him no one would believe I was Alex. Then he gave me the shot and said that in thirty minutes even I wouldn't know who I was. So I grabbed his gun and got away. I woke up later. In the snow."

"And that's where Agent Sawyer found you?"

Agent Sawyer. Zoe tried not to think about the look in his eyes when Hottington and his swarm of commandos appeared overhead.

"Yes. That's when Agent Sawyer found me."

She looked around the nondescript room in the nondescript building and fought the feeling that she was once again waking up with no clue where she was or what was going on. She was once again waking up alone.

"What happens now?" Hots probably thought she was asking about Kozlov or Collins or Alex. He didn't know she was talking about dinner. And where she was going to sleep and when she was going to go home and what was she going to do when she got there?

And Sawyer. She still hadn't seen Sawyer. Talked to Sawyer. "Will Agent Saw—"

There was a knock on the door, and a young woman entered, rolling a large suitcase and carry-on.

"Excellent! Thank you, Sims. Right on time," Hots said then turned to Zoe. "Agent Sawyer asked that we go ahead and retrieve your luggage from Paris. And there's a jet standing by to take you home."

The words sounded fine, but then she heard them. *Luggage. Jet. Home.* "Agent Sawyer . . . asked for that?"

"Oh yes." Hots gave an indulgent smile. "Insisted on it. We'll have more questions for you, eventually. But for now, you can relax.

You're safe, Zoe. You're free. You must be eager to get back to your old life."

Her old life.

"Now, come on. Let's get you on the jet."

On. The. Jet.

"But I thought . . ." Zoe trailed off, because what did she actually think was going to happen? That she and Sawyer were going to ride off into the sunset together? Covert and undercover and kiss for the rest of their lives? It was ridiculous. It was insane. It was . . .

Not a danger bang, the little voice in the back of her mind whispered. No. But that didn't mean it was forever.

Six days after passing out in Paris Zoe was finally waking up. To the real world. And her real life. To whatever was supposed to happen next. She didn't have to run anymore, but that didn't mean she knew where to go. Chances were good no one was going to shoot at her tomorrow, but that didn't mean it wasn't scary. Her entire memory was about trying to stay alive, but Zoe was just starting to realize she had no idea how to live.

Without Sawyer.

She honestly didn't know whether to be heartbroken or furious as she followed Hots into a hall then past a railing that looked down on a massive space teeming with people. It looked like something from the movies—a command center filled with screens and computers and people yelling things like, "Where's my satellite?"

Was Sawyer down there? she wondered. Had the CIA dragged him back to Langley? Was he under arrest? Or did he just not care?

"We're right out here." As Hottington pushed open a big metal door, a cool wind blew against her face and it occurred to Zoe that she had no idea how long she'd been in that windowless room. She didn't even know where she was, she realized as soon as she stepped outside and saw the big, nondescript building on the edge of what looked like a private airport. A jet was idling on the tarmac a hundred yards away, and it was all Zoe could do not to dig in her heels because something was wrong. Something was missing. *Someone* was missing.

Because Sawyer had told her he loved her; but then he'd had somebody pack her bags and ordered a plane. He'd told her he loved her. And now he wasn't even going to say goodbye. *Was this goodbye?*

The jerkface.

"I have to tell you, Zoe"—Hots was still beside her, wheeling her luggage—"I'm impressed. You handled yourself extremely well. I doubt even Alex could have done better. I'll have to read your books." He gave her a smile, and Zoe felt herself start to blush because the Duke of Hottington had that effect on a girl.

"And"—he stopped and leaned closer—"I must say, I'm especially grateful to you for looking out for our man on the inside."

It must have been the fatigue because Zoe wasn't exactly sure what he was saying. "Excuse me?"

"He's one of the best MI6 has ever had. So thank you. I don't know what I would have done if we'd lost him." A mischievous glint filled his eye—one that spoke of inside jokes and flirty touches and the kind of charm that could make a woman's pants just melt away. It was all overwhelming and . . . familiar. So familiar that she struggled against a sudden wave of déjà vu.

And maybe that's why she didn't see him—didn't feel him—until a deep voice said, "He has to say that. He's my dad."

chapter sixty-five

HER

Zoe was aware, faintly, of Hots saying something about luggage and airplanes, but she wasn't paying attention. She was too busy watching Sawyer walk across the tarmac, running a hand through thick hair that would someday go salt-and-pepper like his father's. His father . . .

"The Duke of Hottington!" she exclaimed. "*The Duke of Hottington . . . is your father! Gasp!*"

He shook his head and flashed his quickest smile—the one he didn't even know he had. "I don't understand any of the things that you just said."

"I couldn't remember his name so I called him . . ." She trailed off and waved the words away. "Never mind."

She looked at Sawyer's rolled-up shirtsleeves, dark stubble, and tired eyes. She remembered walking through the streets of Paris and making a list, calling him the hottest guy she'd ever seen. She was wrong, of course. He was more than that—so much more. And she tried not to think about the suitcases he'd had collected—the jet that was waiting to take her away.

She didn't want to think about any of the things that were real, so she just said, "Am I going to have to use your courtesy title now? Are you Viscount SexyPants? Is that—"

"We really should have someone check out that head wound."

"But . . . you're not British," she said, like that was the only thing that mattered when, in fact, it was the only thing that didn't.

"I am, actually. I'm both. My father was MI6. *Is* MI6. And my mother was American. I didn't mean to lie. But by the time I realized you thought I was CIA it felt like it was easier to just go along with it. I'm sorry."

Apprehension filled his eyes—like he wasn't asking forgiveness for what he'd done. He was asking for what he was doing.

"You don't have an accent."

"Don't I, love?" And there it was. *The accent.*

"No. Gasp. Put that thing away."

"What?"

"You can't just go around with an accent like that. And with your shirtsleeves rolled up? Are you trying to give me a heart attack?"

Sawyer did that thing where he grinned down at the ground, and Zoe's heart really did stop beating. Which was a good thing. Maybe that would keep it from breaking.

"Was any of it real?" The words slipped out and her voice cracked. Everything cracked. Because the jet was still idling . . . Still waiting . . . Still ready to take her to the other side of a whole, entire ocean. "Was any of it . . ."

"Oh, lady. All of it was real." His palm was warm against her cheek, and she wanted to throw herself into his arms and burrow in like . . . *the kind of animal that burrows*, she thought, cursing herself for not being able to come up with a far better analogy. But her eyes were too wet and her throat was too hot and everything was too much, all of a sudden.

It was too much and not nearly enough.

So she slipped her arms around him and felt the rise and fall of his chest—the pressure of his fingers as his hand cradled the back of her head. It was exactly what he'd done in Paris, but this time it was a different kind of pain shooting through her.

"Don't cry, lady." He wiped her wet cheeks and looked down into her eyes, and she saw the truth. He wasn't sending her away because he didn't love her. He was sending her away because he did. "I swore I'd do what's best for you. Always. And you'll be safer . . ." *Far away from him.*

Spies don't get a happy ending, she had to remind herself. Right before she asked *but what if they could?*

"Come with me." She pulled back and looked up at him.

"What?"

"Get on the plane. Now. Just . . . come with me."

He stumbled back like he'd been hit. "I can't—"

"Can't?" The word was sharp and ragged. It was going to make them both bleed. "Or won't?"

He didn't answer. But he didn't have to. Zoe saw the truth in his eyes—that she could fight Kozlov and Collins and even Alex. But she was no match for the little boy who was still lining up dominoes on the cabin floor, waiting for them to all fall down. So she didn't even try.

"Okay then, Mr. Spy Guy." She forced a smile. She cocked a hip. "I know you must be busy—"

"Zoe—"

"Bad guys to shoot . . . Safe houses to blow up . . ."

"Sweetheart, please—"

She couldn't let him speak. She couldn't meet his gaze. She couldn't stop him or save him or change him. So Zoe did what she'd been doing her whole life: she saved herself.

"I'll say my goodbyes and get out of your way."

Was that pain on his face? Or fear? Maybe sadness. She couldn't tell. She'd known so many Sawyers by that point, but she had no idea how to read the man in front of her. Her eyes started to burn when she realized she never would.

So she leaned against him one last time, felt his arms go around her, and breathed him in.

"Thank you. For the dancing and the lingerie strangling and the . . . all of it. Thank you." She went up on her toes and pressed a kiss to his cheek, lingered a heartbeat longer than she should have. "I'll never forget you."

And then she walked away.

HIM

Sawyer's brain wasn't working right. Neither were his legs. But his heart was the most messed up of all as he stood there, telling himself it was for the best.

His life was always changing and ever dangerous. Kozlov might have been dead, but there was always some new Kozlov, waiting in the wings. He loved her, but Zoe deserved more than a lifetime of constantly looking over her shoulder. Zoe deserved everything.

Someday, she'd meet a nice man with a nice job and they'd go on nice dates to nice places where absolutely no one would try to kill her. Sawyer already hated the bastard.

He felt a presence beside him but didn't turn.

"That drive is going to do a great deal of good," his father said but Sawyer couldn't take his eyes off Zoe. "From what I can tell, we'll be able to roll up most of Kozlov's organization and a few other relevant parties. You should be proud of yourself."

Sawyer didn't feel anything. His goal was to never feel anything ever again.

"She'll be safer in the States, you know." *Away from Sawyer.* "She has a life there." *Apart from Sawyer.* "She deserves a chance to go back to her world." *Without Sawyer.* "And you deserve . . ."

"What do I deserve?" Sawyer snapped.

He knew what his father would say. That they were from different worlds and destined for different lives. That he barely knew her. But his father was wrong. Because Sawyer *did* know her. He knew her smiles and her laughs and her gambits. He knew her silly eccentricities and her fears. And he knew who he was when he was with her. He liked that guy—was just getting used to being him. And he was going to miss him so much when she was gone.

I'll never forget you.

Sawyer squeezed his eyes shut and wondered how long it would take to get very, very drunk. Then he felt a grip on his shoulder.

"You deserve to move on," his father answered slowly. *Without Zoe.* "It's hard to do this job if your heart's not in it."

Sawyer brushed off his father's hand. "You're only saying that because you never loved my mother."

"No." His father's voice was ragged, like he was barely brave enough to admit, "I'm saying that because I did."

Sawyer wanted to turn and gape but he couldn't look away from the woman who was almost to the plane. She might stop. She might turn around. And he didn't want to miss it.

"The world is full of bad guys, son."

"I know—"

"So when one of the good guys gets a chance for a happy ending, he should take it."

Sawyer started to lash out—to rage. He wanted to make someone bleed, but then he heard the words. "What?"

"You should take it."

"What . . ." Sawyer was hearing things—seeing things. From the moment he saw his father in that chopper he'd known this moment was coming—that he'd have to let Zoe walk away. Make her leave. Keep her safe. He'd known that love and covert operations don't mix. He'd known it his whole life, but his father was standing there, looking at him in a way he never had before. Somber and pensive and . . . wistful.

"I thought she was better off without me." His father's voice cracked. "Your mother. But if I could do it all over again, I'd do it differently, son. I'd do it all differently."

Sawyer's blood went cold. "You don't mean that. You can't . . ."

"I didn't appreciate either of you until it was too late. *For me.*" He looked down at a watch that was way too flashy for a secret agent. "But by my calculations, *you* have about two minutes . . ."

Sawyer didn't say another word. He just ran.

HOW TO WALK AWAY

A List by Zoe Sterling, Acclaimed Author and Known Idiot

- Move right foot.
- Move left foot.
- Start a new book about the Duke of Hottington, a

notorious rake who is still in love with the woman he
met years ago while working as an agent for the Crown.

- Don't get bangs.
- Keep breathing.
- Keep moving.
- Don't look back. And don't even try to remember.

"Zoe!"

The jet was twenty feet away now. She could make it. All Zoe had to do was climb those stairs and look out the window and wait for the credits to roll on her grand adventure. She could do her crying later. There wasn't a doubt in her mind she'd cry for the rest of her life.

"Hey, lady." Zoe heard the words on the wind and felt sure she must have dreamed them. "Zoe, wait! Stop!"

And then she did stop even though "keep moving" was right there—it was number six on the list.

"Zoe?" And there he was, tall and dark and dangerous. He was so dangerous in so many ways she'd never expected.

"Did you . . . uh . . . forget something?" She tried to make her voice sound normal. She tried to force a smile.

"This." The kiss was quick and soft and sweet. It wasn't the kiss that came at the end. It was the kiss that came at the beginning, and that's what made her give up any pretense of not crying. Of not breaking. The jerkface.

And then his breath was on her wet cheeks and he was pulling her against his chest. She hated that, too—that she was going to get his shirt all wet. At least the sky was dark. It looked like rain. Maybe he wouldn't know they were tears.

His hands cradled her face, gentle and warm and strong. "I can't ask you to stay, sweetheart."

She pushed free and glared up at him. "Oh, you've been very clear—"

"But I can't let you get on that plane—"

"Then why did you order it?" She didn't know whether to laugh or cry or scream, so she did a little of all three.

"Because I'm in love with you."

"Well, I'm in love with you, too!" They were doing that thing again where the closer they got, the louder they shouted, tension reverberating between them like a wave until, finally, it crested, crashing over Zoe. Sweeping her out to sea. "But that doesn't matter, does it?"

"Oh, sweetheart. It's the only thing that matters." He tried to dry her eyes with his sleeve because she was crying harder now. Stupid traitorous eyes.

"I'm not your sweetheart," she said.

"We've been over this. You're my everything."

And that was the part that broke her. Maybe it was stress or exhaustion or the sheer weight of the past few days finally leaving her body, but she let him pull her closer.

"So if the offer still stands, I'd like to get on the plane *with* you. And go home. With you. And be with you. For however long you'll have me."

The words were sinking in—the reality and the promise and the realization—"I don't know where my home is."

"Then we'll go to mine," he told her.

"Where's that?"

"Wherever you are."

She leaned her forehead against the hard wall of his chest and felt his arms wrap around her—pull her tight. She didn't want to see his face when she admitted, "I know the bad guys are gone, but I'm still scared, Sawyer. Because I still don't know who I am."

Forget the tears, she was going to get his shirt all snotty. If he still wanted her after this . . .

"I do. I know you. You're the woman who is strong and tough and funny and sexy as hell. You're mine, lady." He smoothed her hair. "Remember that morning at the cabin? When you said I made you sleepy? Well, you didn't. You made me forget. About all the bad things that have happened and the even worse things that I've done. You made me forget. So please. Please let me spend the rest of my life helping you remember."

He touched his forehead to hers and she felt herself get wrapped in a cocoon of warmth and safety and hope. The sky opened up overhead but she didn't even feel the rain.

"What about Kozlov? And all the Little Baby Kozlovs waiting to grow up and take his place? What about your job and . . ."

"First, never say the words 'little baby Kozlovs' ever again. Second, I'm out, lady. I talked with my dad, and . . . It's time someone in our family got a happy ending. Now, if you don't love me anymore . . . Or if you love me but you still don't trust me, okay. I'm just asking for a chance. Just the chance to spend the rest of my life earning you."

And, oh, how they broke her, the perfection of those words and that moment and that man. And they scared her. Because—

"What if I'm not enough? What if you walk away from your very important life doing your very important job and you wake up one day and think *I gave all that up . . . for her?*"

"I've risked more for less."

"What if it turns out I'm just a woman with a night guard who hasn't washed her hair in a week and whose entire friend group is fictional?"

"Then that's exactly who I want."

She remembered the man on the mountain, reaching for her, anchoring her. Keeping her safe. She remembered holding on and never, ever wanting to let go.

"I'm never going to be Alex."

And then he laughed—she actually felt it in her chest and on her lips. "Thank goodness."

"What if . . ." But she couldn't think anymore. Couldn't worry. Couldn't wonder. So she said, "What if I have to get home to my husband?"

He bristled and glared, but managed to say, "Pretty sure Alex would have mentioned if you had one of those."

"Or my boyfriend. My big, brooding, territorial—"

"I can take him."

"How about my seventy-two cats?"

"I love them."

"My nine iguanas?"

"Not a problem."

"What if I'm addicted to knitting and blew all my money on extremely high-end yarns?"

"I have savings. And I look amazing in sweaters."

Yeah. He probably did, she thought as he wrapped her in his arms and blocked the rain she didn't even feel anymore. The jerkface.

"I don't know what your life was, sweetheart. We'll figure that out together. I just have one question. What do you *want your life to be*?"

Zoe must have had an answer to that question at some point. A dream home and a dream guy and a dream life. She'd made her whole life about the pursuit of happy endings, but as she looked into the eyes of a man who had thought he'd never have one, she saw her blank past and empty future for what they were: clean slates. And fresh starts.

So they stood there—a woman with no history and a man with way too much—and there was really only one thing to say. "I think I'd like to be Mrs. Michaelson?"

Slowly, he reached into his pocket and pulled out a silver ring. "That can be arranged."

ZOE

"They're here!"

Zoe rolled over and felt the cool sheets beside her. It had been months since she'd woken to a cold, empty bed, and she had to admit she didn't like it. One of her favorite things about her new life were the mornings. Waking slowly beside Sawyer who, it turns out, was a cuddler. Who knew? They'd lie side by side for hours, talking about their lives before and their life after, but on that particular morning, the bed was empty and the loft was cold, so she wrapped herself in an old quilt and padded, barefoot, to the stairs.

She could feel the cold air from the open door, but he had a cardboard box in his hands and was grinning up at her like it was Christmas morning.

"Close the door," she called, and he kicked it shut before carrying the box to the fire.

"Get down here!"

"Fine," she grumbled. "Let me find a—"

He was already pulling a knife from his boot because he was still Sawyer and she wouldn't have had him any other way.

She nestled beside him on her side of the sofa. Because they had sides. They had routines. And habits. And inside jokes and fights and making-ups and everything. They had everything. And Zoe didn't think about what she didn't have and couldn't recall.

It was coming back. In pieces. She'd remembered her mother, who taught English at a fancy boarding school in France, and her father, an American engineer who did something with luxury German automobiles. They'd had their daughters late in life and then one of them had almost died. Zoe. Zoe had almost died. And her mother's full-time job had become keeping her alive.

Don't run, Zoe.

Don't fall, Zoe.

Don't die, Zoe.

She hadn't. In fact, she had gotten very, very good at not dying. But she hadn't been very good at living. Not until—

"You ready?" he asked. He winked. Then she kissed him. Because she could. And he kissed her back because he couldn't not.

"I'm ready," Sawyer said as he sliced open the box then looked down at the advanced reading copies of the debut novel from Z. S. Michaelson—the pen name of a husband/wife writing team that was shrouded in mystery.

Sawyer was still smiling when Zoe slipped onto his lap and wrapped an arm around his shoulders. His stubble was deliciously rough on the smooth skin of her neck as he kissed her.

"Are you sure about this?" she asked for what she swore would be the final time. "You could go back under. MI6 would take you back in a heartbeat. That was your life, and you don't have to leave it just because—"

He tossed the book aside and flipped her onto her back and nestled between her legs. "Does it feel like I'm not completely happy with where I am right now and what I'm doing?" He peppered her skin with little kisses and she forgot what they were talking about.

Then, suddenly, he pulled back. "I think we need to reinstate Naked Thursdays."

"It's Tuesday."

"Every day is Naked Thursday if you try hard enough." He was just starting to kiss the smile off her face when she heard the floorboards creak. A gun cocked. And a voice said, "Get off my little sister."

In the next moment, Sawyer was pushing Zoe down into the couch cushions and coming up with his third favorite gun, spinning and pointing it at . . .

"Alex?" Sawyer shouldn't have sounded surprised. Zoe just had the one sister, after all. But when your only in-law jumps off a mountain and falls off the face of the earth, a guy has the right to be leery.

"Hey, stranger. Why don't you put that gun down?" The words were casual but the tone was cool. Dangerous. *He's still dangerous*, Zoe thought and made a mental note to go all swoony about that later.

"Why don't you?" Alex asked as she walked around the end of the couch and Zoe got her first look at her sister.

Her hair was blonde now—lighter than Zoe's. And longer than Zoe's. And . . . well . . . prettier than Zoe's . . . Alex was still superior to Zoe in all the ways that didn't matter. Because now Zoe knew what she hadn't known before: that Alex might be harder but that had never made her stronger and it never, ever would.

"Hey, Zo." Alex's tone was light but her eyes were sad as she slipped the gun into the pocket of her jacket. "Had to make sure he wasn't killing you."

"Nope. Very much . . . uh . . . alive." Zoe glanced at Sawyer but he looked as confused as Zoe felt because Alex was here and armed and looking at the cabin's steepled roof and toasty fire like she'd just come over for tea.

"Good job getting off the grid. The Agency doesn't know this place exists."

"And we're gonna keep it that way, right?" Sawyer warned.

"Relax, tough guy, your secret is safe with me. I only found you because I was tracking . . ." She pointed to the box. "Don't worry," she added quickly. "No one else will put it together."

"So . . . long time no see," Sawyer went on in that deceptively friendly tone that was like a dog that didn't bark and didn't growl but you'd have to be a fool to pet him. "Where've you been? Who've you killed?"

And Zoe saw them—the words that Alex wouldn't say. She was the strongest woman Zoe had ever known, but something in the past few months had changed her, tilted her earth on its axis, and was threatening to spin her off into the void.

"Alex." Zoe clawed and pushed and, finally, Sawyer let her out of the couch cushions. "What's wrong? Where have you been? What-ever it is we can fix it. Is it the Agency? Another mole? Terrorists? Double agents? Rogue scientists? Is it a robot army? What have you been running from, Alex? Whatever it is . . ."

It was like a spark from the fire sprang up and caught inside of Zoe. She couldn't touch it or feel it but she knew it was there and, if she wasn't careful, that it would burn her sister to the ground.

But Alex just looked . . . annoyed. "Long story short, I'm in an enemies-to-lovers situation." Alex took a deep breath. "And I think I'm gonna need your help."

acknowledgments

All books are team efforts—this one more than most—so I have to take a moment and acknowledge the incredibly generous and talented people who got me through the last year.

First, I need to thank Nicole Fischer, Madelyn Blaney, Laurie McGee, and the team at Avon for their wisdom, patience, expertise and, most of all, for taking a chance on Sawyer and Zoe. And me.

I'm now nineteen books into my career, and none of them would have been possible without Kristin Nelson and the team at the Nelson Literary Agency. Thank you for holding my hand as I made this jump.

Thank you to Shellie Rea, assistant extraordinaire, and to my wonderfully supportive family.

Finally, the greatest gift of my career has been the amazing community of writers, readers, and friends that I've somehow been welcomed into. So thank you to Carrie Ryan, Rose Brock, Sophie Jordan, Sarah MacLean, Lindsey Leavitt, Jen Barnes, Marianne Mancusi, Diana Peterfreund, and Michelle Wright for always replying to my frantic texts and keeping me sane.

But, most of all, I have to thank Rachel Hawkins, who not only let me borrow the surname of Sterling but also told me the exact thing I needed to hear at the exact moment I needed to hear it. This one is because of you.

ALLY CARTER is the bestselling author of novels that have epitomized action-adventure YA romance for more than a decade. From the spy-centric humour of *I'd Tell You I Love You, But Then I'd Have to Kill You*, to the globe-trotting glamour of *Heist Society*, and the non-stop thrill ride of *Not If I Save You First*, the name Ally Carter is synonymous with hilarious action and heart-pounding romance. She is also the writer of Netflix's No. 1 hit *A Castle for Christmas*. Now she is bringing her trademark style and voice to the adult rom-com market.